I0675432

Wild On the Red Carpet

HOLLYWOOD REBELS AND ROMEOS
BOOK THREE

OLIVIA JAYMES

WILD ON THE RED CARPET

Copyright © 2017 by Olivia Jaymes

ALL RIGHTS RESERVED: The unauthorized reproduction or distribution of this copyrighted work is illegal. Criminal copyright infringement is investigated by the FBI and is punishable by up to 5 years in federal prison and a fine of $250,000.

All characters and events in this book are fictitious. Any resemblance to actual persons living or dead is strictly coincidental.

Wild On The Red Carpet

Tyler Gaylord is a world-famous movie star and one of Hollywood's most notorious playboys. He enjoys the company of beautiful, willing women as long as they don't misunderstand the rules. There will be expensive gifts, champagne-soaked parties, and passion-filled nights. But there will be no love or talk of forever. No offense to the lovely ladies, but he's simply not a commitment type of guy.

Wilhemina "Billie" Oliver is a struggling actress who lives in Tyler's guest cottage. She's also his best friend and the only person he trusts to tell him the truth. She'd do anything for him, and he'd do anything for her. No questions asked. The one thing she won't let him do, however, is help her career. She'll make it on her own, or she won't make it at all.

To win the role of his dreams, Tyler needs to appear happily married. The director doesn't believe that a serial womanizer can play a character deeply and passionately in love. So, of course, Tyler turns to his best friend Billie to help him out. They already spend all their time together, so nothing will change but her last name.

It's the perfect solution, and it's not like he asked her to help him bury a body or anything. So why is she being so difficult?

CHAPTER
One

GIGGLING AND BATTING HER EYELASHES, the slightly tipsy blonde in the low-cut dress leaned closer and ran her hand up Tyler Gaylord's jean-clad thigh while at the same time showing off her assets under the flashing colored lights of the nightclub. Tyler doubted this was the first time she'd made a move like this. She was too smooth and practiced, confident even, of his reaction. In fact, he didn't even recall exactly how he'd ended up here on this sofa in the corner with her hand on his leg. He'd been talking to a cute little redhead and then suddenly she was gone and this one was sitting next to him.

It didn't matter though, not really. For the most part the fans were all the same. There were a few exceptions but they were too far and few between to worry about, their numbers statistically insignificant. The females wanted to brag that they'd slept with a movie star. He wanted a respite from the unholy demands of his career. As long as they didn't expect more than one night he was happy to give them the fantasy. It was when they had bigger expectations that things went awry.

"Let's go to your place," she said in a husky, come hither tone he could barely hear over the loud techno music. The floor vibrated under his feet and his ears were going to ring later. "I know just what you need to help you relax."

Taking a sip from his whiskey, he grinned lazily. "I'll just bet you do, darlin'. You're probably an expert."

"He's already relaxed. He doesn't need any help."

Sighing, Tyler turned toward the voice. A voice he'd heard pretty much every day for the last five years - either in person or over the phone. "Awww, baby. You never let me have any fun."

His best friend and nagging conscience Wilhemina "Billie" Oliver put her hands on her hips and shook her head. "You have more fun than any one man should be allowed. Which brings me to why I'm standing here. You have a photo shoot tomorrow and you need to get some sleep. The real kind where you don't wake up with bags under your eyes. Let's get a move on."

Knocking back the last of his drink, he shrugged at the blonde. "What can I say? She's the boss."

Billie wasn't his actual boss, but she thought she was and he went along with it. Most of the time. The fact was she was usually right about things so he was smart to listen to her.

But apparently the blonde wasn't going to give up easily. Clinging to him like a vine, she shot a nasty look over her shoulder toward Billie before looking up at him with sheer adoration.

"Come on, baby. A little while longer isn't going to make any difference. This party is just getting started."

Rolling her eyes and sighing loudly, Billie checked her watch. "He's been partying for a week straight. Now I'm leaving, Ty, and you can come with me or stay here. It's not my job to drag your half-drunk ass out of nightclubs but I'm taking the limo, so good luck getting home."

She wasn't fucking kidding either. The last time Billie had threatened to leave him she'd done it and he'd had to call an Uber to get him home, which had cost him sixty bucks, an autograph, and a selfie that ended up on Instagram with the caption *Tyler Gaylord drunk as a skunk*. His publicist had bitched about that for weeks. That is until the next time Tyler had given him something else to have a stroke about.

"I'm coming so don't leave without me. Keep your panties on."

Another heavy sigh from Billie. Funny how she did that a whole bunch around him. It was kind of a habit. Staggering to his feet, the blonde kept a hold of his arm. Persistent.

"Baby, don't leave. Forget about her," she said with a sneer. "She doesn't look like she's enough woman to handle a man like you."

Not that he wouldn't enjoy a cat fight between the blonde and Billie...because he would...but it wasn't a good idea. Billie would kick this girl's ass from here to Barstow and back. She could be meaner than a snake and damn if she didn't play dirty. The last time he'd wrestled with her on the floor of his television room she'd kicked him in the balls because she didn't want to watch *Star Wars* for the two-hundredth time.

"Oh, for fuck's sake," Billie ground out, tucking her phone back in her tiny purse. She'd explained to him long ago that women had different handbags for different occasions. "I'm out of here. See you tomorrow."

Just like that, she'd turned on her high heels and strode out of the VIP section of the very loud and incredibly dark Hollywood nightclub. If the limo was already at the entrance, she'd be on the road in less than five minutes.

Tyler managed to peel the blonde's hands off of him, all the while wearing the smile he was so famous for. "Sorry, but I'll have to take a raincheck. Duty and all that. I'll call you, okay?"

Nodding eagerly, she stopped trying to pull him back. "You will? That's coo–" She wasn't as dumb as some of the others because she immediately jumped up from the sofa they'd been reclining on. "Wait, you don't have my number. How are you going to call me?"

Tyler didn't answer, instead slipping into the crowd and disappearing in the mass of bodies, all his attention trained in front of him. He needed to catch up to Billie before she left without him. Dammit, he wasn't letting her get away with this again. He caught a glimpse of the white and silver dress he'd helped her pick out and the long sable-colored hair she'd pulled back into a ponytail. Reaching out his arm, he captured her wrist with his fingertips.

"Baby, slow down. I'm coming with you. Don't have a cow. You're impatient as hell tonight. I should have left you at home."

Stopping in the middle of a crowd, she gave him an incredulous look. "I wish you had but you begged me to come to this stupid nightclub opening. I would have happily stayed in tonight but you said you needed the company."

Tyler grinned at her feisty nature. It was one of the reasons he adored her. She didn't give a rat's ass who or what he was. Movie star or ditch digger. Billie Oliver treated him exactly the same, never letting him get away with anything. It was the number one reason they were such close friends. She was truly his best friend and he didn't use that term lightly.

He rubbed his chin, playing dumb. "I don't remember begging."

She flicked him on the side of the head, not hard enough to cause any pain but enough to get his attention. "Then you ought to see a doctor because you might have had a series of small strokes. You begged me to go. On your knees, no less. Do you know your name and what year it is?"

He leaned down so he was speaking softly into her ear. "I'm Batman and it's the Year of the Rooster."

Billie never stayed mad at him for long and tonight was no exception. Her scowl had turned to a smile and she was openly laughing at him. "Close enough. Can the Dark Knight help me wade through this crowd? The limo should be out front waiting for us."

"My pleasure, baby girl. Hold tight and I'll get us out of here."

Good to his word, he had them standing on the sidewalk in less than ninety seconds. He tucked them both into the limo before leaning back against the leather seats and closing his eyes. Billie was right. He had been partying hard this week, but he'd been celebrating finishing a movie. When he was working, he *worked*. He didn't drink much or stay up until all hours. He focused on the job at hand and buckled down. He loved being an actor and he never took the privilege for granted. He was one lucky son of a bitch. But in between he liked to cut loose a little.

"You look like hell," Billie said bluntly, grabbing a bottle of water from the bar in the back. "Drink this. You don't want to be dehydrated tomorrow for the photoshoot. It will show in your skin."

He chugged down half of it in one gulp. "I have been burning the candle at both ends. Thanks for coming with me tonight."

Billie nudged him with her knee. "Not mad at me for dragging you out of there? She was pretty."

Tyler only had vague recollections of the woman's face.

"They all are. And I'm not mad. You're right. I have to be up early in the morning."

Snorting, Billie kicked off her shoes and wriggled her toes. "Blondie looked like the man-eating type. I think you got out just in time. You might have made the newspapers in the morning but not the gossip columns."

It was a running joke between them that he met so many people a certain percentage of them just had to be serial killers. Clearly they'd watched too much television.

"How do you think she would have done it?" he teased, finishing off the water bottle.

"I know how I would," Billie drawled with a grin. "Say goodbye to the family jewels."

Covering his package with his hands, he pretended to cower and grimace. "Say it ain't so, darlin'. Have I pissed you off that much? I thought I've been quite charming these last few weeks."

Tyler had always been a pain in her ass but she didn't complain all that often. Most of the time she'd been very patient. More so than he deserved.

"No one could ever accuse you of not being charming."

She didn't make it sound like a positive attribute though so he changed the subject. He already knew how she was going to react.

"I want you with me at the shoot tomorrow."

"No."

Billie was so predictable sometimes.

"You work for me."

"You don't get to do this, Tyler." She wagged a finger in front of his nose. "I am helping you out because you are between assistants. I am doing you a favor, that's all."

"I'm paying you."

At least he thought he was. Shit, maybe he needed to call his accountant. It would be just like Billie to work for free.

"You're not even sure about that, are you?" She was openly laughing at him now. He was predictable too. At least to her. "You're thinking that you need to call your accountant but tomorrow you'll just tell me to do it."

"So am I?"

"Paying me? Yes. But I'm still not going tomorrow."

"I want you there. You know they're going to put me into some stupid ass outfits and you'll keep me from saying something I shouldn't."

"Your publicist will be there. It will be fine." She paused for a moment. "I have an audition tomorrow."

Immediately straightening, he smiled and pulled her in for a hug, burying his face in the sweet-scented crook of her neck. "Baby girl, that's fantastic. Why didn't you say so earlier? What's the role?"

Turning away, Billie shrugged. She was in defensive mode tonight and he should have noticed it right away but he'd been too damn self-absorbed. She only acted like this when she was nervous. "It's not a big deal so let's not overdo it. It's for a recurring role on a series. Just a small thing, you know, a few lines a week."

"You'll knock it out of the park. Do you want to run lines? We can rehearse a little bit."

"No," she said quickly, shaking her head even before he'd finished asking his question. "I want to get a good night's sleep. I only have a couple of lines for the audition tomorrow. I think my sparkling personality is going to be much more important and I want to be at the top of my game. It's been a long time since I worked."

Tyler remembered her last role over six months ago. A small part in an indie movie. Billie had been great but the director had been a douchebag, trying to get into her pants. When she'd said no her scene hadn't made the final cut of the film. Tyler still wanted to punch that smug bastard's lights out. This business was cutthroat and for all Billie's tough-girl act she had a soft heart.

"I shouldn't have made you go out tonight. Damn, woman, why didn't you tell me before?"

"Because it's not a big deal," she explained in her most patient tone. Reaching into her purse, she pulled out her phone and pressed a few buttons. The gates of his Holly-wood Hills home swung open. "I'll stop by later tomorrow to see how the photoshoot went."

The limo pulled around to the back of the mansion where the guest cottage was located.

"Stay in the house with me tonight."

The vehicle door swung open and the driver extended a hand to help her out. "If I come up to the house you know what will happen. We'll stay up all night watching movies and eating junk food."

Those were some of his fondest memories. Since Billie had moved into the guesthouse five years ago, they'd become as close as family. Tyler captured her hand before she was able to escape into the cottage. "Hey, break a leg, cutie."

He wanted this part for her badly. She needed the ego boost and had been down in the dumps about her career the last few months. This was just what the doctor ordered.

"Thanks. Have fun tomorrow."

He knew he'd hate every minute of playing dress-up but he smiled for her anyway.

"You and me. Dinner and a Lakers game tomorrow night. Are you in?"

"I'm in." She tapped the top of the limo twice. Their special signal that everything was good. "Now get out of here and get some sleep or they're going to have to slap an inch of makeup on you tomorrow."

Tyler waited until she was inside the cottage and the lights were on. She waved from the front window and then and only then did he let the driver close the limo door and drive around to the kitchen entrance. Someone had to look out for Billie and since she appeared to have no one in her life, he'd decided not long after they'd met it was going to be him. She pretended she didn't need anyone but that was just her way.

She was the little sister he'd never had, and he was closer to her than just about anyone else on this earth. There wasn't anything he wouldn't do for her and vice versa. She wouldn't ask him what he was doing with a dead body; she'd just grab a shovel and start digging.

He'd trust her with his life. Hell, he'd trust her with something far more important.

His career.

CHAPTER
Two

BILLIE'S PHONE buzzed insistently for the fourth time that day and it was only noon. There was no name displayed on the screen but she knew who it was and she simply was not prepared to deal with that conversation in her current mental and emotional state. Hitting the decline button, she sent the call to voicemail just as her agent's assistant called Billie's name.

"You can go in now."

Putting her phone on silent mode, Billie straightened her shoulders and took a deep breath, thinking positive thoughts. The audition earlier in the morning had gone well, better even than Billie had hoped for. She had a strong feeling she'd been called here to meet with her agent because she'd been cast in the role.

Ina Jackson sat behind her modern chrome and glass desk, looking as chic as her office in a cream and black dress with high-heeled Louboutins. Her light brown hair had been artfully highlighted and then styled into a sleek chignon that showed off her strong bone structure. She screamed style right down to her perfectly plucked eyebrows. This was Hollywood after all, full of beautiful people. Even the guy who bagged Billie's groceries looked like a blond Adonis.

Ina beckoned to her. "Come in. Have a seat. I have a lunch meeting in thirty minutes at The Ivy."

The Ivy was the place to see and be seen. Known as a hangout for celebrities, there were always a few paparazzi staked out ready to take a few photos for the tabloids.

Clasping her hands together, Ina leaned forward in her chair. "So let's talk honestly. The producers thought your reading went very well. I'm not surprised. You're a good actress, which is why I represent you."

Adrenaline surged and Billie had to steel herself to stay still. This could be it. The break she'd been waiting for. "Thank you. I think it went well too. The part just felt so natural to me."

Ina ran her manicured nail over the surface of the desk. "However, they have a few concerns and I have to admit that I share them as well."

Billie's heart dropped to her feet. What the hell? Calling on her acting ability, she remained outwardly cool, crossing her legs and wearing a small smile. "Concerns? Such as?"

"Have you given any thought to my suggestion from last year about having a boob job? Plus it looks like you've spent too much time in the sun without sunscreen. You have freckles on your nose, shoulders, and arms. You need some intensive skin treatments. Just say the word and I can have you in a private, discreet clinic tomorrow morning.

They can do the surgery and the skin peel all at the same time. You stay there a few days and then recover at home."

Ina had broached this subject with Billie before and received a chilly reception. Billie had as many issues and insecurities as the next person but she'd long made peace with her breasts.

"I don't want a boob job. I didn't want one last year and I don't want one now. My boobs are fine. They're better than fine. They're great. I may not be a D-cup but I haven't had any complaints."

Not that Billie had dated lately. In fact, her social calendar had been sparse in the last year. It was hard to keep a boyfriend around with Tyler as her best friend. Men didn't like to compete and never seemed to understand that she was just a friend to the movie star. They always assumed she was sleeping with him.

Scratch that. *Everyone* assumed she was sleeping with him.

Ina checked her phone before turning her attention back to Billie. "You've had one now. The producers thought your reading was good but they're concerned you don't look glamorous enough."

"The role is for a waitress," Billie replied, exasperation in her tone. "How glamorous do they want her to be? Just how big do her boobs need to be?"

"It's their show and they want boobs."

Billie wasn't enjoying the way Ina was looking at her, like there was something wrong with her and not this fucked-up town.

"I'm not getting a boob job."

Ina heaved a sigh. "You're not understanding what I'm

saying. This isn't a gentle suggestion like last year. If you want to work in this town, you have to play the game, Billie. Frankly, no one gives a shit that you're a good actress. We have thousands of those in Hollywood. You have to be willing to do what needs to be done."

"Is this what you think too? You think I should do it?"

Billie had a real phobia about doctors and hospitals. Nothing good ever seemed to happen in a hospital, at least when she was there. And she didn't give a rat's butt that it was a private clinic. It was the same thing and it probably had that smell. Antiseptic and illness. It was always the same and she wanted no part of it. If her life hung in the balance, she'd have the surgery but this was elective. If other women wanted to do it, that was awesome, wonderful, fantastic. No judgment here. But her? Not going to happen. She had to psych herself up for a week just to have her yearly physical.

"I think if you want to work, you need to have it done." Ina threw up her hands. "And since you're not willing to use your relationship with Tyler Gaylord to get ahead—"

"Stop," Billie commanded, her anger rising. "Stop right there. He's my friend and doesn't deserve to be *used*."

Ina stood and gathered up her purse and phone. "Think about what I've said. The part is yours if you want it but only if you have the surgery. Billie, you're a good actress but you have to think about your appearance. It's what will put you over the top of other good actresses with mediocre looks. Honestly, I don't think I can get you any roles if you're not willing to do this so you need to think hard and make the right decision. Now I need to go or I'm going to be late."

Billie just wanted her agent to say what she fucking meant.

"Are you saying you're not going to represent me if I don't have the boob job?"

Ina smiled sadly. "I think that you and I have come to the end of our professional relationship. You're a sweet person and I wish you all the best. I really do, Billie. But this business might just be a little too shark-infested for you. Maybe it's time for you to go back home to your family and get married, have a few kids. Be like everyone else. Where do you come from? I don't think you ever said."

It was like taking a punch to the solar plexus. In one fell swoop she'd lost a role and her agent. To add insult to injury, Ina wanted to shuffle her out of town. Billie stood on shaky legs and put her purse strap over her shoulder. She'd walk out of here with as much dignity as she could muster. No way would Billie allow Ina to know how much this moment hurt.

"Nowhere. I don't come from anywhere."

It wasn't the whole truth but certainly there was nothing there to go back to. The only home she'd truly known was with Tyler, and even he didn't know where she came from. And if she had anything to say about it, it would stay that way. The past was best left where it was.

CHAPTER
Three

THE DESIGNER CLOTHES Tyler was currently wearing were definitely not his style. He was more comfortable in jeans and t-shirts but the magazine had him in bespoke Italian suits that cost more than the mortgage on his childhood home.

"Everything's going great," his publicist Garrett enthused, slapping Tyler on the back during a break as they changed up the lighting. "The photos look fantastic."

Even Tyler had to admit they looked good. He might not be a fan of the stuffy clothing but the photographer knew what he was doing.

"I'd rather be at a Lakers game."

"And you will be, just as soon as we finish here." Garrett's gaze darted over to the group changing the lighting and then back to Tyler. "Listen, we need to talk when you're done. I just need a few minutes of your time."

That was never a good sign. When Garrett needed to

talk to Tyler it was usually because the shit had hit the fan in the tabloids.

Tyler grinned and mentally ran through the last week of partying. It had actually been fairly tame compared to a few years ago. He wasn't as young as he used to be. "What did I do this time?"

"Nothing," Garrett chuckled. "You're not in trouble. We just need to talk, that's all."

At the end of the long day under the hot lights, Tyler put on his own comfortable clothes and let Garrett lead him to the bistro next door where they both ordered a cold beer. With every minute that passed, Tyler was growing more suspicious. Normally, Garrett was straight and to the point. He didn't dance around what needed to be said.

"You need to spit it out," Tyler said after they'd exhausted several topics including the weather and how the Lakers were going to do tonight. "Obviously this is bad news because you wouldn't hesitate to tell me something good."

Garrett sighed and pressed his lips together. "You're a damn good actor, Tyler, so telling you this isn't easy. The whole situation isn't fair."

"Life rarely is."

Despite his casual reply Tyler was on high alert. There were dozens of irons in the fire when it came to his career and some were highly dependent on each other. One problem and there could be a nasty domino effect.

"It's Ron Weller. He's not interested in talking to you about the lead in his next film."

Weller was the hottest director in Hollywood at the moment and he was going to direct a movie that Tyler desperately wanted to be a part of. A book adaptation, it was the story of a small town outcast as he navigated life's ups and downs. The role spoke to Tyler and he knew that he could do the character justice. He'd told his agent Josh that no matter what he had to play that part. He'd do it for free if he had to but it was his role.

Tyler's fingers tightened on the cool surface of his glass. "Why isn't Josh telling me this?"

"Because of the reason Ron doesn't want to talk to you."

"It's the *Thunder* movies, isn't it? I know they're not great cinema–"

Garrett waved his hand in the air. "It's not that. It's you, buddy. He doesn't want you in his movie because of you."

Feeling like a boulder had fallen on his head, Tyler struggled to make sense of his publicist's words. "Me? What the hell did I ever do to him? I only met him once at an after-Oscars party, for fuck's sake. Did I hit on his wife or something?"

Garrett rubbed his temple and grimaced. "Funny you should say something like that because that's kind of the reason he doesn't want you."

Tyler's brows shot to his hairline. "Are you saying I slept with his wife? Because I'm pretty sure I didn't."

"No, you didn't," Garrett assured him, placing his palms flat on the table. "But you know Weller's reputation, Tyler. He's a stickler for the smallest details. He told Josh that he didn't think that a man who has never been in love can play a man who is so desperately in love he'd give up his own life. He's looking for an actor who has loved deeply and made a commitment based on that love."

"It's called acting." Tyler slapped his thigh and growled. "What makes him think I've never been in love before?"

The look on Garrett's face was priceless and would have been hilarious in any other situation. "Well...have you? It must have been a long time ago."

"Okay, I've never been in love," Tyler admitted, although it pained him to do so. It was his own private business and it shouldn't be the criteria for a fucking role in a movie. "But I've loved things. Surely that counts."

Tyler had a dog when he was a boy that he was positive he'd loved more than some men loved their wives. He'd seen how some husbands treated their significant other and it was downright shameful.

Garrett shook his head. "He wants an actor who has settled down and made a commitment. He specifically said he doesn't want a hard-partying horn dog carrying this picture. You have a reputation, my friend."

Hard-partying horndog. Wasn't that special?

"Basically he wants some boring married guy? That's what you're telling me?"

This was *his* role. He'd felt it in his bones and deep in his gut. He could make this character come alive but he couldn't even get a damn meeting with the director.

"Rob said that if you had never been in love you wouldn't know how to act like you were in love. The other stuff was just additional reasons not to talk to you or have you audition. He doesn't want trouble on his set."

Tyler wasn't going to lose this role because some tight-ass director couldn't see past the hand on the end of his arm. He'd never been trouble on any set. When he was immersed in a role, partying was the last thing on his mind.

He'd acted like a junkie and never been one, he'd acted like an assassin and never killed anyone, he'd even been a vampire and never drank blood. Surely he could act like a besotted fool when he'd never been in love. He'd seen it in others and that was part of acting. Mimicry, for Christ's sake.

"So he wants me to be married, or at least engaged?"

Garrett nodded. "But you're not so you need to let this go. They'll be other movies."

Yes, but not like this one.

There had to be a way. He'd never married because he'd never met a woman he trusted that much. Until...

Could I? Should I? Nothing would change, not really. They'd still hang out together but now she'd wear a ring. No difference. Maybe she'd even let him pay for a few things or help her career.

"Call Josh and tell him to get Weller back on the phone. Tell him I'm engaged to be married but we've been keeping it quiet. That should loosen his shoelaces."

Garrett's eyes were as wide as saucers. "Are you?"

Frowning, Tyler was already checking his calendar on his phone. "Am I what?"

"Getting married," Garrett repeated. "Because that would be news to me and I'm your publicist. Are you even dating anyone?"

"No, but I would never marry the women I've dated. I'm not that stupid."

If they hurried with the wedding plans they could say

"I do" by the end of the summer. Filming on the picture began after the first of the year.

"I know I'm going to regret asking this question but who are you going to marry then? You can't just randomly choose someone at your local grocery store, Tyler. You can't order up a wife like a pizza."

People always assumed actors were stupid, and most of the time Tyler deliberately let them think just that.

"I know. If Weller and the world are going to believe it, it has to be someone that I've been photographed with in the past. Plus, it has to be someone that I could actually spend time with and won't drive me up a wall."

Scraping his fingers through his hair, Garrett groaned as recognition dawned in his eyes. "Jesus, Mary, and Joseph, she's not going to do it. There's no way in hell. Billie is going to tell you to take a long walk off a short pier."

"I'll beg."

"She'll say no."

"I'll offer her money."

"She'll kick you in the balls."

"She does that anyway." The more Tyler thought about the idea, the more he liked it. It was the perfect answer. "We've always been there for each other. This time won't be any different. Give Josh a call."

Inwardly Tyler wasn't nearly as confident as he sounded. Billie was going to find hundreds of excuses to say no but she was his only hope. He'd throw himself on her mercy and if that didn't work...

He'd better figure out a plan B,C, D, and E. Failure was

not an option. This was his movie. The director just didn't know it yet.

CHAPTER
Four

AFTER BILLIE'S CRAPPY DAY, the last thing she wanted to do was go out but she'd already agreed to it last night, and a promise was a promise. Unless she had a dangling limb or was puking up lunch, Tyler was going to hold her to it. He was in his "party" mode that usually lasted about ten days to two weeks after he returned home from a movie set. In about a week he'd settle down and be more normal but right now he wanted to have as much fun as possible after having his nose to the grindstone for so long.

Disgusted with the day, Billie had taken a nap before getting ready for the evening. Luckily tonight she could dress casually in jeans and flats so it wouldn't take long to get ready. She was applying a final coat of mascara when she heard Tyler at her front door. As usual, he didn't bother to knock, simply barging in and yelling her name. She'd gone around and around with him about this behavior and clearly she was wasting her breath.

When she came out of her bedroom his head was in her pantry and all she could see was his well-shaped rear end.

"Are you eating my food again?"

Straightening, he grinned and took a bite out of a cookie. "I like to think of it as our food."

"The same way you think of my front door? This is my home and it would be nice if you knocked once in awhile. What if I hadn't been dressed?"

He popped the second half of the cookie in his mouth. "I wouldn't mind that. You know I own this cottage, right? I'm your landlord."

The best one she'd ever had but it still wasn't okay.

"Even landlords can't just stroll in whenever they want," she argued. "I swear I am going to change the locks someday."

"You weren't saying that the day I *strolled in* and found you in a pool of blood on the floor."

She remembered that day vividly. She'd been standing on a chair trying to access a high cabinet over the refrigerator when she'd reached a little too far, lost her balance, and landed awkwardly on the cold, hard tile. She'd bumped her head and cut her arm on the way down and she'd lain there for quite awhile because the room had spun every time she tried to get up. It had been sheer luck that Tyler hadn't been away on a movie set and had come by to check on why she wasn't in the main house for their training session. That incident had set off this behavior and she didn't see an end in sight. He was over the top protective of her and even more so since then.

"I appreciate that you were there to help me, I really do.

I'm very thankful that you were home and not away on a movie set."

He'd also taken to calling her every single day when he was away, sometimes more than once. *Just to check on her.* She had to admit that she enjoyed how he cared for her. It was something she hadn't had growing up.

His expression had softened. "I'll always be here for you, baby girl. Always. Just like you are for me."

That last part was said in a hopeful tone, which was strange because they'd long ago vowed to be there for each other through thick and thin.

"Something on your mind?" she asked, leading him out of her tiny kitchen and back in the living room. "You sounded...unsure a second ago."

Checking his watch, he appeared uncertain as to how to answer. Billie had seen this mood before. He had something to say but he didn't want to say it. "If we don't leave soon we're going to miss tipoff."

"It's up to you, but I bet the Lakers will play whether we're courtside or not."

He still looked unsure. "You really don't mind? I guess I'm not much in the mood for a game tonight. Can we just order some dinner and hang out?"

"It's fine. Do you want to stay here or go up to the house?"

"We can stay here." He pulled out his phone. "The usual?"

The usual was a hell of a lot of food but Tyler liked to have leftovers. "Sounds good. If you want beer or wine, you know..."

He'd have to go back to the house or run to the liquor store. Billie didn't drink.

"Soda's fine. Let's find something to watch on television."

He was going to pretend he didn't want to talk. That was fine. She'd just wait him out. They'd done this dance before. He pretended there was nothing bothering him and she pretended he was right.

It was over an hour later when his tongue finally loosened up. They'd demolished a large pizza and watched half of *When Harry Met Sally*. It had been her turn to pick the movie tonight and he'd given her a long-suffering sigh even though she knew he liked the film too. Maybe not as much as she did, but he enjoyed it all the same.

Harry and Sally were singing *Surry With the Fringe on Top* in a Sharper Image store when Tyler pressed the pause button on the remote control.

"I've got something on my mind that we need to discuss."

Geez, finally.

"I thought so. I'm listening. Is everything alright?"

They were both reclining on a stack of pillows strewn on the floor in front of the television. Tyler sat up, rubbing his palms together in a nervous gesture.

"It's not but it can be," he replied rather ambiguously. "And I need your help. I know it's a lot to ask but you're literally the only one that can help me."

Jesus, this sounded serious. Even his expression was sober and frightening. Her heart lurched in real fear that he might be sick or dying or worse. He was the closest thing to a real home and family that she'd ever known.

"If you need a kidney or part of my liver, it's yours. You know that."

Did he need bone marrow? She'd give him that too. Anything as long as he'd be okay.

"I need your hand."

What? That didn't make any sense. He had two perfectly good ones attached to the ends of his arms. They were twice the size of her own and much stronger.

"My hand? I'm not following you."

His gaze dropped to the floor and then back to her, his blue eyes intense. "I need your hand in marriage, Billie."

The world stopped spinning on its axis and the noise of the outside world dimmed. All she could hear was a buzzing sound in her own ears and she was pretty sure that was the sound of her brain draining out of a hole in her skull.

Obviously, she'd heard incorrectly.

"Can you say that again?"

Her question had come out choked and mangled but then she was rarely this up-ended by Tyler. Normally he was as predictable to her as the tides.

"I need you to marry me, babe. The sooner, the better."

Is he pregnant? Wait, no. He can't be. Am I pregnant?

"That's what I thought you said."

That's when a horrible thought occurred to her. Had Tyler...fallen in love with her? Had he been carrying some imaginary torch for her all these years and only tonight had screwed up enough courage to say something... All unrequited love like the movie–

Whoa. This was Tyler Gaylord.

Not some lovelorn hero in a chick flick. She was

barking up the wrong tree if she thought he'd been pining for her ass all this time. Something else had to be at play here. But she had to be sure.

"I can't believe I'm asking this but...are you...you know...in..."

Shit, she couldn't even say the words out loud but he seemed to get the idea because his eyes widened and his face split into a grin. "Baby, relax. This is not a declaration of love and devotion here."

She could breathe again. "Whew. Well, that's a relief. You had me scared there for a moment."

His smile disappeared and that earnest expression was back. "But you know I love you, right? I'm just not *in* love. You know what I mean? I don't do the hearts and flowers thing. It's just not me."

Now she was annoyed. It was ego-deflating to hear him vehemently deny that he was desperately in love with her. Not that she wanted him to be, because she didn't. She and Tyler didn't have that kind of relationship. It might have been nice though if he had a little crush or something.

He'd never even tried to get her into bed. Not once since the day she'd met him. She was possibly the only women in the greater Los Angeles area he hadn't come on to. When she thought about it, it was kind of hurtful. She was attractive and had excellent hygiene. She was also conveniently located, living less than a hundred feet from where he slept.

"I got it," she replied curtly. "Now do you want to tell me - clearly, please - what's going on here? Since when do you want to get married at all, let alone to me?"

He held up his hands in surrender. "I can explain it but

please hear me out all the way until the end. This is important."

Gritting her teeth, Billie nodded. She had a million questions but she'd hold them all until he was done. Whatever was going on had Tyler rattled. She'd never seen him like this. He acted almost like he really did want to get married which she knew was pure bull.

Tyler Gaylord was many things. Handsome, sexy, talented, funny, sweet, caring, and a pain in the ass. But he definitely was not the marrying kind. He wasn't even the faithful kind.

He was Hollywood's quintessential playboy and he loved every minute of it.

CHAPTER
Five

TYLER HAD LAID out his quandary for Billie. He'd explained about the movie role, although they'd discussed it before and how much he wanted it. He'd explained about the director Ron Weller and how he didn't think a person could act in love unless they'd actually been in love, plus his preference for actors who had settled down and didn't party. Then to put the cherry on top of the sundae, Tyler had explained that the only person he could possibly stand to be around that much was her. He'd thought she'd be complimented.

"It won't even change things all that much, babe. You can even keep your last name if you want."

She was looking at him as if he'd lost his mind, which he was sure he hadn't. It was the smartest idea he'd ever come up with. It was perfect. She was perfect.

"What do you mean things won't change? Dear Lord, we'll be married." She shoved at his shoulder. "That's a change. A big one, idiot."

"It doesn't have to be a big change."

She shook her head, her eyes wide. "Have you even thought this through? I mean, I know you're impetuous but this is beyond anything you've ever done. Let me ask you this...after we're married...where will I live?"

That was a silly question. "With me, of course. Husbands and wives live together."

"So that would be a change. How about another question? Would I travel with you? Because that would be different."

Billie was throwing up roadblocks where there didn't have to be any. "Sure, if you want to. If you weren't working. Why wouldn't you travel with me? And you have traveled with me, Billie. You've visited me on several movie sets."

"So that would be another change," she stated. "Already we have two big changes. I'm sure there are more."

Why was she making this so difficult? Couldn't she see how this would help not just him but her as well? She hated to take any assistance in her career but being his wife would give her connections that could make all the difference.

"Billie, I know I'm asking a lot but I cannot lose this role. I just can't."

Cocking her head, she regarded him steadily. "Do you? Do you really and truly understand what you're asking because I'm not sure you get it. Marriage is a commitment even if as you say it won't be forever. It's still a promise that I would make to you."

Was she worried about not being allowed to date other

guys? Love and men had never been high on her priority list in the past.

"You're not even dating anyone, are you?"

That was apparently the wrong question to ask because her face turned red and she jumped to her feet to pace the small space.

"No, I'm not but you didn't know that for sure and you've already assumed that I'd say yes. Why on earth did you think I'd say yes to something like this, Tyler?"

Swallowing hard, he was beginning to see that she wasn't thinking about this as some run of the mill request. He knew it was major but she'd give him a kidney. Was a marriage license a much bigger deal than a kidney? "Because we always said we'd do anything for each other. This is much less of a risk than burying a body for me or giving me a vital organ. It's just a piece of paper, Billie."

Abruptly she stopped pacing, her fingers pressed against her temples. "It's marriage. Do you even know what that means? We'd get up in front of witnesses and say vows."

He was starting to see what it meant to her. "It wouldn't be forever."

"That makes it worse."

He threw up his hands. "Make me understand here because you've lost me. I'm asking you to marry me to help me get what is probably the most important role of my career. You wouldn't have to be married to me for the rest of your life. How many Hollywood marriages survive? Just a couple of years. I'll make sure you're well taken care of when it's over. Whatever you want. You name it."

Her face had gone pale and she took two steps away from him. "Are you trying to buy me, Tyler Christopher Gaylord?"

The shit had really hit the fan when Billie used his middle name. He was in some big fucking trouble and he needed to step carefully.

"It would be a business arrangement, baby girl, so of course you would be compensated. Think of it as the ultimate acting gig."

Sitting back down, she buried her face in her hands for a long moment before looking up at him. "Let me try this again. First, I'm upset that you told your publicist that we're engaged without speaking with me. It was high-handed and presumptuous. Pretty much all the things that you are. Second, despite my background and lackluster family situation, I do take something like marriage seriously. It's...sacred. You say vows in front of family and friends. You sign a paper and make promises. I'm not sure I can do that knowing I don't intend to keep any of them. Jesus, Tyler, your parents have been married like forty-five years. How can you take this so lightly?"

This was turning out to be much more difficult than he'd pictured.

———

Clearly Tyler had been hit on the head at some point during the day and now he was suffering from a serious break with reality. He wanted to get married. To her - Billie Oliver. But not for forever. Just for awhile. Just long enough to make a movie and promote it. Maybe attend a few award shows.

Billie wasn't a naive Hollywood virgin. She knew the drill. Relationships were often more business out here than emotional. Girls and guys calculated what and who could give them a leg up in the industry and they considered it the cost of doing business. She was proud of the fact that she hadn't slept her way into a role and she wanted to keep it that way.

But that brought up another question she was afraid to ask... Did he expect them to have sex? Was he planning to be faithful? Because Tyler Gaylord couldn't go too long without some intimate female companionship. She'd seen that with her own two eyes these last five years. He had a high sex drive. Like Mount Everest high.

Right now, his expression was contrite but hopeful. "Listen, I'm sorry that I told Garrett that we were engaged but it honestly never occurred to me that you would react like this. Shit, you're ten times more practical than I am, always thinking about business and being professional. I figured if I hadn't thought of this, you would have."

Tyler made a good point. It was something that she might have come up with and suggested, the difference being she wouldn't have put herself forth as a candidate.

"I admit it's not the worst idea in the world," she replied carefully, not wanting him to get his hopes up. The answer was still a resounding no. "But can't you hire someone to do this? I can think of a half a dozen actresses off the top of my head that would give their fake boobs to do this. Hell, they'd pay *you*."

He was already shaking his head no. "No way am I

going to get involved with some actress who is looking for the main chance. I've seen that go south more times than I can count. The only way I would do this is with someone I can trust implicitly. That's a short list, babe, and you're at the top of it."

As gratifying as it was to hear that, she wasn't going to marry him.

"Tyler," she began again, needing him to understand. "I love you. You know that, right? And I've always said that there isn't anything I wouldn't do for you, but I guess we found a limit. Marriage is in a whole other category, karma-wise. It's not something you play with even though I know here in Hollywood people do it all the time. I just can't vow to love and honor you until death do us part while at the same time planning our divorce a few years later, after you win your Oscar."

He sat across from her, placing his large hands on her knees, the warmth from his skin seeping through the denim of her jeans. "Babe, I love you too and no matter what you decide I always will. But I'm begging you here. Do you want me on my knees?" He dropped to his knees, making her want to climb over the back of the couch and hide. When he was like this he was hard to refuse. "I'll beg and plead. This role feels like it was written for me. I can feel this character in my bones and heart, deep down into my soul. If you don't want a contract that specifies an end date then we'll just play it by ear. Heck, we might even really enjoy being married to each other. We can have so much fun, babe. Even more than we have now because we'll be together. Parties, travel, movies. I'd love to work with you. We can do it all but you have to say yes."

For a moment she was tempted. The part about working with Tyler was something she'd always wanted. He was a consummate actor and she'd played opposite him when she'd helped him rehearse but never in a real, live production.

Reaching out, she cupped his face in her hands, tears pricking the back of her eyes. Disappointing Tyler was the last thing she wanted to do but how could she do something that deep down she felt was wrong? This wasn't how she'd pictured being proposed to.

"I just can't," she said softly, watching his expression fall. "I've never said no to you, Tyler. Not about something important, anyway, but today I have to do it. Marriage isn't a toy you take out to play with whenever you get the urge. It's a commitment that I don't take lightly. When I get married - if I ever get married - I want it to be because I can't imagine spending the rest of my life without that other person. I want them to be my soulmate, the reason I breathe and get up in the morning. I want to be head over heels, helplessly in love. I'm so sorry. So very sorry."

Sitting back on his heels, he gazed down at the floor. "I never realized what a romantic you were, babe."

Shrugging awkwardly, she swallowed the lump that had taken up residence in her throat. Her little speech had shocked her as well. "I guess I am. More than I knew."

Raising his head, their gazes collided as his fingers tightened on her legs. "I'd do anything to make you happy, Billie. I know I don't look it but I think I could be a decent husband to you. I'd treat you right."

He'd try but would old habits come back to haunt them? As one of the premiere movie stars in the world, rules simply didn't apply to him like they did to other mortals.

Standing, she rested her palm on the top of his head, struggling to keep the tears at bay. Saying no to the one person in the world who had treated her like family was tearing her apart. It would have been easier to give him part of her liver.

"I think you should go."

He also rose to his feet, his arms falling to his sides, his shoulders slumped in defeat.

"Promise me you'll think more about this."

It was almost funny if it hadn't been so tragic. "I doubt I'll think of little else."

Tyler turned and walked out of the cottage without another word but she knew this wasn't over. He hadn't reached the pinnacle of his career by being a quitter. Tyler Gaylord had more than his share of perseverance and grit. He'd be back after he thought of something else to sweeten the pot. She'd need to be ten times stronger to resist.

Or maybe he wouldn't come back. Maybe he was done with her. By saying no had she ruined the only good thing she'd ever had in her life? Had she just broken her own home?

CHAPTER
Six

WIPING away a few tears that had leaked from her eyes, Billie wandered into her tiny kitchen and dug into her chocolate stash that she hid behind the box of granola bars in the pantry. Tyler had quite the sweet tooth and would have devoured her dark chocolate candies if he'd known they were there.

Since she didn't smoke or drink, sugar was her only indulgence and she needed the comfort that chocolate always brought. Even when she was a child, a candy bar had been a decadent but rare treat.

He hates me now.

That might be a tad dramatic but he was disappointed. His expression had said it all and he'd left here sad and deflated. Apparently he'd been sure she would say yes and she couldn't really blame him in a way. The idea was practical and for Hollywood it wasn't all that outlandish. It was good business, really.

But...it sure as hell wasn't how she'd pictured being

proposed to. Like a merger or a real estate deal. There'd been no romance, no confession of feelings. Just a list of all the reasons they should and how they would both benefit. She'd been shocked by her own reaction to his proposition. The sensible, practical woman who pried him out of night-clubs and made sure he didn't eat his weight in candy would have said yes. Who knew she had this flighty, romantic little girl inside of her that wanted a prince on a white horse? Fat chance of that happening in Tinseltown.

Certainly there were good reasons for marrying Tyler. Career-wise she would benefit. He had all sorts of contacts in the business and another agency would quickly pick her up despite Ina dropping her earlier today. Personally, he was a good and kind man, generous to a fault. They had a great deal of fun whenever they were together, and scarily, they could almost read each other's mind. There was no lying or subterfuge between them. Tyler was honest as the day was long and she was too.

Maybe too honest, though. He'd never pretended to be anything other than what he was. A playboy. A partier. When he was working, no one put their nose to the grind-stone harder than Tyler did but when he was between pictures he liked to have fun. Sometimes with her and sometimes with the myriad of women that always seemed to be hanging around him. He was a chick magnet and he attracted all kinds. Even some crazy ones. She'd shooed more than a few of them away and called the cops on the ones that couldn't take no for an answer.

It pained her to remember when she'd first met him. His prior tenant in the guest house had decided to move to New York City to work on Broadway. She'd met Kyle at a kickboxing class and they'd hit it off. When he'd seen where she'd lived, he was appalled at the dangerous neighborhood and the high price tag. Immediately he'd given her a key to the guest cottage and told her she could move in at the first of the month. Desperate, she hadn't questioned it. So when Tyler Gaylord showed up at her front door while she was unpacking her dishes she'd been shocked.

Then scared he was going to throw her out.

Because Kyle hadn't told Tyler that he'd moved Billie in as a replacement. She'd been the one to tell Tyler about Broadway and how Kyle had hated where she lived and given her a key. She was sure she was going to end up on the streets but Tyler had simply nodded and said they'd try it out and see how it worked.

At first, he'd left her alone but after a few weeks he'd come down just to see how she was doing. She'd offered him a soda and they'd ended up talking all night. A friendship blossomed, mainly because she'd always been straight with him. She didn't ask him for money or favors and treated him just like he was one of the guys. No better and no worse. It was clear that he'd been hungry for that in his crazy, fame-filled life.

That was five years ago. As far as she knew she was still on probation.

There was also the little secret she'd harbored all of these years, and there was no sense in ever telling him. He didn't need to know.

The first six months she'd lived in the cottage she'd had a terrible crush on Tyler. She hadn't shown it, of course. In fact, she'd gone out of her way *not* to show it so she might have even been a little rough on him. He'd been handsome and sweet, a man who really listened when she talked. Something she hadn't been used to with her background. Her feelings had probably been inevitable when she looked back at that time. However, as she got to know Tyler more and more, her feelings had faded and them morphed into something far different and complicated.

He was difficult at times, and often more child than man. And the women... There were always plenty of them, although not one of them hung around too long. Somehow Tyler Gaylord had glided through his life with his heart untouched. While she thought of herself as a lovely person, she wasn't going to be the wonderful and amazing woman who somehow managed to get to his buried heart and make him fall in love. It just wasn't going to happen. She'd end up heartbroken and crying and she'd had enough of that crap for a lifetime.

It was better that they were friends only.

Now he wanted to throw off the delicate balance that they'd achieved. With marriage. He was so cavalier about the whole thing, thinking that everything would stay the same. It wouldn't and it could ruin everything. She just couldn't lose him out of her life. He was too vital to her happiness and well-being.

The ringing of her phone cut off her melancholy thoughts and she groaned when she saw the display. The same number as earlier. She'd been putting this off but she already felt like shit. She might as well go all the way and feel like hell.

"Hello."

"Billiie, thank goodness you finally answered. I've been calling and calling."

Connie, a childhood friend, sounded out of breath and shaken which immediately put Billie on alert. Frankly she never heard any good news from her old hometown.

"Hi, Connie. Sorry about that. It's been busy here. What's going on?"

She hadn't wanted to ask but Connie wouldn't call unless it was important.

"It's your sister, Sierra." Connie didn't bother with any more pleasantries and went straight to the point. "Brian beat her up again. This time it's real bad. She's got a broken arm and a black eye. A few broken ribs too. The shelter advised her to divorce Brian, change her name, and leave the state. You know, start a new life, but that costs a lot of money. They said she needs to disappear because he'll never leave her alone. The divorce alone will probably be thousands, plus you know he'll fight it tooth and nail. Then to get her set up in a new life with a new name... The social worker said that they have attorneys that might accept lower fees or a payment plan but it's still going to be expensive."

Sierra had a no good, loser husband she'd been with for about seven years. Billie had told her way back then that she needed to dump him but her sister was completely controlled by her infantile husband. Brian *needed* Sierra. He'd cry when she'd tried to break it off. He'd threaten to kill himself. Then she'd married the son of a bitch and things had gone downhill from there. Brian would get drunk, smack Sierra around, Sierra would leave and stay with Connie for a few days, and then Brian would buy flowers and apologize. Cue the cycle to start again.

"Will she really leave him this time? For real?"

"She says she's done and I believe her. This time he threatened to kill her and I think he means it."

Through all of this bullshit she was still Billie's sister, although Sierra might see it differently. The last time they'd been together they'd argued about Brian and Sierra had told Billie she hated her and to leave and never come back. Billie had been trying to convince her sister to come with her to Los Angeles. She'd failed and tried to put the past behind her, but she'd never quite put her sister in the lost cause category. She'd always had hope that Sierra might one day wake up, which was why Billie kept in touch with Connie.

If Sierra was ready to leave the bastard, Billie wanted to help her.

Billie had been saving up for the down payment on a new car. It looked like she'd be driving her 2002 Honda Civic awhile longer. It didn't help that she hadn't had a decent acting job in months. She'd been getting by on temp jobs and bartending at a local place on the weekends. Luckily Tyler charged her almost nothing for the cottage and he wouldn't have noticed if she didn't pay at all. Not that she would ever take advantage of that.

"I have three thousand dollars saved up. I can send that to help."

The impatient exhale of breath into the phone clearly said that wasn't good enough.

"You don't understand. Between the attorney's fees and the new life she needs to start, it's going to be more like twenty-five thousand. Probably more. She left the house with nothing but the clothes on her back. She needs everything new, plus that figure doesn't even include the medical bills and she doesn't have any insurance. Is there anything you can sell?"

More tears - this time for a different reason - squeezed through Billie's tightly closed lashes. Frustration warred with anger at the situation that had been festering for years. It might as well be twenty-five million. The only thing Billie owned was her car and that wasn't going to fetch more than a grand or two, and she couldn't even think of selling it. A person couldn't live in Los Angeles without transportation.

She had some clothes, mostly what Tyler had bought her over her objections, but she wouldn't get much for them.

There had to be some way but at the moment Billie had no idea what to do. She'd lived on the edge, paycheck to paycheck her entire life.

"I don't know what to say, Connie. I just don't have that kind of money."

"We have to do something. She can't go back to him, Billie. He'll kill her next time."

Billie had been saying that very thing for years. She was protective of her sister even though most of the time she tried to forget she had that other life in her past. She was all about living in the present. Even Tyler didn't know about Billie's family. She was pretty sure he thought she was an orphan. Most of the time he'd be right. Billie's mother had passed away after hitting a tree while driving drunk, and she didn't talk to Sierra any longer because that asshole didn't like for her to speak to anyone that might say something against him.

"Let me think on it. I'm sure there's something we can do."

Billie wasn't sure at all but it had all been dumped into her lap to be solved. It wasn't Connie's mess to clean up, Sierra wasn't capable at the moment, Billie's mother was in the great hereafter, so that just left Billie.

"Call me if you figure something out. It needs to be soon too because she's getting out of the hospital tomorrow morning. She has to give the attorney an answer in a few days plus he's going to want a retainer of some sort to keep working on the case. There's a social worker that can help us but we need to get a plan together."

Ending the call, Billie tossed her phone aside and stared up at the ceiling. She wanted Sierra to get away from Brian. She'd wanted that for years. Now there was someone who could help her with that but it cost big bucks. Money that she didn't have.

The fact was the Oliver family was fucked up. This was one of the big reasons why Billie didn't drink. She wanted to be in control at all times. Her mother had been addicted to booze and it had cost her everything.

It was up to Billie to do something. But what? Sell a kidney? It was the only thing of value she had.

Wait...a kidney.

A terrible, horrible thought came to Billie. One she didn't want to even think about.

What am I willing to do for my family?

CHAPTER
Seven

TYLER HAD SPENT the last several hours replaying the conversation with Billie over and over in his mind. When push came to shove she was far more important to him than a role in a movie - no matter how desperately he wanted it. While he didn't think there would be another game-changing part like that for him he also knew he'd never find a better friend than Billie. He was disappointed that she'd said no but her happiness and well-being was his top priority. He couldn't help it that he thought she'd be better off letting him help her instead of struggling for money and roles as if she didn't have any connections in Hollywood.

So now he was nursing a full-bodied Cabernet while trying to come up with ideas that might sway Billie's decision. If she wouldn't take anything for herself would she change her mind if he vowed to make a huge donation to the local children's hospital? They were both involved there personally, making appearances and reading to the kids.

Or perhaps he should simply leave her alone and think of another way to get the role. If Weller knew who Tyler truly was he might come around.

And pigs might sprout wings and fly over the Hollywood sign while TMZ reports it live.

Tyler wanted this role in spite of Ron Weller, not because of it. The man was definitely not an actor's director, worrying more about schedules and budgets than he did the creative process of filmmaking.

"You should really lock your door. Just anyone could come in."

Billie's soft voice pulled him from his reverie and he sat up from where he was sprawled on the couch and placed his wine glass on the coffee table.

"If we were married you could remind me to lock the door every night before we turned in."

Rolling her eyes, she sat down on the cushion next to his. "That's something to look forward to. Lock the door. Turn down the thermostat. Put out the cat."

This was the Billie he knew and loved. "We don't have a cat."

She curled up comfortably, her feet tucked underneath her bottom. "I guess we could get one, although I have allergies."

"Maybe a dog," he suggested, keeping the conversation light on purpose. Hope had once again flared to life inside of him but he didn't want to push and scare her off. "I had a dog when I was a kid."

"You never told me that."

He hadn't, but why was a long, drawn-out conversation that he didn't want to get in to. His past was one of the reasons he'd wanted this role so badly.

"His name was Scout and he was the best dog ever."

"Scout's a good name for a dog."

They simply sat there for awhile not saying anything but the silence spoke volumes for them. There was a tension that hadn't been there before. A question hanging in the air like a blinking neon sign that neither could ignore. Billie was the first to give in and speak.

"I may have changed my mind about your earlier offer."

She had Tyler's complete and undivided attention.

Caution. Proceed slowly.

"That's good news but it sounds like you still have a few reservations. Want to talk about them?"

He held his breath waiting for her reply.

"No contract," she stated firmly. "We agree to the details and shake hands like the friends we are. I won't have a contract in my marriage."

"Agreed," he said quickly. If all her demands were like this it was going to be easy.

"You have to promise you won't embarrass me in the press."

Stiffening, Tyler couldn't help but feel offended. "Do you honestly think I would do anything to hurt you, babe? Really?"

Billie shook her head. "Not on purpose, but sometimes your partying can get out of hand. And the women. There are always women, Ty, and there are always paps when the women are around. I don't want my name dragged through the mud because you were out with a couple of fans dancing the night away. You'll need to be discreet."

There wouldn't be any females once they were married but he was getting the idea that Billie wouldn't believe him even if he wrote it in his own blood. Actions were always more important to her. He'd simply have to show her that he knew how to behave. He'd promised her to be a good husband and he would be.

"Agreed. I would never do that to you. You have my word. Anything else?"

Shifting on the cushions, Billie chewed on her thumb- nail. "We only get married if we absolutely have to."

"I'm not following. What do you mean *only if we have to*?"

"Being engaged might be enough. If you get the part we can just tell everyone we're putting off the wedding until after the shoot."

Tyler didn't want to scare her any more than she prob- ably was already was but she needed to go into this with her eyes open. "Babe, I was actually thinking we would get married this fall. That would give us time to put together a kickass wedding but not so fast that people would think I knocked you up."

Apparently that thought hadn't occurred to her and her eyes flew wide. "Pregnant? Do you think some people will think I'm expecting?"

"Only if we hurry into the marriage. Besides, I'm not going to rob you of a great wedding, Billie. I remember what you said about wanting a fairy tale wedding and I'm going to give it to you."

Tyler was ready to fight with her on this. They weren't

going to slink away to Vegas or something even worse like they were ashamed.

"I do not remember ever saying that but I guess a fairy tale wedding is appropriate for a make-believe marriage. But still...if you get the part before the wedding, we could postpone it."

He could argue with her about needing her for film promotion when it was released and then awards season but he'd already won a major battle tonight. That was a fight for another day.

"Okay, is there anything else? So far you haven't mentioned anything that's a deal breaker for me."

Tyler watched as Billie's hands wrung together, turning the knuckles white.

"Fifty...thousand."

It took him a moment to realize she was talking about money because she so rarely would speak with him about anything financial.

"That's it?"

The question came out before he could stop it. Frankly when he'd mentioned giving her compensation for doing this he'd thought of a much larger number.

Like one million. Or two.

It was her turn to look offended. "I'm not a gold digger, Tyler. This isn't about the money for me."

Daring to touch her, he reached out and placed his hand over hers, prying the fingers apart. At the rate she was going she was going to rip all ten of them out one by one. Her hands were cold but what was that old saying? Cold hands, warm heart?

"That number is actually far too low, babe. It would be

an insult to the time and effort you'll be putting in on my behalf. Make no mistake, I know that I am the one benefitting the most from this and I want to make this more equal."

"I'm not asking for any more."

She never asked for anything and it was the number one issue they argued about. She never let him do shit for her. That was the first thing that was going to change when he got his ring on her finger. She was going to learn to accept a little help now and then.

"I know that but fair is fair."

He didn't like that she wouldn't look him in the eye. It wasn't like her at all and it made him slightly suspicious. In fact, she'd never even borrowed gas money from him so her naming a price had him worrying. Was she alright?

"Babe," he began cautiously. "Are you okay? Do you need anything? Are you...sick?"

Frowning, she finally turned to look at him. "No, why?"

"If you need money for an operation or—"

"Stop right there." She held up her hands. "I swear that I am healthy. I just need the money. Is it important as to why?"

No and yes.

No, Tyler didn't care what she did with it but since she barely spent any money at all it was surprising to hear that she needed fifty grand. Maybe she wanted a new car? He'd never let her spend her own money on a new vehicle. It would be his engagement present to her.

Yes, it had him concerned though. Had she picked up a gambling habit? He knew she didn't drink or take drugs.

"How you spend the money is your business, babe."

And something I'll figure out eventually.

She was twisting her fingers together again. "I'd like to have it as soon as possible, if that's okay with you."

Now he was in full-blown worried mode. She was avoiding his gaze and biting her lip. A sure sign she was keeping something from him.

"You know you can trust me with anything," he said gently, wrapping an arm around her shoulders and pulling her close so they were cuddled together on the sofa. "There isn't anything I wouldn't do for you, babe. Anything. Night or day."

Looking up at him with a pleading gaze, she exhaled shakily. "If you really mean that, then the thing I want you to do for me is to let this go. Don't ask me again why I want the money. It's...personal."

When Billie asked him like that there wasn't any way he was going to refuse her request.

"Then I won't," he replied, pushing a stray strand of hair behind her ear. "But I just want you to know that I'm here for you. No matter what. Even if you need something completely crazy like a husband."

A smile tugged at her lips. "That would be crazy. I need one of those like I need a hole in the head."

"We can start with fiancé and work from there." He pressed a chaste kiss to her forehead, something he'd done a million times before, but today it felt different. More like a promise than the comforting gesture it was meant to be. "I'll take care of you, Wilhemina. Please trust me."

Billie might be doing him a favor but he'd make sure she never regretted helping him. They'd have lots of fun, traveling and making movies together. Being married didn't have to change their friendship. It simply meant that they could spend more time with each other. This wasn't about love and passion and that's what made it so fantastic. This was simple, straightforward while those other emotions were complex and messy.

The best thing about Billie was that he wasn't in love with her.

CHAPTER
Eight

BILLIE DIDN'T KNOW what poor banker Tyler had roused out of bed in the middle of the night but she had fifty thousand dollars in her bank account first thing in the morning. He'd taken her seriously when she'd asked for it as soon as possible. She had been thinking *a few days*, but clearly he'd been thinking *a few hours*. Maybe he was afraid she'd back out, but she'd made her deal with the devil and she'd see it through no matter what. Of all the rotten things that could happen to a broke, aspiring actress in this town marrying Tyler Gaylord wasn't the worst. Heck, it wasn't even in the top one hundred of crappy stuff she'd seen. She believed him when he said he'd take care of her but she also knew that sometimes things happened in this life that he hadn't intended.

Padding into the kitchen, she poured herself a cup of coffee and sat down on the back patio of the little cottage to listen to the morning birds as they sang. The air was warm and dry but the sun felt good on her skin. It had snowed yesterday in Wisconsin. If she still lived there she'd be wrapped up from head to toe freezing her ass off.

At least now she could try and help her sister out. Maybe...just maybe...Sierra would finally leave the bastard and start a new life. Like Billie had.

Pushing thoughts of the past away, she instead thought about her new future. Replaying last night's conversation with the man that might just become her husband, she was more than a little mortified that Tyler had brought up the time she'd told him about her dream wedding. She'd lied to him last night. She did remember saying it. It had been when she was still starry-eyed and in love with him. She'd been his date for a wedding and they'd jokingly talked about what they wanted when they tied the knot. Tyler had said he wanted a beach ceremony and she'd said that she wanted a fancy wedding with all the trimmings like the ones she'd seen on television.

It had all seemed so glamorous, especially from her humble background. A big ball gown of satin and lace. Tons of flowers. A tiered cake taller than she was. A huge diamond ring and a handsome groom. An exotic honey-moon that would never end. She'd been a hell of a lot younger and less wise then. Now she was more worried about the man she'd marry than how she'd do it.

And she could do this. It wasn't how she'd planned her life but she'd learned long ago that sometimes fate took a hand. It had brought her here to this little abode and to Tyler. That had turned out better than she could have ever hoped. Now it was taking her in a different direction.

She truly did want to help Tyler, and she wanted to help her sister. This would accomplish both. All she had to do was keep her head on her shoulders and her feet firmly planted on the ground.

I can do this.

She just wished...

Tyler simply didn't understand her reluctance. When she'd imagined getting married - even engaged - it hadn't been a business deal. Marriage wasn't a game to be played with the press and the movie studios. It was serious. The good Lord knew she'd seen her mother take the commitment rather casually and that had been a disaster. How many men had wandered in and out of Sharon Oliver's life over the years? Dozens, at least. Some good but most of them had been losers, drinking just as much or more.

Billie simply wanted one good man that loved her more than anything. If she had that she wouldn't care about the ceremony or the reception.

The sound of familiar feet stomping through her house pulled her back to the present and her reality. She was officially engaged to Hollywood's biggest playboy. A man-child wrapped in a sexy shell. It was anyone's guess whether she and Tyler would even be speaking to each other in six months, let alone still be friends. But she hoped so.

"You didn't knock again," she said with a sigh as he stuck his head out of the sliding glass doors to her tiny kitchen.

"You're right I didn't." Scowling, his gaze raked her head to toe. "You're not dressed."

That wasn't precisely true. She was wearing a pair of soft cotton pajama shorts and a tank top along with a pair of white socks because her feet tended to get cold at night.

"I know I'm going to regret asking this but dressed for what? Did we have something planned today?"

Tyler had that look in his eyes. The one that said he did indeed have a day of activities planned and she simply had to go along with him. Except this time she couldn't really say no because...she did have to go with him. He was her fiancé.

He lifted her from the chair and placed her on her feet. "We have a busy day, babe. We need to get you an engagement ring and then start making a list for the wedding. Plus, we have to call my parents and tell them the news. They're going to be thrilled. They adore you. Then we have a meeting with Garrett to talk about some photo ops to get the public warmed up to the idea of me being a married man." Bopping her on the nose, he took her now empty coffee cup from her. "And we can't do any of that in your pajamas. You get dressed and I'll get you more coffee."

A ring. His parents. Photos. She'd known it was all coming but somehow she'd thought she might get a day or two to get used to the idea. No such luck. When Tyler did something he did it all the way. Full out and balls to the wall.

"I doubt your parents are going to believe this. Why don't you tell them the truth? Surely they deserve to know."

"They wouldn't understand but this will make them really happy. They're always telling me I should marry you."

To Billie's horror, they often did it while she was sitting right there. Still, it was nice that they weren't going to be upset about the engagement.

I still can't say wedding or marriage yet. I'll stick to engage-ment for awhile.

He led the way back into the house and poured her another cup of coffee, his expression wary. "Is there...is there anyone that you want to tell? You know...back home? Maybe an old friend or a distant relation?"

She'd never told Tyler about her family, content to let him think she didn't have any. It was far easier and she'd never wanted his pity. He came from loving parents and had a middle-class upbringing while her early years hadn't been nearly as idyllic. Billie was pretty sure he didn't even know where "back home" even was. She'd referred to the Midwest and her childhood in the vaguest of terms and he'd allowed it, seeming to understand that she didn't want to discuss it.

She had a few friends she wanted to tell and eventually she'd tell Sierra. If her sister was even speaking to her, which at this moment wasn't the case.

"Everyone can find out when the photos of you buying me a ring hit Twitter."

He looked like he might argue but then he nodded. "Whatever you think is best."

She took another fortifying sip of her coffee. There wasn't enough caffeine in the world for what they were going to do today. This was going to cause a frenzy in his fandom.

"Give me thirty minutes to get ready and then we'll go."

As if half an hour would prepare her for what was about to happen. All hell was going to break loose.

CHAPTER
Nine

THE MOST EXCLUSIVE jeweler in Beverly Hills lived up to its reputation. The private room in the back Billie and Tyler were ushered into was opulent but understated. Tyler made a mental note to thank his friend Sam Collins who had recommended the establishment. He'd called ahead and they'd been able to accommodate his request quickly. In an effort not to discuss prices in front of Billie he'd given the discreet manager his price range ahead of time. Nothing would be brought out for her to see that was over his outrageously huge budget. Nothing under it, either. If he knew Billie, and he did, she'd try and get out the door with the smallest, cheapest engagement ring this joint sold.

He was not going to allow that to happen. This ring was going to be photographed by dozens, if not hundreds of paps, and seen in magazines all over the world. He wasn't being immodest when he said that the wedding of Tyler Gaylord was big news. No one - himself included -

had ever thought it would happen. But here he was acting the role of besotted groom-to-be.

The manager, Harmon, who appeared to be helping them personally, offered up wine but Billie demurred. She didn't make a big deal about not drinking alcohol but he'd never seen her do it. There was a story there he was sure but he hadn't pressed her for it. He'd always assumed she had one or more parents who drank to excess. Not that he would know that, either. She was decidedly closed-mouthed about her childhood. That had been fine when they were best friends hanging out at Laker games but she was going to be his wife and he ought to know more about her.

Harmon, a slight man in an expensive suit, sat across from them, a big smile on his face. When Tyler and Billie left here, the man would have bragging rights that he'd outfitted the Hollywood golden couple of the year with their wedding rings.

"So did you have anything in mind?"

The question was directed at Billie but when she didn't answer immediately Harmon turned to Tyler, which wasn't much better. Tyler hadn't given it any thought other than he wanted her ring to make a statement.

"We want an engagement ring for Billie and wedding bands for the two of us."

Harmon nodded as if that cleared everything up. Maybe everyone came in here as clueless as he was. "Matching bands? Yellow gold? Platinum? White gold?"

Tyler didn't know shit about jewelry but he'd heard enough from his actor friends Max and Nate who were both married to know the basics. Platinum was the most expensive.

"Platinum."

Harmon's eyes lit up. "Ah, platinum. Excellent taste. Were you thinking platinum for the groom's band as well?"

Billie shook her head, finally joining the conversation. "Whatever he wants is fine."

They were back to him again. "I'm open to be persuaded."

That seemed to make Harmon happy so he pulled out a black velvet tray of sparkling diamond rings, each one more ostentatious than the last. "We have an excellent selection of platinum wedding sets but if you don't see anything you like today we can always design something for you and have it made. I can also assure you that these stones were ethically sourced. Did you have a particular cut in mind?"

Of course Billie didn't, so they spent what felt like the next ten hours looking at rings, although it was probably less than forty-five minutes. In the end, she had narrowed the selection down to two rings. One was a simple eight carat princess cut stone and the other was a smaller six carat emerald cut with small diamonds on the band. She kept going back to the smaller diamond but for some reason she wasn't ready to say it was the one.

"Do you like it, babe? Try it on again," he urged.

Nodding, she slid it on her finger and held it up for his inspection. He hadn't ever noticed her hands until now but they were small and dainty, with manicured nails polished in a light lilac shade. Yet he knew from personal experience that those same hands were strong and capable. He'd seen her take down a man in self-defense class and also helped him prepare an elaborate meal for their friends. It was that contradiction that fascinated him. One minute she was a young actress that needed his protection, the next she was a warrior who didn't need anybody.

"It's like it was made just for you," Harmon gushed. "There's a matching band for that."

The manager dug into a cabinet and pulled out another tray of rings. It only took a moment for him to locate what he was looking for and he slid it onto her finger before handing Tyler a larger, much heavier platinum band.

"I think this will fit you, Mr. Gaylord. Why don't you try it on?"

For a moment Tyler hesitated but then plucked it from Harmon's grasp and slid it on his own ring finger. The weight of the metal was more than he'd imagined and for a split second the fit was far too tight, almost cutting off his circulation before relaxing and allowing the blood to flow again. Except that rings didn't shrink and grow at will and this one hadn't budged on his finger. It had been all in his mind.

The fingertips of his other hand passed over the cool metal and he couldn't seem to drag his gaze away from the ring. There it was. Real and solid. He was really going to get married and he was going to do it with Billie. They would say vows and wear rings. They would belong to each other because of their promises and a piece of paper.

Maybe he should take this marriage stuff a little more seriously than he'd originally thought. She was right that it wasn't something you play with. It should mean forever ideally, although for him the thought was ludicrous. He could give her honesty, fun, happiness, material wealth, and fame. Wasn't that enough? In return, all he needed was her loyalty.

"Are you okay?" Billie's sharp tone broke through his daydreaming and he jerked his head up to gaze into her concerned eyes. "We don't have to do this today, you know."

Had she recognized his momentary panic? The heavy mantle of responsibility he would wear as her husband? She'd talked him out of getting a cat a few years ago because she hadn't been sure he could keep it alive. Now he was going to have a wife.

"It's fine. I was just thinking about how these would photograph. Is that the ring you want?"

Her fingers curled over the ring, covering it from his sight. "I know you probably want me to have the other one. It's bigger and will show up in pictures better."

It would but it was more important that she have what made her happy.

"So? Is that the one you want?" he repeated, a smile tugging at his lips. "If the paps can't see that ring I'll buy you a big necklace and earrings to go with it."

Harmon almost swooned but Billie just scowled, of course. "You'll do no such thing, and yes, this is the one I want." She pointed to the band on his own finger. "Is that what you want?"

Was it? Never in his life had he thought he'd be picking out a wedding band.

"It's okay but I'd like you to pick out my ring. Whatever you like."

It was a cop out but Billie did have great taste. She'd chosen the prettiest wedding set they'd been shown today.

Reaching down, she tugged off his ring and handed it back to Harmon. "I think Tyler needs something far more traditional. I think he needs a gold wedding band. Plain and old fashioned."

In a flash a yellow gold band, heavier than the last, was slid on Tyler's finger. Jesus, he'd feel good and married with this one. There's be no forgetting he was committed.

That's a good thing.

His phone buzzed in his pocket and for a second he thought to ignore it but then decided he needed the distraction. It was a text from his publicist Garrett and Tyler began to smile. A wedding ring wasn't so bad after all. He and Billie had been spotted on the sidewalk coming into the jewelry store and it was all over social media.

The campaign had begun. Bring on the rings and the preacher.

———

They ended up at a furniture store after ring shopping. Billie's finger was currently bare as her set had to be sized and it would take a few days, but already news of Tyler Gaylord's visit to a jeweler had spread through social media like wildfire. There were paparazzi waiting for them when they exited the shop and Harmon had been beside himself with happiness. It meant a bunch of free publicity for his store.

As usual, Tyler completely ignored the press following them and focused all of his attention on her. When he wasn't checking his phone, that is. He was in an especially festive mood today since his plan seemed to be working. Everyone wanted to know if the unashamed playboy was finally settling down.

"What are we doing here again?" Billie asked, keeping her head down as the sound of cameras clicking filled her ears. Once the doors closed behind them it was much quieter but she still had a feeling of unease like she was waiting for a shoe to drop. An expensive Manolo Blahnik or maybe a Louboutin.

"Married people get new furniture," Tyler said as if explaining himself to a child. "We're getting married so here we are."

That was all well and good but Tyler's home was completely decorated by a famous designer that had supposedly worked for royalty in London. What was Billie going to pick out? A new spice rack?

"Do you need new furniture?" she asked, trailing after him as he strode confidently through the store. "Are we looking for something in particular?"

Tyler stopped so abruptly she almost ran into the back of him. They were now in the bedroom furniture section. Oh shit. This was the part of the deal she'd been trying not to think about.

They were going to be married.

Maybe for two or more years.

Tyler wasn't going to go that long without sex.

Which was why she'd asked him not to humiliate her in the press but in the back of her mind she'd known this was looming. It would be easier if they simply slept with each other than with other people. She could already hear Tyler's voice in her ear saying that very statement.

"Pick something out." Tyler pointed to an old-fashioned four-poster bed in a dark oak. "How about this one?"

She needed to get out of here. Immediately, if not sooner. She simply wasn't ready to deal with this.

"Fine. Let's get that one."

Anything as long as they could leave.

Frowning, Tyler shook his head, urging her closer to the bed which suddenly took on so many other meanings besides getting a good night's sleep. "You didn't even look at it."

No, she hadn't and yet she was being plagued by thoughts of the two of them on that bed. Thoughts she shouldn't be having. This was Tyler. Her buddy and pal. Her crush was over long ago and now she made fun of his carnal pursuits. It threw her entire world into flux to think she might be one of them in the not too distant future.

Shrugging, she studiously kept her gaze on a cherry-colored dresser. "Sure, I did. It's fine. Whatever. Just a bed."

Tyler was scowling at her and then his forehead smoothed and a gentle smile took its place.

"It's just a bed, babe. It doesn't mean anything."

"Then it doesn't matter which one we choose."

Leaning down, his lips came so close to her ear she could feel his warm breath on her skin.

"Nothing, and I mean nothing will ever happen in that bed or in our house, or anywhere else for that matter, that you don't specifically want. This is all on your timetable, Billie. You're in charge whether it's two days, two weeks, or two years. So please pick something out that you like and feel comfortable with. I want you to be happy when you move in. I want you to think of it as your home."

As comforting as those words were - and they were - it was all a little too much. First the rings, then Twitter, and now a bed. It was far too intimate and she couldn't deal with any more.

Which is why she thought up an excuse that he might actually believe.

"I can't possibly make any more purchase decisions on an empty stomach. I'm starving here."

Smiling that smile that had graced millions of magazine covers, he placed his arm around her shoulders and led her back the way they'd come.

"Then I guess I better get you fed then. Burgers or pizza?"

After the morning she'd had? Both. With extra everything. She deserved it.

CHAPTER
Ten

BILLIE DIDN'T HAVE many friends in Hollywood other than Tyler but the minute the news of the engagement hit it felt like everyone she'd ever met or talked to crawled out of the woodwork, all claiming to be her best pal.

Dinah Everett, however, wasn't one of those people. She really was a good friend, although she and Billie didn't get to spend much time with each other. Dinah had finally made some traction in the acting business and she'd been working on a show for the BBC in London for the past six months. Unfortunately, the show had been cancelled so Dinah was back for an audition - a small part in a blockbuster.

So when Billie called Dinah with the big news, a lunch invitation was the most natural thing in the world. There was no worrying about whether it was because the person genuinely liked her or it was some ploy to get closer to Tyler. Dinah also wasn't much for the whole "being seen" attitude so they'd eschewed the trendy hot spots and ended up at a small, quiet cafe in East Hollywood that served great food.

"If we get photographed here this cafe is going to become the 'in' spot for celebrities," Dinah teased as she slid into her chair opposite Billie. "I put on an extra coat of mascara in case we end up on TMZ."

Billie had been on TMZ with Tyler several times, especially at the beginning of their friendship when the press hadn't been sure whether she was a girlfriend or a friend who happened to be a girl. When they'd discovered she was the latter instead of the former the gossip rags had left her alone.

No such luck now.

"I think I got out of the house without being seen," Billie grimaced. "It's like a feeding frenzy. You would think no one had ever become engaged before."

Dinah laughed, her eyes sparkling with mirth. She was a pretty girl with long auburn hair and green eyes. Casting directors called her cute but she said she wanted to be glamorous.

"Tyler Gaylord has never been engaged before and that's a big deal, my friend. Now tell me how this happened. You never mentioned anything was going on with Tyler when we talked, although I don't blame you for the secrecy. I'm sure you just wanted it to be private as long as possible."

Billie didn't like keeping things from her friends. Dinah was a good person and she deserved the truth but that wasn't an option. Not right now, anyway.

"It was kind of sudden," Billie explained as vaguely as

possible. "One minute there was nothing to tell and the next..."

Dinah could fill in the blanks with her fertile imagination.

Clapping her hands together in delight, Dinah sighed. "That's so romantic. Like in a *When Harry Met Sally* kind of way. So have you set a date yet?"

Fiddling with her napkin, Billie shrugged. "We've had a few discussions. Tyler suggested the end of summer."

"That's soon. You'll have to get moving on the wedding preparations, unless of course you're going to elope to Vegas or something."

"Tyler wants a big wedding."

Just saying it felt strange. Tyler wanted a big wedding. Or rather he said he wanted it for her.

"I would imagine if I'd waited as long as Tyler, I would want the whole kit and caboodle too. Are you on board with it?"

Excellent question. Billie had decided to just go with the flow when it came to all of this because she knew from experience that when Tyler had an idea in his head talking him out of it was almost impossible. Almost was the key word. If she really put her foot down he'd give in. If there was something that was important to her, Tyler always made sure it happened.

"I don't mind," she replied. "I'm sure this will be my one and only marriage so I might as well do it up right, but I really have no idea where to start. Where to have it, what to wear. We're going to need security too, I would imagine."

The logistics to keep it a secret or at least to keep out the paparazzi would be a nightmare.

"Billie, you can hire people for this. They have experienced wedding coordinators that will take care of all of it." Dinah tapped her chin in thought and then smiled. "I can dig up a few names for you. I swear every wedding I've attended in the last five years the wedding planner has shoved their business card in my hand. Do I look like I want to get married?"

Dinah had just come off a bad breakup with a guy in London who had *accidentally* slept with his neighbor. At least that was how he'd described it. And since it was an *accident,* he felt she ought to not make a big deal out of it and simply forgive him. Dinah had walked out and never looked back.

"No, you do not but you have a great idea. Tyler and I need someone who has done this before. Added together we have zero experience with planning a big event." Billie took a deep breath. "I was kind of hoping you'd be in my wedding. You know, my maid of honor."

Billie had considered her sister Sierra but with all her problems with her husband, the impending divorce, and basically hiding out she had her own problems. Big important ones that eclipsed color schemes and hors d'oeuvre selections. Sierra didn't need the added responsibility of looking at wedding dresses and planning a bachelorette party. Perhaps if Sierra was willing she could be a bridesmaid. Assuming Sierra decided to speak to Billie again after years of silence.

First I have to tell Tyler I actually have a family.

Dinah's mouth fell open in surprise. "I'd love to. But

don't you have any family you'd rather have? You've never talked about family but I assume you have some. You weren't hatched from an egg."

Had Tyler assumed that as well?

"I do have family but this isn't the right time to be asking them to put any energy into my wedding. They're dealing with their own issues right now and it's taking all of their attention."

"You know what? If you were marrying anyone else in the world, you'd have Tyler as your Dude of Honor. That's so cool, Billie. You're literally marrying your best friend. It's so romantic."

And weird. But then so was the thought of Tyler standing by her side when she married another man. Not one day since she'd met him had she thought about getting serious with someone else.

But I'm totally over him. It's just his personality. He consumes every waking moment just by being Tyler.

"Dude of Honor?" Billie tried to laugh it off. "I bet he'd love the title."

Dinah's brows shot up and her eyes grew wide. "Can you imagine the bachelorette party he'd throw for you? It would be epic."

It would be broken up by the cops and everyone loaded into a wagon to take them to jail.

"I think I'd pass on that," Billie replied. "The last party he threw at the house I had to shoo a horse off the patio."

"Your neighbors have a horse?" Dinah laughed.

"I only wish they did. I have no idea where it came from."

"I missed it all when I was in London. Are you two having an engagement party? I won't miss that."

All Billie needed was one more thing to worry about.

"Let me get a handle on the wedding and maybe we'll talk about it."

Dinah signaled the waiter for a refill on her drink. "I just have to tell you that I think you and Tyler are going to be very happy. Everyone has been rooting for you two to get together and now it's happened. Billie and Tyler forever."

Forever. Why did that sound so ominous?

CHAPTER
Eleven

WITH THE NAMES and numbers of three wedding planners in hand, Billie headed back home after her lunch with Dinah. Tyler's car was in the driveway along with a vehicle that Billie didn't recognize. A quick check of the calendar she was keeping for him until he found a new assistant told her it had to be the interviewer from a national men's magazine. Personally, Billie found the publication rather misogynistic with its half-naked pictures of simpering females on the cover and inside but Garrett insisted it sold movie tickets to the right demographic.

One of Billie's jobs was to help visitors to the door when their time was up. Tyler was fun and likable and people enjoyed his company. Sometimes that meant they didn't know when it was time to leave. It even happened with insiders in the movie business. All Billie had to do was stick her nose into their interview and remind Tyler of his next appointment.

Which he didn't actually have but it served to help the interviewer wrap things up. Tyler's image was one of a good guy and Garrett didn't like him to be the enforcer. Billie however didn't mind it a bit. So with practiced ease, she breezed into Tyler's living room but found herself rooted to the spot in front of the doorway.

Tyler and...some woman...were sprawled out on the floor in front of the television watching a movie, on their stomachs and way too close together. The female had a hand on Tyler's back as if giving him some sort of massage, which was of course ridiculous because he'd just had a massage the day before and could call up his favorite masseuse at will any time of the day or night.

He'd promised. Billie should have been grateful he'd stayed faithful for almost a week. It wasn't a record for Tyler but it still was longer than she'd imagined.

Stepping farther into the room, her pulse sped up and her stomach churned. She wanted to smack her erstwhile fiancé and then kick him in the balls. "There you are. Your next appointment is in ten minutes, Tyler."

Tyler was not a stupid man, although he sometimes liked to act that way so he had to know the situation looked bad. Lifting his head, he grinned when he saw Billie, rolling away from the female.

"Hey, babe. We're watching *Double Indemnity*. Tara has never seen it before."

Calm. Controlled. Cold. That's what she needed to be.

"Great film. Maybe we can lend her the Blu-Ray then."

Tara, all blonde and tanned like the perfect little Californian, took her sweet time taking her hand off of Billie's man. She even ran her fingers down Tyler's back as she did it, gazing at Billie the entire time.

A challenge? For real? He's newly engaged, bitch.

"That's a great idea," Tyler replied, leaping to his feet and snagging the disc from the player. "Tara, you can keep this one. I'll get a new one. Everybody who loves movies should have a copy of *Double Indemnity*. Consider it a gift."

A parting gift. Time to go.

Gathering up her laptop and purse, she accepted the movie from Tyler with a sweet smile.

"I don't mind returning it. Maybe we can meet for lunch or a drink so I can give it back."

Quirking an eyebrow at the man that had asked her to marry him only a few days before, Billie waited for his answer. Apparently, his survival instincts were strong because he chuckled and shook his head.

"Billie and I are going to be pretty busy with all the wedding preparations, the promo for the new movie, and of course the comic book convention. I won't have time to meet again, but I think you got some good quotes, right? And please keep the movie. Like I said, everyone should own a copy."

Tara pursed her glossed lips. "That's right. You're getting married. Have you set a date yet?"

Somehow Tyler had sidled to Billie's side and placed an arm around her waist, pulling her closer. He had to be able to feel how rigid she was holding herself and his fingers tightened on her hip. "As soon as I can get this angel down the aisle. I can't wait."

Billie inwardly gagged but to anyone else he sounded genuine.

Swinging her purse over her shoulder, Tara's smile had disappeared. "You're a lucky woman."

Tyler didn't let Billie reply. "I'm the lucky one. Billie is one of a kind."

"I'll just bet she is," Tara said in a low voice as she slipped past Billie and Tyler. "I'll send the draft to your publicist. Thanks for the movie. I'll see myself out."

"You're welcome," Billie replied with a saccharine smile, waving to the woman's retreating figure. "Have a nice day."

Moving away from Tyler, Billie headed into the kitchen to grab a bottle of water. She could hear the roar of an engine as the reporter sped down the long driveway, leaving her alone with her fiancé.

"You're mad," Tyler said flatly, dogging her heels as she went out onto his back patio and sat next to the pool, studiously trying to keep her emotions in check. Yelling wouldn't help the situation.

"Why would I be mad, Tyler? Have you done something that would make me angry?"

She hated this passive-aggressive bullshit and it wasn't her style in the least, but then she'd never been the bride to be of a major movie star before. Was it expected that she'd turn a blind eye to his flirtations?

Fuck that.

"Don't. Just don't." He sat down on the edge of her lounge chair. "Since when do you hide that you're pissed at me? Just say it."

Taking a sip of the cool water, she ran through her options. She could, indeed, chew him a new asshole or she could just let this all go. They weren't really together, after all.

But she couldn't let it go and she didn't want to examine why too closely.

"I'm pissed at you."

He inched over a little more, crowding her on the lounger. "Now we're getting somewhere. You're mad about that woman but you have to know that nothing was going on. Hell, I'm not attracted to her at all. It was just business. I gave the interview and then she wouldn't leave. I was happy when you showed up."

It was probably all true. Women came on to him all the time and he barely acknowledged it. He was definitely a player but even Tyler Gaylord couldn't fuck every single female that was interested. He had to have time to work, sleep, and eat too.

"She had her hand on you," Billie said through gritted teeth. "You said you wouldn't embarrass me. Just so you're aware, that's embarrassing. She thinks you're available."

"I can't imagine how she could," Tyler declared with a shake of his head. "I spent two hours telling her how amazing you were and that I couldn't wait to get married. As for her hand being on me, she'd just done that when you walked in and I frankly didn't know how to get her to stop without making it a humiliating moment. For her. Garrett doesn't like that shit."

The only reason Tyler would spend so much time extolling Billie's virtues is because he was trying to get that meeting with the director. He had to persuade everyone in Hollywood and beyond that he was deeply in love.

"You've never been engaged before. I think Garrett

could cut you some slack on pushing away grabby females when you're supposed to be committed to one woman. That's the point of all of this bullshit, isn't it? We're supposed to be convincing the world that Tyler Gaylord, the biggest man-whore on the planet, has finally settled down with one person."

Her voice had gone up quite a bit at the end, telegraphing her tumultuous state of mind. Normally she was the calm one in their relationship but she didn't feel relaxed in the least.

"Because honestly if you can't extricate yourself out of that kind of situation," Billie went on. "I just don't see how this is going to work at all. Women throw themselves at you a dozen times a day. Am I supposed to just stand there while they hang all over you? Because that's crap, Tyler. You need to man up and step away. I won't let you make a fool of me. I'd rather give the money back and forget all about this."

Except she'd already sent the money to her sister so she couldn't give it back.

His hands came up and cupped her cheeks so she had to look at him, his face inches from her own and his skin rough and warm.

"Listen to me," he said, urgency in this tone. "I would never do that to you. You're my best friend, Billie. You're the most important thing in my life other than my career. I'd walk in front of a bullet for you. "

Swallowing hard, she nodded. "A fake Hollywood bullet."

His hands fell away and she instantly missed the contact. "Are you still mad?"

She couldn't lie. "Kind of. I'd just like to remind you that I didn't ask for any of this. You begged me to do you a favor."

"Because you're the only woman in the world that I trust. Other than my mother." His brow was furrowed and his lips turned down, his expression sad. "But I think you don't trust me. At least not the way I trust you. That hurts, babe."

Tears burned the back of her eyes and her stomach churned. Hurting Tyler wasn't what she'd set out to do. He was the one person who had brought stability into her world. He was as close to home as she would ever get, and when she was thinking straight, she knew in her heart he would never hurt her on purpose.

"I do trust you."

"No, you don't, but that's my fault. It's mine to fix, and I will."

That he cared to do it at all overwhelmed her. Her own family hadn't cared this much.

"How?"

Chuckling, he gave her a lopsided grin. "Now that I don't know. I'm not famous for my brains, baby girl. I'm just pretty."

"Too handsome for your own good."

"Mom says that to me all the time," Tyler sighed. "And she's always right. You are too."

"I know. I got it from her."

Levering to his feet, he nodded toward the house. "I'm going to get changed and go for a run. Want to go with me?"

Normally she would and she ought to. The exercise

would clear her head and drain any residual anger, but then she had a better idea. Peace and tranquility coming right up.

"Actually, I think I'm going to go to the yoga studio down the street. They have a class starting in about forty-five minutes."

She thought he might argue with her but he simply nodded and loped back into the house, leaving her alone. Stretching out her legs, she tipped back her head so the sun warmed her face. It felt good and calming. Summer had always been her favorite season and here in Los Angeles it was pretty much summer all the time. Those long, cold winters back in Wisconsin were still all too fresh in her mind. She'd never been able to get warm. The house had always been freezing and she'd been sick more than she'd been healthy. Day after day, week after week, month after month of being nothing but miserable, sick, cold, and hungry. It wasn't a shock that Billie had chosen somewhere pleasant to run off to.

Would she have been as upset with Tyler if she wasn't already emotionally drained? Between her family and the wedding plans Billie didn't know if she was coming or going. She was constantly worried about whether Sierra was safe, and then this...relationship with Tyler. She'd always been able to handle stress but she might have reached her limit.

She didn't have the luxury of falling apart, however. People were counting on her and it was her job to be the practical one. She'd gone into this with her eyes wide open. Hadn't she?

It was too late to back out now. They'd have the best

damn wedding ever and Tyler would win an Oscar for the film role he desperately wanted. Everything was going to work out.

A Hollywood ending...completely made up and not a bit real.

CHAPTER
Twelve

SWEAT POURED down Tyler's back as he ran along the trail in Coldwater Canyon Park. The weather was warm and dry, perfect for a good workout, and he pushed himself to run harder and faster. He wanted it to hurt, not just because he knew he was getting a good workout. No, he wanted it to hurt because he'd inadvertently hurt Billie and she was the last person in the world he wanted to do that to.

He'd meant it when he said she was the only woman besides his mother that he trusted. That she'd been hurt by his carelessness was inexcusable. He hadn't thought the pretty reporter's actions were a big deal. Women came on to him all the time and he didn't think much about it. Unless he was interested, which in this case he wasn't. Her hand on his back hadn't seemed important, but it had been important to Billie and that meant it was important to him. He could see her point. Even though he knew it was meaningless, other people - the reporter included - wouldn't understand.

Because the one thing he'd learned since becoming famous was that the people around him tended to make his every action about them, even when it couldn't possibly be. They thought his smiles were for *them* specifically, that his thank you speeches were gratitude for something *they* had done. When he took selfies with them it was because he wanted to be closer to *them*, get to know *them*, become friends or more. There were many people in Hollywood who took credit for Tyler's success but they weren't anywhere to be found when blame needed to be doled out.

But not Billie. Even when he was specifically thanking her for some wonderful kindness she didn't make it about herself. That's why he trusted her. She didn't want anything from him. Well...except for fifty grand. She'd wanted that and the why was still bugging the hell out of him. He'd figure it out eventually. In the meantime, he had some groveling to do.

Gasping for breath, he stopped and bent over, his hands on his knees. His lungs hurt and the sweat dripped into his eyes, but he was smiling at the pain. He was only halfway through his run but it had served its purpose. He had an idea of how to make things better with Billie.

———

Tyler wasn't quite finished when he heard Billie's footsteps in the hallway. It turned out both he and Billie had more clothes than he'd thought and with all the calls he'd received about the upcoming promo tour it had taken him longer than he'd planned to move them.

"What are you doing?"

Billie stood in the doorway of his bedroom. Frowning. Considering the bed was covered with her clothes he would have thought it was obvious.

"Moving you in."

Wearing a casual track suit over her yoga outfit, her hair was clipped up and her face was devoid of makeup. She must have come upstairs straight from class. Her eyes widened and she finally seemed to notice the stack of garments on the mattress.

"Moving me in?" she repeated, giving him some serious stink eye. "I don't think I'm following you."

He hung up a handful of her sundresses in the huge walk-in closet before answering.

"When I went for my run I thought about what you were saying. How we might not be a real couple but people certainly are going to perceive us as one. I want you to know that you have my loyalty and I also want everyone else to know it. How could they possibly believe it if you were still living down in the guesthouse? We're a couple now and I agree that we need to start acting like it. So I moved all my stuff into one of the spare rooms and I moved your things in here. I want you to feel like this is your home, Billie. I think it might go a long way toward making you feel like you can trust me. That you're important."

Her mouth had fallen open and she didn't seem to know how to answer so he decided to help her a little bit.

"Are you still mad?"

She shook her head. "No."

"Do you hate me?"

A smile bloomed on her pretty face. "No."

"Do you wish you hadn't agreed to help me?"

Her gaze softened at his query. She was such a gentle touch but she tried to pretend she was tough.

"No."

"I just want to make you happy, babe. I know that I don't know shit about love and relationships but I'm trying."

"I know," she said softly. "Did you really move out? That doesn't make any sense, Tyler. Why didn't you stay here and I could move into a guest room?"

He'd thought about that briefly but it hadn't seemed right. "I want you to feel like this is your home so putting you in a guest room wouldn't solve that. You're not a guest, you're my fiancée."

"So now you're the guest?"

He shrugged. "I could sleep on concrete, you know that. It doesn't matter to me. Besides, we already know that this is my home. Now we need to convince you that it's yours too. What do you think? I'm separating your clothes by type. Slacks, blouses, dresses, formalwear but if you want I could do it by color or something."

Tentatively, as if there was a monster in the closet, she stepped closer and peered in. "Oh my God, you're really organizing things. I don't usually bother with that."

He'd noticed that when he retrieved her clothes. How she found anything he wasn't sure. Because he had so many clothes for different occasions he had to be organized. A former assistant had set up his system so all he had to do was stick to it.

"I think you'll see this is easier. You'll be able to find things much faster."

She pulled a face, laughter bubbling from her lips. "You can just say it. I'm a slob. I have no organizational skills whatsoever while your wardrobe is catalogued on index cards."

"I have many more clothes than you do, which by the way I left quite a bit here in the closet. I only moved the clothes that I wear a lot but there's still plenty of room for your things, although that might not be the case six months from now. When that happens I'll move all of my stuff out or we can take over one of the spare rooms and have a giant closet for two built."

Billie appeared dazed, which wasn't her usual demeanor. "I can't believe you did this for me."

"Technically, I'm not done yet."

Her brows shot up and she groaned. "Wait one cotton pickin' minute. Where is my underwear? Tyler Gaylord, did you run your grubby paws all over my panties? You pervert."

Closing his eyes, he laid his hand on his heart. "It was almost a religious experience. I swear angels sang in the distance and a white light shone brightly like a halo around your undergarments."

"That was your dead relatives warning you not to do it and that I'd kill you with one of your golf clubs." She slugged him in the shoulder with one of her fists but not hard enough to really hurt. "I can't believe you were up to your elbows in my lingerie drawer. Ick."

He managed - barely - not to remind her that in a few months he was going to be her husband and he'd have his grubby paws on more than just her panties. In the last few days he'd found that the idea of sharing a bed with Billie was something he was looking forward to.

Like... a lot. He'd always been attracted to her, but of course he'd never acted on those feelings since they were buddies. But now it was different. He was supposed to want to have sex with her and that had freed a whole bunch of carnal feelings that he'd been keeping deeply buried. Way deep. Now, however, they'd popped up out of the ground like vampires or zombies.

Tyler loved giving Billie a hard time and she always returned the favor but he was going to have to come clean. "As George Washington would say, I cannot tell a lie. I have all of your hanging clothes moved into this room plus all of your folded ones like shorts and t-shirts, but I saved your lingerie drawer for last. Your unmentionables remain untouched but mentioned. After I finished these I was going to make that one last run down to your house."

Blowing out a breath, she rolled her eyes. "You just saved your own life. I will do it myself." She turned to walk out but paused. "You know this doesn't solve anything, right? I mean, it helps and you were sweet to do it but the issue is still there."

She knew the truth as well as he did. "There are women who want me for all the wrong reasons but I don't care about them."

Her chin lifted defiantly. "But you'll sleep with them anyway. You'll take what they offer."

"I *took* what they offered. Past tense. I slept with them,

but you know that I never made any promises to them. They always knew it wasn't serious for me. I never led any of them on. But I made a promise to you and I intend to keep it."

Her shoulders slumped in defeat. "It's still more complicated than this."

"Trust always is," he agreed without hesitation. "It's a start, though. I begged you to help me and you said yes. I won't let you down. Just like I know you won't let me down."

"I just wish–"

She broke off, shaking her head.

"You wish what?"

"I wish," she sighed. "That you understood that more is going to change than my last name. You're taking this so casually as if everything is the same. It's not the same, Tyler, and you don't seem to see it. It's hard to trust someone that is in deep denial. Our lives are changing right before our eyes and you're pretending it isn't happening."

He didn't know what to say to that. Sure, things were changing a little but it wasn't the end of the world. The main part of their lives was staying the same.

"You act like nothing will ever be the same. You say you don't regret helping me but your actions don't match your words, Billie. If you want out, just say it and stop acting this way. Hell, the world wouldn't blame you for breaking off our engagement. They think I'm a pussy-hound who can't be trusted with the female population so you dumping me will fit right into their narrative."

He could hear the tabloids sharpening their knives.

They'd like nothing more than for him to be humiliated and shamed.

"I don't want to dump you, I just want you to understand that things are going to change. People are going to treat us differently. We might even treat each other differently."

He threw up his hands in surrender. "If I admit that you're right can we move forward? Billie, I want us to be happy but you have to meet me halfway. I'll stop looking at everything as perfect if you stop trying to only see all the pitfalls."

Her expression softened and she turned to look into the closet again. "You did a nice job organizing this."

"I'm not done yet. Why don't you get the rest of your clothes and we'll finish this together? Then I'll take you out to dinner."

From the smile on her face she wasn't going to say no. "We'll end up on Instagram."

That was pretty much a given these days.

"Fuck 'em. Let's just live our life and not worry about what other people are thinking or doing."

A novel concept in image conscious Hollywood. Dealing with people's perceptions of him was a full-time job, one he was happy to let Garrett do. Tyler just wanted to work and be happy. He wasn't all that concerned about whether some nameless, faceless person reading a tabloid rag somewhere approved of who he was marrying or what he was wearing. He'd seen other actors who did and it only served to make them crazy and burned out.

"I want a cheeseburger. And fries. And cheese on my fries."

Food wise, they really were a bad influence on each other.

"And a hot fudge sundae," Tyler said, wrapping his arm around Billie and leading her to the bedroom doorway. "Now go on and get the rest of your clothes so we can go eat. Now I have a craving for chili cheese fries."

Watching her retreating figure, Tyler heaved a sigh of relief. He'd headed this small crisis off at the pass but he had a bad feeling that this was simply a battle and not the war. There would be more and he only hoped he'd figure out how to handle his soon-to-be wife. He needed her...more than she needed him. Making her happy meant that she wouldn't back out of their deal, but even more she deserved to be happy. She'd always been there for him and he was determined to be the same.

First on the list had been moving her in. Second? A boost to her lagging acting career. She'd kick up a fuss and tell him she didn't want the help but he wouldn't take no for an answer. Tyler was going to give Billie her dream. He'd make her a star.

CHAPTER
Thirteen

TYLER GULPED down a glass of orange juice as his publicist droned on and on about the upcoming movie promo tour. He and Garrett were meeting this morning out on the patio and he wasn't sure what the point of this was, to be honest. He'd done a myriad of these events and they were pretty much all the same.

Smile pretty for the cameras. Shake hands. Say complimentary things about the cast and director. Talk about how great the studio support for the movie had been. Gush about the beauty of the locations and how nice the locals were. Be humble when asked about any awards he might win for the role. Don't get too drunk at the parties. Smile some more. It wasn't rocket science, so he wasn't too sure why Garrett felt the need to go over tiny details that Tyler didn't give a shit about and didn't affect him. Time to cut to the chase.

"I get it," Tyler cut in, stopping the unending flow of words from Garrett's lips. "You know, I've done a few of these tours in the past. I've even done a few specifically for the *Thunder* franchise. Are they doing something new and different this time?"

His face turning red, Garrett cleared his throat. "No, not really. I just... Listen, I wanted to talk to you."

"That's all you've been doing for the last thirty minutes."

Garrett exhaled noisily and rubbed his chin, his gaze darting all over the screened-in patio but never quite looking Tyler in the eyes. "I want to talk to you about something else."

"Then talk. You've never spared my feelings in the past so let's not start now."

Luckily Garrett had caught Tyler in between work projects so he was relaxed and patient. If it had been forty-eight hours or less before the tour or the start of a movie, the reaction might have been much different.

Opening his briefcase, Garrett pulled out a manila file folder. "When you told me that you were going to ask Billie to be your wife...well...I thought I'd better do a thorough background check on her. You know, make sure she doesn't have any major skeletons in the closet that could come out and bite you in the ass later and ruin your image and career."

Tyler's blood ran cold and a muscle jumped in his jaw. The mere idea of Garrett digging into Billie's past looking for dirt infuriated him. He shouldn't have taken it upon himself to do this without discussing it with Tyler first.

"I should fire you right here and now," Tyler said through gritted teeth. He fisted his hands under the table and didn't even bother to try and look cool and unbothered. He was pissed as hell and he wanted his publicist to know that he'd fucked up royally.

"I did it for you," Garrett replied, holding his hands up as if to ward off a punch in the face. "It's my job to protect you, Tyler, and I take that seriously even if you don't. You've worked hard for your success. Do you want to do something stupid that will ruin it all?"

Regarding the folder like it was a poisonous snake, Tyler pushed right back. "Are you saying you found something out about Billie that would ruin my career? Because I seriously doubt it. I've known her for the last five years and she leads a boring, quiet life. Hell, I've been in much more trouble than she has. You should be lecturing me about ruining my own career."

"I do on a fairly regular basis," Garrett said, shaking his head. "But I'd be derelict in my duties not to check Billie out. Yes, you've known her for the last five years but what about before?"

"What about it?" Tyler had had just about enough of this. "If it's that far into the past who really gives a rat's ass? Did you find out she's secretly a drug dealer? No, wait. Maybe she's a high-class madam for an escort service in her spare time. Can't be that. It must be that she's secretly a genius computer hacker that just pretends to like expensive shoes. I can't believe you went behind my back and did this. I thought you liked Billie. She deserves better from you, man. She's made your job a shitload easier these last five years, that's for sure."

Garrett looked like he wanted to cry but Tyler wasn't going to cut him any slack. What he'd done was dog dirty. "I know she has and I appreciate it. I adore Billie, you know that. But you pay me, Tyler. My first loyalty is to you."

"Then you shouldn't have done this," Tyler shot back. "I never asked you to."

His publicist and friend simply nodded. "No, you didn't but I did it anyway. I have to live with that."

That folder was still sitting between them.

"I can't believe you can even look Billie in the eye after this," Tyler said. "She really liked you and she was always on me about listening to you. Do you think she'd tell me to listen to you now?"

His expression sober, Garrett nodded. "Actually, I think she would. She'd want the best for you."

"She is the best. She's the best person I've ever known." He pushed the file back toward Garrett. "I don't care what's in there. It won't make a difference. We're already engaged and we're going to be married. Whatever you think you've found doesn't matter."

Garrett pushed the folder back toward Tyler. "I'm not saying you end things but we can mitigate any damage–"

"Just fucking stop," Tyler grated, trying hard to control his anger. He didn't want to be mad at Garrett but what he'd done was beyond the pale. "What damage? Are you saying you found something on Billie? I don't believe that."

"Look through what I've found and decide for yourself." Garrett tapped the file. "You don't know everything about the woman you're about to marry, Tyler."

Tyler was well aware of that fact but he also knew without a shadow of a doubt that he could trust Billie with his life. Her integrity was far better than his own. There might be something in her past that wasn't shiny and

wonderful. The way she avoided talking about her childhood was a huge clue, but that didn't mean she wasn't a
good person.

"Whatever I need to know, Billie will tell me. I'm sure of
it. I don't need your file of skeletons. What human being
could stand up under the scrutiny that the public puts
people through? I've got a few bony bastards in my closet
too, remember?"

"Yours are minor," Garrett argued with a sigh. "Billie–"

"Don't," Tyler shook his head. "I will not sit here and
hear a word against her. Not when she's not allowed to
defend herself. How in the fuck do you even know what's
in that folder is true?"

"It's true," Garrett said quietly. "It's not horrible but I
just think you should know. Before you marry her. Before
some reporter finds it and then we're on our back foot
trying to defend it in the press. That's all I'm asking, Tyler.
Just be aware of it."

His publicist pushed back his chair and stood, looking
like there was a hell of a lot more he wanted to say but
Tyler was in no mood.

"I'm leaving that with you." Garrett nodded at the
folder. "Read it. Don't read it. Whatever. But I'm of the
opinion that you should know more about Billie than what
cheese she likes on her hamburger. You're one of the
biggest movie stars on the planet. The films you've made
are some of the highest grossing in history. You're riding
high, my friend, but don't get too comfortable. There are a
lot of people that would love to take you down to the level
of us lesser mortals. They'd love to make your life difficult
and drag you through the mud whether you and Billie

deserved it or not. When someone is as successful as you are, you're a target. I'm just trying to protect you. Don't shoot the messenger."

Scraping his hand down his face, Tyler suppressed a frustrated groan. Garrett was only trying to help but he still should have talked about this before he did it.

"I appreciate what you're trying to do but whatever is in this file? Billie will tell me. I know she will."

Garrett gave him a crooked smile. "Maybe you're right. I hope you are."

"You think I'm making a mistake. Marrying Billie."

"Actually, I think it's the smartest thing I've ever seen you do," replied his publicist, that smile growing wider. "She's a hell of a woman and the only one that can handle you. I'd get her down the aisle as soon as possible."

That didn't make any sense.

"I don't understand you. If you think that, then why this?" Tyler poked at the folder on the table. "If you want me to marry her what's in here can't be all that bad."

"She's not an assassin for the Mafia," Garrett mocked. "All I'm saying is the press is going to dig around in her past and we should be ready. They'll take any youthful indiscretion and blow it out of proportion. I also think you have a right to know about your future wife's past."

Tyler shook his head. "Listen, it's not that I disagree with you. It's just this wasn't the way to go about it. You probably don't know but I've never actually asked her about her life before I met her. I should probably try that first, don't you think?"

"Are you going to ask her?"

"Eventually." Tyler shrugged as if it didn't matter to

him in the least but he had to admit his curiosity was peaked. What was in that folder that Garrett was so fired up about? What did he think Tyler needed to know? "We'll talk. I'll tell her my secrets and she'll tell me hers. It'll happen in our own time."

Although that moment was rapidly approaching. His publicist had a valid point. The press wasn't going to be easy on Billie. Or him. He was a target and he'd pulled her into his orbit, so now she had a bullseye smack on her forehead too.

Garrett turned and left, leaving Tyler sitting at the patio table with the folder. A file filled with details about Billie's life. Maybe even the reason she'd needed the fifty thousand. Because he was her best friend he wanted to know everything about her, but he also wanted to respect her privacy. If he knew anything about Wilhemina Oliver it was that she was a straight shooter, as honest as she could be. If there was an incident that he needed to know about, she'd tell him. She knew this business as well or better than he did. In the meantime, this folder was far too tempting and also kind of sleazy. He couldn't violate her trust like this.

Picking it up, he strode toward his office at the front of the house. He'd bury it in one of the drawers there. Out of sight, out of mind.

However, he needed to add one more thing to their wedding checklist. Ask about her past and then talk about his. It was far past time that they learned some of the more personal details about each other. After all, she was going to be his wife, maybe for a long time. If they had fun and the relationship was good, did they even need to get a divorce? Garrett was right. Tyler should marry Billie as soon as possible. Good thing they were meeting with the wedding planner in a few days.

Another item on his to-do list. Give Billie the wedding of her dreams.

CHAPTER
Fourteen

THE NEXT FEW days passed quickly for Billie as they prepared for Tyler's promotional tour for his last *Thunder* movie. It seemed like forever since he'd wrapped filming but the release was almost upon them. She'd thought Tyler might be sad to say goodbye to his famous alter-ego Bobby but he seemed fine with the end of the movie franchise. There might be other installments but Tyler's contract was up and he wouldn't be a part of any future films.

As a newly engaged couple, she and Tyler would be traveling to New York City, London, and Toronto in addition to the premiere in Los Angeles. That meant she needed clothes, which had started a whole new argument with her movie star fiancé. He'd insisted on purchasing clothes for her along with all of the accessories like shoes, handbags, and jewelry. She'd said *no* of course. She paid her own way.

Tyler wasn't one to give in easily, however, and he'd argued that the only reason she needed the clothes was because of him and the movie. Therefore, he should pay for it all. They'd gone around and around about it until they'd both been red in the face. Tyler had pulled the marriage card at the end saying that he was going to be her husband and her money was his money and his money was her money. That was all well and good except she didn't have any money so it was hardly fair.

He'd opened his mouth after she'd said that as if he was going to point out that she did indeed have money. Fifty grand worth. But instead of saying anything he'd stayed silent, making her feel more guilty than ever. She had to find a way to tell him about her family, but so far every time she'd tried the words simply wouldn't come.

Eventually, she'd given up because it was easier than explaining what she'd done with the money and he'd made a valid point whether she was ready to admit it or not. They were a couple now - albeit a make-believe one - and couples shared things. Couples did nice things for one another and helped each other. It would have been churlish to refuse. It did make her feel slightly better when he told her that a famous designer had offered to dress her for the events and parties. At least Tyler wouldn't be footing the bill for expensive dresses she'd only wear once.

This morning, however, she had a renewed sense of urgency to come clean about where she'd spent the money. If they were going to be - heaven help both of them - husband and wife, she was going to have to part with a few personal details no matter how distasteful.

They'd gone for a run early this morning and then shared breakfast on the patio before she took a shower and dressed for the day. There was still one small obstacle to talking with Tyler and that was their appointment this morning. The wedding planner was coming over to talk to them, making this entire situation even more real than it already was. It felt like a runaway freight train speeding down the tracks and she was standing in its way holding up a useless sign that said *Slow Down*. The massive train didn't give a crap that she was nervous. It had a life of its own, pretty much like her deal with Tyler. With the press coverage and the expectations of fans all over the world, stopping it now would be almost impossible. Not completely out of the question but damn hard. She couldn't just end things and walk away unscathed. Not in this town. To add insult to injury, no one would seriously believe it had been her that had called off the wedding, not Tyler.

Frankly, she kept whipping herself back and forth like a flag in the wind. One moment she was content with marrying - or at least being engaged - to Tyler. The next she was furtively looking for a way out, panicked that her friendship with him would be ruined. That was her greatest fear...losing him and the love he'd shown her. As flighty as he could be, he'd brought stability into her life.

Dressed in a teal blue sundress and low-heeled sandals, Billie made her way down the long staircase and out onto the patio where Tyler was chatting with a blonde in her late thirties to early forties. It was hard to tell in Hollywood. She could very well be over sixty. Her hair was styled into a sleek bob and her makeup was perfectly applied. Houston Callaway had come highly recommended and knew how to keep a secret. This wouldn't be her first big name wedding and Billie was looking forward to depending on the woman's expertise.

Tyler beckoned to her. "Come meet our wedding planner."

The introductions were made and Billie settled into a chair next to Tyler so they were both facing Houston on the other side of the table. Billie wasn't sure where to start but luckily Houston wasn't shy. She plunged right in without a lot of small talk.

"First of all, congratulations to both of you." She spied Billie's ring. "What a lovely engagement ring. You have excellent taste."

"I can't take any credit." Tyler smiled and shook his head. "Billie picked it out."

Houston nodded approvingly. "Just gorgeous. Now let's get started. Before we dig down into the details I want to get an idea of what kind of wedding you're looking for. A small intimate ceremony on the beach? Or a lavish event with hundreds of people? Something in between? Or perhaps you're not sure but you know you want it to be in the evening? Whatever you have in your head I want to hear about."

"Whatever Billie wants," Tyler said firmly. "I don't care what it costs. I want this wedding to be everything she's ever dreamed about."

Tyler appeared to have said the magic words. *I don't care what it costs.* Houston was beaming from ear to ear and her eyes were sparkling. Billie wondered how often the planner heard that in this town of dreams. This probably wasn't the first time, nor would it be the last.

Billie laid her hand on Tyler's arm. "I'm sure we can

have a nice wedding without hocking the crown jewels. As for what I have in my mind, well, to be perfectly honest I'm not sure what I want."

"That's not true," Tyler said, frowning. "You told me you wanted a big wedding to rival the royal ones you saw on television."

Houston was smiling again but Billie was going to have to burst her bubble.

"I did say that," she admitted. "But that was five years ago and I've grown up a lot since then. I don't need a huge production. I want something elegant and tasteful, not cheesy or over the top."

"We can absolutely do that for you, Billie," Houston replied. "How about we start by talking about the mood? When you picture your wedding, is it night? Or daytime? Are you inside or outside?"

"It's night," Billie said, surprising herself with the answer. She hadn't realized that's what she wanted, but an evening wedding with candles and a starry sky sounded perfect. "And inside. I don't want to have to worry about the weather. But it would be nice to have an outside area so people can get some fresh air."

Houston nodded and scribbled a few notes. "That's great. This is good information. Have you started your guest list yet? Do you have any idea how many people you're thinking about inviting? Just a ballpark figure would be fine."

"Not yet," Tyler replied. "But with all the people we know I would imagine the number won't be small and intimate. I'm going to throw out two or three hundred but it's just a wild guess at this point."

Two hundred people? Was he expecting her to invite half of that number? She didn't know that many actual human beings and she sure as hell didn't like that many enough to invite them to her wedding. Her number was somewhere around twenty or twenty-five.

"The sooner we get that number the sooner we can book a venue." Houston flipped through her notebook. "Do you think you can get me at least the preliminary number by Monday? Then I can have a list of possibilities to you by Wednesday. Would that work for you?"

It wouldn't take five minutes for Billie to write up her list but getting Tyler to sit down and do it was a whole other story. She practically had to strap him to the kitchen table when Garrett sent over boxes of photos to be auto-graphed. He was too hyper to stay still for long.

"I can do that," Billie said, arching a brow at her fiancé. "Tyler?"

"Sure can," he replied cheerfully. "No problem. Having the venue list before we go would be helpful."

Houston smiled and folded her hands. "Which leads me to my next question which you're probably surprised I didn't ask up front. What date are you looking at?"

This was Tyler's question to answer. Billie was content to wait and see if they actually needed to get married but he was adamant that they needed to be together for more than just getting this role. There was filming, promotion, and hopefully awards season, and he wanted her by his side for all those, not that she wouldn't have been anyway. She simply would have been doing it as his best friend.

"Late summer or early fall," Tyler said firmly. "But if you can't do it by then we can go as late as the holidays. I want us to have some time for a honeymoon before I start my next film after the first of the year."

If he snagged the role. Of course if he didn't get this one, there were always more movies. A stack of scripts showed up to the house every Monday morning by messenger from Josh, Tyler's agent.

Houston made more notes, not seeming too worried about the aggressive timeline. A timeline that scared the ever-loving crap out of Billie. It was happening too quickly and she couldn't control it.

It was that runaway train again barreling toward her at the speed of light. She was going to end up road kill at this rate. She either needed to get out of the way or get with the program and the former wasn't really an option.

Reaching down into her oversized leather bag, Houston pulled out a stack of glossy magazines and slid them across the table. "I always bring these to our get-to-know-you meetings just in case the bride and groom aren't sure what they want. These are yours to keep, so look through them and see if anything strikes your fancy or anything makes you gag in revulsion. I think it will help you decide what kind of wedding you want. In the meantime, I'm going to be looking at what venues are available during your preferred time-frame. Can we set something up for Wednesday? I'd like to talk about color schemes and dresses in addition to venues. You'll need to get going on that as your timeline is short."

The three of them agreed on ten o'clock Wednesday morning and Tyler rose from his chair and escorted Houston to her car. Billie took the opportunity to pick up one of the magazines and page through it. It was all dresses, flowers, cakes, tuxedos, and even honeymoon destinations.

"We should look at those," Tyler said from behind her. He hadn't lingered long seeing Houston out. "But I meant what I said. I want you to have whatever it is that you want."

Twisting in her seat, she faced him, really looking at him for the first time this morning. For a man that had managed to avoid love and commitment for almost thirty-nine years he didn't look concerned in the least about his upcoming nuptials.

That worried her. It was the same old complaint. He wasn't taking this seriously, although he'd said he would try. He simply didn't get that this was *marriage.* Legal and everything. Frankly she was tired of reminding him.

She flipped open another magazine and the photo showed a cake that had to be at least eight tiers high. "I don't know what I want but I think this might be overkill. How about I look through these two and mark the pages I like and you do the same with these other two? Then we can compare."

"Deal." He picked up the magazines but his gaze was on Billie. "Are you okay? You've been acting strangely this morning. Are you coming down with something?"

Holding up her left hand, she ran her fingers over the ring, the diamond cold and hard but glittering brightly in the sunshine. "I'm acting weird because we just met with a wedding planner. You and me, Tyler. I'm freaked out and I'm a little worried that you aren't the same. Did you take a handful of Valium this morning or are you in deep denial?

You're going to lose your bachelor status and I would think you'd be sweating over that."

Smiling so that his dimple peeked out of his cheek, he leaned his hip against the table. "I think maybe you're more freaked out than I am, baby girl. You're holding onto your single status like it's a life preserver. I know you think I'm going to be a lousy husband but I told you that I'm going to help you trust me. You won't be nervous after that."

She slapped the magazines down on the table with a huff. "You're not nervous in the least?"

"Nope, and do you know why?"

I sure as hell don't.

"Why?"

"Because I have faith that marrying my best friend in the whole entire world is going to be fine. We've worked every issue we've ever had out and we'll work the future ones out as well. It's going to be okay and we're going to be happy. I'll make sure of it."

This was so Tyler. "You can't make another person happy. It isn't possible no matter how much we want it."

Leaning down, he planted his hands on either side of her, trapping her with his arms so their faces were inches from one another. She could feel his warm breath against her cheek and she shivered despite the temperature.

"Seems like you've decided to be miserable and that this is going to be a disaster," he replied, his intense blue gaze making her squirm. "No offense, babe, but you've been a real downer since accepting my marriage proposal. If you don't want this, then we'll call it off. You can keep the money. But if we're going to do this can you smile every now and then? Jesus, Houston probably thinks I have a gun to your head. You're not a hostage so stop acting like one. You keep saying everything is changing but from what I've seen you're the one who has changed and not for the better. I miss my best friend."

Straightening, he turned and strode back into the house leaving Billie rooted to her chair, reeling from his anger.

No, he hadn't been angry. He'd actually been rather calm, but sort of sad. Honestly, she missed *being* his best friend. She'd been so intent on being his fiancée she'd forgotten to be his pal and his confidant. He was right about her attitude as well. She'd been a real bitch to be around and she didn't even like herself at this moment in time.

It all changed now. Picking up the magazines, Billie began looking through them. For real this time. She was going to be the happiest bride in California, maybe the entire West Coast. Tyler deserved better than what she'd been giving him. They were going to be friends again.

Who just happened to be engaged.

CHAPTER
Fifteen

TYLER DIDN'T REGRET what he'd said to Billie out on the patio after the meeting with the wedding planner. He'd needed to say it and it was long overdue. What he did regret, however, was the timing. She was already feeling raw and overwrought about the wedding plans. She was overwhelmed by it all and she was upset that he wasn't too. She was nervous and she wanted him to be nervous with her. She was scared and she wanted to know she wasn't the only one. He understood that but he'd learned in his life that worrying didn't get him anywhere. It didn't solve a damn thing; it only festered and made him second guess his actions. It was better to decide the course and stick to it, making corrections along the way. He and Billie would be fine but she needed to get out of this death spiral she was in, constantly looking for the worst case scenario.

If he had it to do all over again he would have picked a better time. Maybe after a good dinner when they were both relaxed in front of the television. Or after a particularly hard workout when she was too exhausted to argue with him. Too late now. He'd gone off on her and she was probably pissed off at him. To make it up to her he'd gone through the wedding magazines and marked all the pages that he liked. Perhaps if she thought that she wasn't going to have to make all the decisions alone it might put her in a better mood.

Descending the stairs, the aroma of charred beef tickled his nose and his stomach growled in approval. Billie was grilling and it was the most heavenly smell in the universe. He'd missed lunch today because of meetings with his agent and business manager and his mouth watered as he turned into the kitchen where she was slicing a tomato.

"Hamburgers are on the grill," she said, barely turning around, but her tone was cheerful and friendly. "I also made some fruit salad and some homemade fries with sea salt. It should be ready in a few minutes."

This was a pleasant surprise. He'd assumed they'd go to a restaurant where they'd make awkward conversation until one or both of them broke down and apologized. They were never able to stay mad at one another long.

"I love your fries," he replied, placing his hands on her shoulders and dropping a kiss on her cheek to test how far this friendliness went. In the past she wouldn't have blinked an eye at his behavior. "I'll go check on the burgers. Do you want cheese on yours?"

"Absolutely." She waved her knife to the other counter. "I already pulled it from the refrigerator and sliced it up."

Grabbing the neat stack of cheddar slices, Tyler headed out onto the back patio to the outdoor kitchen. It had been one of the major selling points of the house he'd purchased sight unseen. He'd given his business manager a list of must-haves while off making movie after movie and this home was what had been selected from that criteria. He hadn't even decorated it himself. His people had hired a designer and he'd come back exhausted and bleary-eyed to a brand-new home that he'd never seen before but was move-in ready.

He liked the house but if he were truly honest he would have moved a long time ago if Billie hadn't been living in the guest cottage. He'd always wanted to live at the beach and if Billie wasn't so spooked about everything changing he'd suggest they start looking for a home in Malibu.

Stopping abruptly in the doorway to the patio, Tyler surveyed the scene before him. Something was clearly going on. The outside table where they ate most of their meals had been set by Billie. Nice dishes, not the paper plates they usually ate from. Flowers and candles. Music from the discreet speakers in the wall. She'd even put a few of his favorite beers on ice.

It almost looked romantic which was silly because they didn't do romance. They were buddies. Pals. He didn't think about Billie that way.

Except she had looked very pretty in the short sundress that showed off her long and tanned legs. She'd left her hair down tonight and it came down to the middle of her back like a silky dark curtain. He didn't often think about how Billie looked but it was times like these that reminded him that she was a beautiful woman.

He was going to be her husband and suddenly that took on all sorts of meanings that it didn't have before.

He'd been rather flip about sharing a bed with her but that's exactly what they were eventually going to do. He hadn't thought that he cared whether it was sooner or later but he found that he did. Quite a bit. Sooner was much better and it didn't have anything to do with the fact that he hadn't slept with anyone in awhile.

It had everything to do with her.

Friendship and sex. It was a powerful combination. So many men only had one or the other.

He checked the burgers and added the cheese and had just placed the platter of cheeseburgers on the table when she joined him, a bowl in each hand.

"Are you ready to eat?" he asked, watching her closely. He'd known this woman for five years and she didn't set a semi-fancy table for cheeseburgers and fries. There was more going on and he couldn't wait to find out what it was.

Settling into a chair, she pushed the bowl of fruit salad toward him. "Starving. The burgers look great."

"You did most of the work. Thanks for making dinner."

Awkward. This was terribly awkward. They weren't people who did small talk. Soon they would be discussing the fucking weather.

They ate mostly in silence, the music in the background soothing to his frazzled nervous system. He didn't want Billie to hate him but it appeared that's exactly what he'd done. Perhaps this nice dinner was to soften the blow of telling him she was breaking things off.

Billie popped a fry in her mouth. "It's supposed to rain tomorrow so we might not get to go on a run."

Weather. Shit. He couldn't take this anymore.

Swallowing a bite of melon, he placed his fork on his plate with a clatter. "Just for fuck's sake yell at me, baby girl. If you're mad, say it so we can get past this. I can't take the passive-aggressive bullshit."

Instead of letting loose on him, Billie calmly dabbed at her mouth with a napkin before replying. "I'm not mad at you. I'm mad at me. That's why I made dinner tonight. I wanted to show you that I'm sorry and that I'm going to try harder." She sighed, her lips turning down. "I miss you too."

"I never went away, babe."

"I was pushing you away." She dropped her head into her hands for a long moment and then finally looked up. "I'm so freaked out about losing you as a friend if this all goes sideways. I don't think you realize how important to me you've become. You're practically my whole world."

She'd choked on the last words, her moss green eyes bright with tears. A pain ripped through Tyler's heart and it was all he could do not to leap over the table and pull her into his arms and tell her everything was going to be okay. He'd rather cut off his own arm than let Billie be unhappy for even a second.

In fact, what the hell was he waiting for? Why was he just sitting there? This was his best friend and now fiancée. He should comfort and care for her. He started to rise but Billie shook her head and waved him back into his chair.

"Don't. If you come over here I won't be able to say what I need to say, and it's important that I do."

Fear clawed at his insides and he had to force himself to stay seated and not panic. He'd been right when he came downstairs. Something was definitely up with Billie.

"You're important to me too," he said, trying to keep his tone soothing. Her lips were trembling and she'd paled as if in fear. "You're my best friend, babe. I'd die for you. You know that, right?"

She tried to smile and laugh. "I don't want to test that theory. I just need to tell you something, okay? And I need you not to react until I'm done. Can you do that for me?"

Probably not. He wasn't known for his patience but for her he'd try. She hadn't even told him what it was yet but already he was nervously sweating, his heart pounding against his ribcage.

"I will. What do you need to tell me?"

Straightening her shoulders, Billie took a deep breath. "I have family. Not much of one really but I do have one."

Honestly he'd always assumed she didn't have a soul in the world, perhaps an orphan. She'd never once mentioned anyone and only referred to her life before Los Angeles in the vaguest of terms. She hadn't wanted to talk about it and he'd respected that. His mind couldn't help but drift back to his office and the file folder he'd shoved in one of the drawers. Out of sight but not out of mind. Was she about to tell him what was contained there?

"Okay," he said cautiously. "I have to say that I'm kind of surprised."

Gobsmacked was a better word, but whatever.

"I have a sister," she confessed, her gaze studiously avoiding him. "A twin sister."

Freakin' twins? She had a twin? What in the ever-loving fuck?

"A twin?" he repeated. "You've never mentioned her, Billie."

Her head snapped up when he used her name, which he didn't do often. She had to know that although he appeared calm he was becoming increasingly upset. How could she have had a fucking twin sister and not mentioned that to him in the last five years? It made a mockery of how close they were supposed to be.

Rubbing the back of his neck, he pushed his plate away. Food was the last thing on his mind. He wanted to hear Billie's story.

"Maybe you should start at the beginning."

CHAPTER
Sixteen

THIS WAS ten times harder than Billie had thought it would be. Clearly Tyler wasn't happy with her and she'd barely begun to tell her story. By the time she was finished he was going to be livid.

"We were poor," Billie began, watching his expression carefully. "Like dirt poor. I never met my father and my mother drank too much. We didn't have a lot of food and other necessities that people take for granted."

Like clothes, heat, and medicine.

Scraping his hand down his face, Tyler sighed. "Aww, baby girl. I'm so sorry."

Billie shrugged awkwardly. "You don't have anything to be sorry for. It's not your fault. It's just the way it was."

"What about social services? Didn't they intervene?"

"A couple of times but they'd send our mother to parenting classes and Alcoholics Anonymous. Things would get better for a little while and then she'd start to drink again. She'd get fired from whatever crappy job she'd been able to get and the cycle would start all over again. By the time Sierra and I were about eight years old we were taking care of Sharon, not the other way around."

Tyler frowned. "Sharon?"

"That was my mother's name. I didn't call her Mom. She never encouraged that. She didn't like men to know she was old enough to have children."

Suppressing a shudder, Billie thought about all the "uncles" that had drifted in and out of their lives. Thankfully none had abused her or Sierra but they'd been losers, every one of them, and they hadn't done Sharon a bit of good, pulling her down into the gutter with them.

Tyler was angry. His lips were pressed together so tightly they had a white outline around them and a muscle worked in his jaw. Tears burned behind her eyes at the thought that he might be mad at her for keeping this secret.

"Where is your mother now?"

Her throat tightened painfully and she had to clear her throat a few times before she could answer. "She died about three and a half years ago. She got drunk and ran her car into a tree. The paramedics said she died instantly."

His mouth hanging open, Tyler placed his hands on the table as if to hold onto something solid. "How did I not know this? I don't remember you taking a trip for your mother's funeral. Did you not go?"

She remembered that time well. It had cost her every single cent she'd saved since hitting Los Angeles. Luckily she'd just been in a movie and was living in the guest cottage for almost nothing. "I did go, although there wasn't a service or anything. Someone had to claim the body. I had her cremated. You were in Toronto shooting a *Thunder* movie."

"And you never mentioned it."

He didn't phrase it as a question because they both knew the answer. She hadn't told him for a myriad of reasons. Hopefully she could get him to understand what she'd been thinking.

A few tears of fear slipped down her cheeks and she swiped at them with her fingers. "You had this wonderful and loving childhood, Tyler. Your parents adore you and were there for you, like moms and dads are supposed to be. I never had that and I was ashamed of what people might think about me. For the longest time I blamed myself. That maybe if I'd been a better daughter or more lovable Sharon wouldn't have to drink every day. I know now it's a load of horse shit but at the time I really believed it. When I came to Hollywood I wanted a brand-new start with my past behind me."

"As if it didn't exist," Tyler murmured. "As if you as a child didn't exist. You obliterated every sign of her and became a new person."

"Basically? Yes," Billie agreed. "I didn't want to be poor, cold, and hungry anymore. I wanted to be beautiful and glamorous. I wanted to have the life that I'd seen on television so I came to the place were dreams are literally manufactured."

She waited as patiently as she could while Tyler digested all that she'd revealed. His anger wasn't as palpable and had changed into a sort of sadness. She hadn't wanted his pity either but it was preferable to his rage.

"Where is your sister?"

This was the more complicated part and honestly, she'd rather keep silent about it but she'd decided that she would tell him the truth. That meant all of the dirty details.

"That's the second part of this story," Billie finally said, carefully choosing her words. "Sierra reacted to Sharon's drinking differently than I did. She always had boyfriends because I think she needed to feel loved. Eventually she met her current husband and he's a fucking loser who verbally and physically abuses her. I tried to get her to leave him but she never would and eventually she got tired of the arguing. On the day that I showed up to her house to bring her with me to Los Angeles she ordered me out of her life. She said she hated me. I haven't talked to her since but I do occasionally speak with a mutual friend who still lives in Wisconsin."

"Wisconsin?" Tyler's brows quirked. "So that's where you come from. You always just said the Midwest which could be anywhere from Nebraska to Ohio. Of course all of this explains why you don't drink. I've wondered about that."

But he'd respected her privacy and never asked. "I drank some in high school as well, but I didn't really enjoy it and after seeing my mother and her long line of men I figured it was a bad idea to do it. I didn't want to go down that road. I wanted a better life."

Sierra had too but she'd never had a chance. A few bad decisions and it went sideways.

Tyler looked at her now, his intense gaze almost stripping her bare as if he could see all the way inside of her mind and heart. "She's your twin. You have to miss her a great deal."

A sob caught in Billie's throat and she rubbed at a few stray tears. "Sometimes it's as if I've lost a limb. We weren't identical twins but we were close. We spent almost all of our time together growing up. We were a team and she was my best friend...and then suddenly she wasn't anymore. I knew I had to leave and make something of my life."

Tyler's smile was gently. "Babe, I think you've looked back a whole hell of a lot. You might not have said anything to me about this but I know this had to have been in the back of your mind all these years. I'm sorry you haven't talked to your sister."

She hadn't cried this much in years. Certainly not since she'd met Tyler. "She hated me then and maybe she hates me now. I don't know. I do know that I must be a horrible person for getting out of there and leaving her."

"If you didn't leave you might have ended up the same. It's not terrible to want a life for yourself. You tried to help her."

"Did I try enough?"

Tyler ran his fingers through his hair, leaving it sticking up on its ends. "It's been my experience that people have to help themselves and that sometimes you have no choice but to walk away. If she wouldn't let you help her it would be cruel to ask you to stick around and watch her destroy her life with a man that hurt her."

That's pretty much what it had been like. At some point, Billie's survival instincts had kicked in and she'd run for her life. The only thing she'd had by then was a crappy apartment she'd shared with three other girls, a wreck of a car, cheap clothes, and two lousy waitressing jobs with handsy male customers. She'd been going nowhere fast. But the guilt of leaving had never quite gone away.

"I'm hoping she'll really leave him for good this time. That's what the money was for. My friend called and said Sierra was in the hospital. Her loser husband had beat the shit out of her and she was so skinny and frail she was having a hard time recovering. Connie begged me for the money to help Sierra pay the hospital bills, get a divorce, change her name, and start a new life. He threatened to kill her next time. That's why I changed my mind and said yes. I needed the money."

Reaching across the table, he captured Billie's hands in his own much larger ones. "Baby, I would have just given you the money. You don't owe me a goddamn thing. Shit, was it even enough? Do you need more?"

Shaking her head, Billie slid her hands out from under his and tucked them into her lap.

"No, it's all fine. Connie says that Sierra is doing better."

"We can go visit her if you want," Tyler offered, looking hurt from her withdrawal. "In a few weeks when she's feeling better."

"I don't think she'll want to see me. She hates me."

Something Sierra had been happy to tell Billie every time they talked.

"I doubt that. That's the situation talking. Once she's away from him, I bet she'll be glad to have her sister back. So will you."

"I'm not holding my breath."

Rubbing the back of his neck, Tyler shook his head.

"That's a hell of a story, baby girl. I have to admit I never would have guessed it."

Billie took a breath and held it, tears squeezing from her eyes. "Are you mad at me? Do you hate me too?"

Tyler was out of his chair so fast it felt backward with a clunk against the tile. Rounding the table, he pulled her up and locked his arms around her like steel bands.

"I don't ever want to hear you say something like that again. Do you understand me? I am not angry. I admit I was at first but now I'm mostly just mad at your mom and the system that let you down. You deserved a better life than that and I'm going to make sure that you get it."

He didn't understand and she had to make him see. Cupping his jaw in her hands, she turned his head so their gazes clashed.

"You already have, Tyler. You're not only my best friend, you're my family. You're my home. That's why I'm so scared about this blowing up in my face. If I lose you as a best friend, it will be the second time in my life. I barely survived the first."

Resting his forehead on hers, they stood like that for a long time as she drew strength from his hold. Everything seemed to fade into the background and all she could hear was the pounding of her own heart. His soft breath landed on her cheek in perfect rhythm and she allowed her eyes to drift shut and her body, that had been so tense before, relaxed against his.

Billie could have happily stayed like this forever but it wasn't the most practical way to spend their days and nights. Eventually his hold loosened and she stepped back, sighing at the loss of warmth. His fingers smoothed down her still damp cheeks before carding through her tangled hair.

"I promise you that I will never leave you no matter what. You're just as important to me as I am to you." He lifted her chin so she was looking into his eyes. "I just wish you trusted me."

"I do. More than anyone I've ever met."

He was already shaking his head in denial. "You believe that but it isn't true. I'm not sure you've ever trusted anyone in your entire life, but now I understand why. I'll say again what I said before. I'll earn your trust. I just know now that it's going to be a hell of a lot harder than I thought it would."

If Tyler couldn't do it, she doubted it would ever happen.

CHAPTER
Seventeen

UNABLE TO SLEEP, Tyler padded down the stairs and into the kitchen, grabbing a bottle of water from the refrigerator. Twisting it open, he took several gulps, wetting his parched throat.

After listening to Billie's woeful tale at dinner earlier he'd experienced a myriad of emotions running through him as he'd tossed and turned, trying to sleep. Anger at her mother for not giving Billie the home she needed, then pity for that same woman who had been the victim of her own human frailties. Not everyone was cut out to be a parent - especially a single parent - and it appeared that Sharon Oliver fell into that category.

Those same feelings surrounded Sierra as well, although they were mixed with a kind of hopefulness. Perhaps this time she could pull her life together and have a future that wasn't filled with fear and pain. Tyler wouldn't mind having ten minutes alone with her abusive husband to help him learn how to treat a woman. He didn't have any patience for a male - he couldn't call him a true man - who mentally or physically hurt a female.

Billie had answered so many unasked questions tonight when she'd told him about her nightmare of a childhood. It explained so much about Tyler's best friend. The independent streak a mile-wide. Her reticence to ask for help. Her fear of trusting another human being although desperately wanting to.

Tyler had a memory of when he was a kid and they'd adopted his beloved dog Scout. When Scout had come to them he'd been pretty skinny and quite skittish. Although not yet even a year old, the puppy hadn't been treated well in his former home. He had a fear of humans that made him shy, hiding under the dining room table when he first arrived at the house. Tyler had sat under that table with Scout for hours, not touching him but simply sitting there and talking to him. Every now and then, Scout would move closer, wanting to be petted and loved until finally he'd allowed Tyler to hold him.

Billie reminded him of Scout, although she might not appreciate the comparison. She hadn't cowered under a table but she'd been hiding her heart for a long time, protecting it. So busy with his own life, Tyler hadn't noticed at first and then when he had he'd decided that it was none of his business.

He hadn't pushed her for details or to go out of her comfort zone. It wasn't in his nature to push for intimate and emotional information about a person's life and Billie hadn't displayed any outward damage from her childhood. She'd smiled and laughed like other people, but with a

certain maturity that was far beyond her years. Their friendship had deepened and he'd thought that she really did
trust him. She kind of did as long as she was in her comfort
zone. But an engagement and an upcoming wedding had
thrown her into unchartered territory. Suddenly it mattered
because if she couldn't open herself up and trust him - for
real - this was going to be one miserable marriage.

And that brought up the big unanswered question.

Was there anything else important that Billie hadn't
told him?

Somehow his feet had carried him into his office and he
sat down at the desk, a voice in his head saying *no* but a
second voice saying *yes*. Tyler dug into one of the drawers
and pulled out the file on Billie that Garrett had given him
and placed it in front of him on the desk.

Closed.

Staring at it for a long time, Tyler's hand finally came
up to flip it open but then fell back to his side. It wasn't
right. His stomach churned and acid rose in his throat. He
couldn't betray Billie by reading the contents but there was
also a vocal part of him that exhorted him to do just that.
Didn't he deserve the truth? They were going to be
husband and wife. Married, for fuck's sake.

A make-believe marriage.

His conscience was chatty tonight, but he was starting
to see what Billie had said about things changing and
marriage being a bigger deal than he'd thought. Even a
make-believe marriage had to be grounded and solid. It
had certainly pulled his blinders off regarding his new
fiancée. They'd been gliding along, just skimming the

surface, but whether they liked it or not they were diving deep and figuring out what made the other one tick.

The folder still sat on the desk, mocking him for being such a wimp. It was practically screaming at him...*open me. Open me.* Learn all of Billie's secrets. Know everything. Take the shortcut and figure her out in one fell swoop.

And it would be a shortcut. The easy way. He wouldn't have to put the work in. He wouldn't make any stupid mistakes with her because of something he didn't know. It was tempting as hell and his hand reached for the folder once again.

No. Fuck no. Don't do this.

For the second time he pulled his arm back as if he'd touched a hot stove. This file...was wrong. Garrett should never have done this. Billie had told Tyler of her past of her own free will. If there was anything else he needed to know, she'd tell him. He wouldn't be opening this file tonight or any other night. If the fireplace had been lit he would have thrown it in and let the flames eat it until it was ashes.

"Tyler, what are you doing up?"

Startled, Tyler sucked in a breath and snapped his head up to see Billie standing in the office doorway. Guiltily, he shoved the file under a stack of scripts, not wanting her to see what he'd been looking - or not looking - at. Billie and Garrett had a good relationship and Tyler didn't want to ruin that by revealing what the publicist had done. She'd be livid and rightly so.

"Couldn't sleep," he said, pretending to leaf through a stack of mail. "I thought I might read through some of my fan mail. What's your story?"

Shrugging, she perched on the corner of his desk and he couldn't help but notice the smooth skin of her thigh and the way the strap of her tank top sagged down, exposing a bare shoulder. His body responded as if she'd stripped naked, rubbed on body glitter and was dancing on a pole in Las Vegas. Shit, she wasn't even trying to be attractive and now he couldn't seem to get away from seeing it every time he looked at her. This was becoming damn inconvenient.

This was *Billie* and he needed to get his dirty mind out of the gutter.

"I woke up and couldn't get back to sleep so I came down for some water and saw the office door open." She smiled and his chest tightened so he could hardly take a breath. What in the hell was happening to him? "I don't suppose I could convince you to leave the fan mail for another day and watch a movie with me instead? I'll even let you choose."

They'd played this game before. She'd let him choose but then when he did she'd make such a sad face he'd end up picking something else. Something she would have chosen. And he didn't mind a bit. He might not know every secret from her past but there were a bunch of things he did know about her.

"*Weekend at Bernie's,*" he said. "You go cue up the movie and I'll pop the popcorn."

Tyler had his best friend back and he couldn't be happier. It was all going to be just fine. He just had to stop thinking about taking her to bed every five minutes.

———

Clearly Billie had made a mistake staying up and watching *Weekend at Bernie's* with Tyler last night. Now she was yawning and bleary-eyed, sucking down coffee as fast as the machine could brew it. She'd even skipped her usual workout because she might fall over in heap on the side of the trail. Tyler, on the other hand, was bouncing around like Tigger, full of energy. Working torturous hours on movie sets had trained him to live on little sleep. Not able to handle his cheery disposition, she'd sent him on his run to get a little peace and quiet while she caffeinated.

She was on her third cup of coffee when the doorbell rang. As far as she knew, they weren't expecting anyone. Then there was the question of how they entered through the gates of the home without the code.

Frowning, she hurried to the front door as the doorbell pealed again. Whoever was on the other side was impatient this morning. Billie opened the door to find a young man maybe in his mid to late twenties with longish brown hair and wire-rimmed glasses. He wore a pair of faded blue jeans and a red and gold Gryffindor t-shirt that looked well-loved. Tucked under one arm was a brown messenger bag stuffed to the gills. He didn't look like the usual fan that jumped the gate but she'd learned that looks could be deceiving. He sure as heck didn't look like a reporter either.

"Can I help you?"

Call the police? Lock the doors and activate the security alarm?

The young man smiled and held out his hand. "I hope I'm not late. I got a little turned around. I'm Curtis. Curtis MacDonald. You must be Billie Oliver."

He knew who she was which was no great feat, considering her face had been featured on several tabloids since the engagement. But Curtis was looking at her like she was supposed to know who he was. Except that she didn't. If she went the honesty route he might do the same.

Billie stood her ground in the doorway, not willing to let him inside to discuss this. "It's nice to meet you, Curtis, but I'm not sure what you're late for. Did you have an appointment?"

"I'm here for the job."

"Job? I think you must be confused. There is no job here."

Curtis's happy expression turned to one of dismay. "You mean Garrett gave the job to someone else? Why didn't he call me?"

Garrett. Crap.

"Garrett told you to be here today?"

Nodding eagerly, Curtis hurried to explain. "He said I was Tyler Gaylord's new assistant. Is that not right?"

Billie pressed a finger to her throbbing temple. "I'm sure it's correct. I just wasn't expecting you today. Come on in."

She stepped back so Curtis could enter and then led him through the foyer all the way to the kitchen in the back of the house where Tyler was standing, sweaty from his run and gulping down a bottle of water.

"Tyler, this is Curtis. He says Garrett hired him as your new assistant. Do you know anything about that?"

Scraping his fingers through his damp hair, Tyler grimaced. "About that, babe. Garrett mentioned it last time

I talked to him but I forgot to tell you. Good news, you don't have to help me anymore."

It was a surprise as she'd thought Tyler was doing nothing to find a new assistant. She should have known he'd have Garrett choose one instead.

"That is good news, especially as we have the comic book convention coming up soon."

Tyler grinned. "That's right and that's the first thing we'll have Curtis do. Confirm all the arrangements for San Diego. Can you...?"

Of course Tyler had no idea where the detailed itinerary was, not that she thought he should. He was busy making the movies and being the movie star. He could pay people to arrange transport at the airport. It wasn't a cost-effective use of his time.

"I can," she confirmed. "Let me give you a tour, Curtis, and then show you the office. I've been filling in but I'm happy to hand over the responsibilities."

Tyler and Curtis shook hands and then the younger man followed her as she showed him around the house and grounds. Hopefully he would last for awhile. Good assistants didn't grow on trees and the really efficient ones were in demand and paid handsomely. The hours sucked and there was little glamour in the job but luckily there was a breed of people that were born to be organized and liked hanging around the movie business.

If Curtis could survive the comic book convention then he could probably survive anything. Billie had never been but she'd heard the stories from Tyler's friends. This year, however, she was going and she had to admit she was a little worried. These were Tyler's most rabid fans, the ones who weren't all that thrilled that Billie had taken him off the market.

Everything she'd done up to now was nothing compared to San Diego. All she wanted to do was survive the trip and not make a fool out of herself. Anything more was a bonus.

CHAPTER
Eighteen

"ARE you sure you're not mad?"

Billie didn't appear to care that Tyler had a guy's night planned with his close friend Sam Collins, but she'd been so sweet lately he didn't want to upset the delicate balance they'd managed to achieve. When she'd said that she was going to get a new attitude, she'd spoken the truth. The last three days had been almost completely normal, hanging out together and having a ball. He felt lucky to have his best friend back.

Huffing, Billie slapped a bookmark into her paperback and sighed. "I am not mad, but I will be if you keep bugging me by asking me that over and over. Why would I be mad?"

Tyler shrugged awkwardly, not knowing how to deal with the situation. It wasn't anything he'd experienced before. "I don't know but I've seen women get pissed off when their significant other goes out with the guys. It's just Sam, you know."

"I know and I like Sam. Have a good time and don't drive if you drink." She rolled her eyes and slapped her forehead. "What am I saying? You're going out with Sam. Of course you're going to drink. Use the car service and don't let anyone take a picture that's going to end up on social media. We have the comic book convention coming up and you don't want to spend three days answering questions about public inebriation instead of the *Thunder* movie."

Billie was well acquainted with his evenings with Sam Collins. She'd participated in more than a few too.

"I am using the car service," he confirmed. "What are you going to do while I'm gone?"

His guilt was rapidly dissolving as he studied her gleeful expression. Far from being upset, she appeared thrilled that he was leaving her alone.

"I'm going to take a long, hot bath. Then I'm going to read my new book in bed. Heaven."

Billie looked damn happy about it too.

"You can do that when I'm here. You don't have to wait until I leave."

"Really? Because last time I tried you knocked on the bathroom door at least three times to ask me what you deemed to be important questions such as 'Do we have any milk?' I'm pretty sure you could have figured out the answer by opening the refrigerator."

Women didn't understand. "I knew we had milk," he explained patiently. "I just didn't know if it was any good. It was the day after the date on the carton."

"Then smell it."

"I don't know how bad milk smells."

"Trust me, you'll know. And how could you get to the age of thirty-eight and not know how bad milk smells? It's not witchcraft, it's common sense."

He shot her his most charming grin. "What can I say? I'm a little spoiled."

"A little? Try a lot." She made a shooing motion with her hands. "Now go have your guy night with Sam. Drink beer. Wrestle bears. Get a tattoo. Call me if you need bail money."

Being married to Billie was going to be no hardship whatsoever. She could make him laugh so easily and she didn't sweat the small stuff.

"Aww, baby girl, that's sweet, but I wouldn't wake you up for that. I'll call Garrett and get his ass out of bed. That's what I pay him for."

She was laughing as he exited the house, climbing into the dark SUV the service had sent. It didn't take long to reach the out of the way bar that he and Sam liked to frequent. It was still Hollywood but a toned-down version. The drinks were overpriced but it wasn't filled with tourists hoping to see a movie star. This place was for locals and for the most part they left Tyler and Sam alone.

Sam was already inside flirting with a pretty young waitress. Or maybe she was flirting with Sam. It was hard to tell at a distance but his friend didn't seem to mind. Sam was the Hollywood ideal of tall, dark, and handsome so there were always women wherever they went. He had been married years before and had been single for the last ten or fifteen at least. At age forty he didn't seem in a hurry to settle down again, always saying that when he met the right woman he'd race her to the altar as fast as he could. Apparently he hadn't met her yet.

Tyler slid into the dark booth across from Sam.

"Sorry I'm late."

The waitress's eyes widened when she took in Sam's drinking buddy for the evening.

"Trouble with the old ball and chain?" Sam smirked. "Did Billie give you a hard time about going out with me?"

Tyler didn't want to have this conversation with the waitress listening in. He'd deal with her first.

He pointed to Sam's beer and chaser. "I'll have the same."

Reluctantly - very reluctantly - she headed to the bar to get his drinks, looking over her shoulder the whole way.

"You better hope I don't tell Billie what you called her because she'll kick your ass into next week. I'll have you know that not only did she not care about me coming out tonight, she almost pushed me out of the house. Apparently she wanted some alone time and I'm cramping her style and not giving her any peace and quiet."

"I would imagine living you with you is like living with a toddler. A happy one but still immature."

They were always busting each other's balls and it looked like tonight wouldn't be any different.

"Because you're so mature?" Tyler taunted. "You might want to rethink that, my friend. Remember that time in New York City?"

Tyler didn't even have to mention which time, although they'd had more than one wild night. But that *particular* crazy evening wouldn't be forgotten very soon.

Chuckling, Sam stroked his chin and smiled at the memories. "That was a great night."

Tyler pointed a finger at his friend. "And it was all your idea, Mr. Maturity. So take your toddler bullshit and shove it up your very famous ass."

The waitress brought Tyler's drinks and tried to linger, brushing his shoulder with her hand as she straightened up. This certainly wasn't the first time some girl had given him an eyeful of her cleavage but it sure didn't feel the same. Before he'd enjoyed the view and every now and then he might even pursue something with the lady in question. But that was before.

His life was now separated into two parts. Before being engaged to Billie and afterward.

It didn't seem respectful to ogle a waitress when he had a beautiful fiancée at home. Of course it wasn't real but that didn't make much of a difference. It still wasn't right and Billie deserved better than a horn dog for a husband. After hearing the story of her childhood, she deserved better *everything* in her life. Period.

The waitress leaned down and placed her hands on the table so her breasts were almost spilling out of her tight t-shirt. "Is there anything else I can get you? My name's Trish, by the way."

Sam quirked an eyebrow at Tyler. "I'm fine but I can't speak for my friend."

Tyler shook his head. "I'm good too. Thank you, Trish."

Her lips turned down in disappointment, Trish wandered back to the bar where a few others patrons sat. Sam watched her as she walked away, her hip swaying, before turning to Tyler.

"You could have had her if you wanted."

"So could you. And you're not engaged."

A slow smile crossed Sam's face. "Speaking of your new status, what's up with that? I thought Billie had more sense than to get romantically involved with you. Did she have a severe blow to the head and get amnesia?"

Sam Collins was one of Tyler's best friends in the world and there wasn't much they didn't know about one another. Lying would be useless anyway as Sam could see bullshit from a mile away. It was uncanny how the man could sniff out a lie.

"She's helping me out," Tyler admitted, his voice low although the bar was loud. It was doubtful anyone would hear them. "Weller won't even talk to me about the role. He wants a man who is settled and in love."

"Weller's an ass. I wouldn't work on one of his sets for all the millions in the world. You need to think twice about whether this part is worth it."

It was worth it. Tyler wasn't afraid of Weller and all his bitching and whining.

"You didn't seem surprised at all. Had you already figured it out?"

Sam shrugged and took another draw on his beer. "I couldn't be sure. It didn't seem probable that you turned your friendship into an engagement in the six weeks since I last saw you but stranger things have happened. Billie's a good woman though, and you're lucky. Are you actually going to get married for a movie role or just stay engaged? A wedding seems kind of extreme but people have married for worse reasons, especially in this crazy town."

"We're getting married," Tyler said firmly. "This is the role of a lifetime and I'm grateful to Billie for helping me."

No way was Tyler going to mention the financial arrangements. That was private.

"I can't imagine that girl ever saying no to you for anything. Or you to her, for that matter."

Shaking his head, Tyler chuckled, remembering the look of horror on Billie's face when he'd brought up the proposal. "Let's just say she didn't say yes right off. I had to use my powers of persuasion."

"Well, I guess I should say congratulations. I actually think you and Billie will make a great couple. When is the big day?"

Damn, this was harder than Tyler had imagined. What if Sam said no?

"Yeah...about that...shit...I was hoping...well...that you might be my best man."

He had his answer when Sam's face lit up. "Fuck, yes. Do I get to throw you a bachelor party?"

Saying yes was a dangerous proposition but it was a tradition. "Sure, just keep our names out of the press. I don't need pictures of all of us with strippers on the cover of the *Enquirer*."

Sam held up two fingers. "Scout's honor."

"You were never a Boy Scout."

"You don't know that for sure." He nodded to the empty pool table. "Now let's go play some pool. How about a little friendly wager?"

Tyler was going to love every second of taking Sam's money.

CHAPTER
Nineteen

TYLER HAD a smile on his face the entire drive back to his home. It had been a great evening of beer and pool, although he'd lost about a thousand bucks to Sam. They'd both agreed to double or nothing next time they got together.

The SUV pulled into Tyler's driveway and stopped at the closed gate, the driver looking over his shoulder to his passenger in the backseat. "You'll need to open the gate, Mr. Gaylord."

Easier said than done.

It shouldn't be this difficult.

Fumbling with his phone, it took Tyler several tries before his fingers finally took direction from his brain and typed out the code. The gates swung open and the vehicle pulled to the front of the house.

I might be more drunk than I thought.

"Safely home, Mr. Gaylord. I hope the ride home was satisfactory."

Kevin was Tyler's regular driver whenever he used this car service and the older man always took good care of him, no matter where they were or what time of night it was. Other drivers had sold Tyler out, talking to tabloids, but Kevin never had.

"Smooth and uneventful," Tyler said, pushing the car door open before reaching into his pocket and pulling out a hundred-dollar bill. The smell of morning dew and fresh earth assailed his nostrils. "Just like I like it."

He handed Kevin the tip and stepped out of the car but his legs didn't cooperate. Stumbling into a bush, he felt Kevin's arms catch him before he fell onto the ground. For an older guy, he moved fast.

"Easy there, Mr. Gaylord. Let me help you to the door."

"Thanks, Kevin. I seem to be having some trouble walking."

It was all because the earth was undulating under his feet, making it difficult to stay steady. When they arrived at his front door, it took another few minutes for him to find his key and slide it into the lock.

I am definitely more drunk than I thought. I need to sleep this off.

The front door finally opened to Tyler's relief and he stepped inside before thanking Kevin. The older man wished Tyler a pleasant evening although it was already four in the morning. Knowing Billie, she'd be up at the crack of dawn just to fuck with him when he had a hangover.

Jesus, I need to get to bed.

Walking carefully through the house so he didn't knock

anything over, Tyler hugged the walls so he could stay upright. The stairs proved trickier but with time and determination he navigated his way to the top and down the hall to his room, stripping his clothes off along the way. By the time he stood naked at the end of his mattress he didn't bother to brush his teeth. They could stay furry for a few hours.

Crawling into bed, his head fell onto the pillow and he haphazardly pulled the comforter over his legs. He might regret this tomorrow but he'd had a good time tonight. A thought ran through his head that he ought to drink some water or take a few ibuprofen for the headache he would surely have but he was too relaxed to move, his limbs like lead.

Time to sleep it off.

———

The light from the window filtered through Billie's eyelids and she groaned softly. She'd never be a morning person. What time was it, anyway? The sun wasn't too high so it couldn't be all that late.

Shifting on the mattress to stretch, she found herself trapped under something heavy and her fingers reached out to brush it away but instead came in contact with something warm.

Very warm.

It didn't take much exploring to realize she was being weighed down by a heavily muscled arm around her waist. The real shock was that she hadn't noticed the face that was buried in her hair at the curve of her neck, the breath smelling faintly of beer and whiskey. There was also something hard and masculine poking into her backside.

That was when she realized her bed partner was quite naked. Unfortunately, so was she.

Choking on her own spit, her heart seemed to cease beating for a long minute and she struggled to suck oxygen into her lungs. What in the ever-loving fuck?

A glance over her shoulder told her the worst. Tyler laid next to her snoring as if she hadn't just silently screamed in horror. This wasn't the first time they'd slept in the same bed, far from it, but it was the first time either of them had been naked. And engaged. The sheet had slid down sometime during the night and his impressively muscled chest with just a smattering of dark hair was on display. Only a scrap of thousand thread count cotton kept his modesty. Not that Tyler had much shame to begin with.

It must have been quite a night for him if he'd been so drunk he didn't remember that he was sleeping down the hall. Shit. How was she going to get out of this predicament without waking him? A better question was how she'd slept through his return last night. She was a heavy sleeper but she would have woken if he'd turned on a light or brushed his teeth. That hot bath must have put her out like a light.

No more hot baths before bed. Ever again.

Slowly, a millimeter at a time, she carefully twisted out from under him, terrified the entire time that Tyler might wake. As long as he stayed asleep she could pretend this embarrassing scene never happened, but it was taking forever to move away from him. At one point she was almost free, but he'd groaned in his sleep and shifted, trapping her in his arms again. At six feet tall, he had the wing span of a pterodactyl and that made it impossible to escape his reach.

After several minutes of sliding around the bed with Tyler, Billie was covered with sweat and exhausted. If anything she was in a worse situation than when she'd started this whole thing. His arm was like a band of steel around her waist, his palm cupping her breast. His erection was poking insistently into her bottom and he was beginning to rub it against her in his sleep. It had been a long time since she'd shared a bed with an amorous male and her body clearly liked the idea. Her pulse had sped up and she was feeling something she hadn't felt in over a year...arousal.

It didn't help that the rough hair on his thighs was brushing her skin and sending tingles to unmentionable places, or that asleep he looked almost angelic when she knew very well that he was actually the devil. His touch was warm and it felt so good to be held. Physical affection wasn't something she'd received much of in her youth and even in her adulthood so she was greedy for it when in a relationship.

Except this engagement is fake. Fake, fake, fake. As in not real.

Her weakness didn't set well with her and it made her all the more determined to get the hell out of this bedroom with at least some of her dignity intact. Instead of inching along and moving carefully, it might simply be better to make one fast move. With any luck he'd turn over and fall asleep, oblivious that she wasn't his latest hookup.

One...two...three...

It was on three that she made her big break, grasping his wrist to keep his arm still as she slid out from under it. She was just about to celebrate her victory when she realized that a pair of blue eyes were staring at her. Puzzled but not alarmed. Not yet, anyway. She, on the other hand, was frantic.

Because while moving out from his hold, she'd dislodged the sheet covering her naked body. Right now she was sitting up on the mattress, bare to his gaze. Billie wasn't a prude, but having her best friend see her naked wasn't an everyday occurrence for her and she could feel a blush crawling up her body all the way to the roots of her hair.

Why doesn't he move or say something? Is he just going to lie there and look?

Just as she thought it Tyler did move, levering up on the bed, his hair sticking out in several directions and a shadow of whiskers on his too perfect face. It wasn't fair that men could look so amazing in the morning.

His gaze ran down to her toes and then back up to her breasts before eventually ending up somewhere in the vicinity of her eyebrows. He was frowning now and she could practically see the wheels turning in his head as he tried to figure out what was going on. Frozen and mortified at first, Billie managed to drag a blanket up over her naked form, shielding herself from his intense scrutiny. She ought to be chilled but instead she felt quite warm. Too warm, really.

Someday they were going to laugh about this. Today was not that day.

"How much did I drink last night?"

Tomorrow wasn't looking good either. How far away was Christmas?

CHAPTER

Twenty

NORMALLY WHEN BILLIE had a problem that she couldn't solve herself she talked to Tyler. But when the problem was Tyler himself that was an issue.

Dinah was her closest female friend so Billie found herself spilling the entire story over lunch only a few short hours after extricating herself - nude - from a bed with Tyler. The details came slowly at first but eventually she couldn't speak fast enough as the whole sordid tale was laid out for her friend. Tyler's movie role. Her sister. The agreement to get engaged and then married. Her moving into the house. The difficult transition from friends to...whatever they were now. And then finally the mortification of this morning. To Dinah's credit, she listened carefully, only stopping Billie a couple of times to clarify a detail or two.

Taking a deep breath, Billie slumped back into her chair. "So that's pretty much it. I had to tell someone."

Dinah nodded a few times, took a sip of her iced tea, nodded again, then signaled for the waitress.

"I'm going to need a cocktail. Then we'll talk. Are you sure you don't want to start drinking? Because now would be the perfect time in your life."

Billie had always sworn she wouldn't drink but she was tempted. However, she doubted alcohol was the answer. It hadn't helped Tyler last night and had only made things worse.

"I'll pass but I am definitely ordering something chocolate for dessert."

"You and me both, sister," Dinah said under her breath as the waitress came and took her order. They didn't say much, silently eating their chicken Caesar salads until Dinah had her Long Island Iced Tea in front of her and she'd had a couple of sips.

"Okay, let's get to this." Dinah placed her palms together and rested her chin on her fingertips. "Let's start with this morning and work our way backward. After he woke up and realized you were both in the bed naked, what exactly happened? You only said you hightailed it out of there with the sheet wrapped around you. That leaves out a great deal of information."

Billie rolled her eyes, remembering it clearly. "You know how Tyler is. He started grinning and that pissed me off. He quickly realized what he'd done but he didn't seem a bit upset about it."

Lifting a shoulder, Dinah laughed. "Well, yeah, he's a guy. Haven't you noticed that?"

Billie had noticed. More so these last few weeks than all five years before combined.

"I'm his friend and he shouldn't be looking at me that way," Billie insisted weakly. "He just shouldn't."

Dinah smiled and waggled her brows. "But now he's more than your friend. He's your fiancé. Were you looking at him, by any chance? Is the...equipment as impressive as it's rumored to be? You lucky dog. I've heard stories."

So had Billie, although she'd tried to not think about them often, if at all.

Fumbling with her napkin, Billie couldn't meet her friend's gaze. "I might have looked. Very briefly. I mean, I couldn't really avoid it. He was right there only six inches from me."

Dinah's eyes went round. "It was more than six inches, wasn't it? I heard–"

"Stop," Billie commanded, cutting of her friend. "I was talking about the distance between us, not his genitals. I didn't see...it. His lower half was covered by the sheet. I...felt it. You know, against me when I woke up."

"Ohhh, a little morning wood. How did it feel?"

"Hard," Billie blurted, her censoring mechanism clearly malfunctioning. "Jesus, I can't believe this happened. Everything was going so good, too."

Giggling, Dinah dabbed the corners of her mouth the napkin. "I don't know about that. I think waking up with a hot guy like Tyler in my bed would be very good indeed. I understand that finding him there was a surprise but you're acting like it's a terrible thing. You're going to marry him, Billie. At least that's what you've promised to do. Married people generally sleep together. You didn't say when you talked about the agreement but is this some kind of no-sex marriage of convenience? If I was marrying Tyler Gaylord I'd make sure I got some of the sugar, if you get my drift."

"I do," Billie replied dryly, shaking her head at Dinah. "It's not a no-sex thing, but I guess I thought I had more time to get used to the change in our relationship. Tyler thinks nothing will change but my last name but I know better. So many things are going to be different and sex is just one of them."

"Taking your friendship to a physical level is a big deal. But can you honestly say that you're not at least a little bit attracted to Tyler? I know that you've seen him at his worst. Drunk, vomiting, farting, just being a jerk at times. Does it sort of put you off him?"

Billie shook her head. "I can see the real Tyler but I can also see how sexy he is too. He looked good this morning."

Dinah rubbed her hands together with an evil glint in her eye. "Now we're getting somewhere. You liked what you saw. So things are heating up between you two because it sounds like he liked what he was seeing this morning as well. Maybe it's time to take the next step. As you pointed out, you've shared a bed together dozens of times. Have Tyler move back into the bedroom. See what happens."

"I'm an actress, not a choir girl. I know what's going to happen. I'm just not sure I'm ready for that yet."

"But you want to," Dinah prodded. "You're starting to see Tyler in a whole new way."

If she was being honest with her friend she might as well do it big.

"When I first moved in with Tyler, I kind of had a crush on him," Billie admitted. "It didn't last long, maybe six months or so, and he didn't do anything to fuel it really, but I guess what I'm saying is that this wouldn't be the first time I've seen him as sexually attractive. It's just the first time that something might come from it."

Dinah's lips twisted into a crooked smile. "Can I be super honest with you? When you and I first met and I found out you were living in Tyler's guest house I kind of assumed you were friends with benefits."

"A lot of people think that," Billie admitted. "I don't care much. People are always going to believe what they want rather than the truth. I guess you figured out it wasn't true without me having to tell you."

"Eventually," Dinah said laughing. "But I still stand by what I said when you told me about your engagement. I think you two make a great couple. I thought it back when I first met you and I still think it now. This may be all for the cameras and publicity but I think it's the best thing that could happen to both of you. You were meant for each other. Friends to lovers. It's the oldest romance trope in the book, Billie. Honest to God, I cannot imagine Tyler falling in love with anyone but you. You're the longest relationship he's ever had with a woman not counting his family members."

That was true. She and Tyler had been constants in each other's lives for a long time.

"We're not going to fall in love. Tyler says he's never been in love and I believe him."

"You both don't have a clue." Dinah took another sip of her drink. "I know it's scary but be open to having a relationship with Tyler. You said that he's keeping his options open if you both like being married. I think that's because deep down he knows that you're the one. Give him a chance to fall in love with you. Stop running."

"I don't think I'm running."

Dinah's brows shot up. "Oh? What did you do this morning?"

"Run," Billie admitted. "Although to be honest it was more of a crawl. I tripped on the sheet. I wouldn't say I left with my dignity intact."

She was fairly sure she'd shot Tyler the moon on her way out of the bedroom door.

"What exactly did Tyler say?"

Groaning, Billie buried her face in her hands. "He was laughing and as I left he said that he was going to drink every single night if it meant he got to wake up with me naked in bed."

"What happened after that?"

"Nothing really. It all pretty much went back to normal except that I couldn't look him in the eye. In the kitchen a little while later I handed him some coffee and a couple of ibuprofen. He thanked me and then we talked about San Diego. I think he knew I was embarrassed so he backed off."

Tyler had always been good at reading her mind but honestly, he wouldn't have had to this morning. Anyone could have seen she was uncomfortable as hell.

"Always putting you first," Dinah pointed out. "Just like a man in love would. He's ripe for falling in love. So are you. You both need a push, though. Like over a cliff. Jesus, I've never seen two people so scared."

"You're one to talk." Billie shook a playful finger at her friend. "You've sworn off men."

"For now. Eventually I'll get back in the ring but not for awhile. Seriously though, what reservations do you have about Tyler? The women? The fame? I know it's not how he treats you."

Was it the women? There were a lot of them. So many. Too many. But Tyler wasn't a pussy hound despite his reputation. He turned down a hell of a lot more women than he slept with and he still managed to have an active sex life. He'd be a wreck without food or sleep if he said yes to every female that made herself available to him, but he'd never made sex the number one thing in his life. It was always the work that came first.

Was it the fame? The loss of privacy? She'd come to grips with that a long time ago when they'd first started hanging out. It was true that now there was even more scrutiny but she wasn't one to read the tabloids. Mostly she didn't care.

"It's the thought of losing him as a friend," she finally said, her throat clogging with emotion at the mere thought of Tyler not in her life. "I don't want to lose that, and I'm afraid that I will."

"Maybe you can have something even better. Let's call it Tyler-plus," Dinah giggled. "Listen to me, just relax and let things happen. Let nature take its course. You might be surprised where it takes you. You agreed to marry the man, you ought to enjoy it."

"You make a decent argument."

"Of course I do." Dinah sipped the last of her drink. "But now that I know the truth, you have to keep me in the loop. I'm going to want every detail."

"On one condition," Billie replied. "I get to call you when things seem overwhelming."

"Phone support twenty-four-seven," Dinah vowed, her

hand over her heart. "I'll be there for you. Now let's talk about the wedding plans. Did you like the planner?"

The conversation turned to the wedding, flowers, cakes, and dresses, but in the back of Billie's mind she was still thinking about this morning. In only a few short weeks everything between she and Tyler had changed.

She couldn't turn back the clock. Forward was the only option.

CHAPTER
Twenty-One

THE FLASH of the cameras had Tyler squinting as he and Billie sprinted from the airport into the limousine, ducking their heads and ignoring the barrage of questions from reporters. It seemed everyone wanted to snag a photo of the newly engaged couple. They'd managed to get out of Los Angeles quietly but there had been a posse of press waiting for them when their little charter jet had touched down in San Diego. It might have been better to simply drive but Tyler became antsy on any road trip more than an hour or so.

They'd arrived for the yearly comic book convention, although this would be Tyler's last since his contract for the *Thunder* movies was complete. While he enjoyed the energy and the ability to be close to his fans, the three days of the convention were also fucking exhausting. Every year after he finished, he took a few days in Hawaii to rest and relax. This time he was taking Billie with him.

His fiancée. That he'd seen naked less than a week ago.

The images of Billie au naturel were burned on his brain as if with a branding iron. And just as permanent. Even when she wasn't right there with him, he somehow came around to seeing her naked in his head.

Go for a run? See Billie naked on the trail.

Have a meeting with his publicist or agent? See Billie sitting on the table, those pert breasts exposed.

Those images - sexy, beautiful, and gorgeous as fuck - were driving him slowly out of his mind. He'd seen a myriad of women nude in his life and not one of them had affected him like Billie had. He was acting like a teenage boy with raging hormones, not the grown man he was supposed to be.

He'd had to force himself to look her in the eye so his gaze wouldn't wander farther south. This morning when they'd been waiting for the car to take them to the airport, he couldn't help but notice her smooth, tanned legs and her subtle curves shown off by the royal blue dress she was wearing. She'd pulled her long, dark hair back into a ponytail that accentuated her exquisite bone structure and emphasized her green eyes.

It was wrong to pant after his best friend. Wasn't it?

Except that she wasn't just his friend anymore. She was his fiancée and she'd be his wife before the end of the year. Maybe this was what was supposed to happen. Tyler hadn't quite been prepared for the wave of desire that ran through him whenever Billie was near him. He'd always thought she was beautiful but this was something different, something far more.

He hungered for her.

That appetite wasn't going to just go away on its own.

The limousine door closed and the vehicle pulled away from the curb and into the flow of traffic. Curtis, the new assistant, who seemed to be doing a great job so far sat across from them, an iPad balanced on his knee.

"We'll get you checked into the hotel," Curtis stated, perusing his list. "Then you have an interview with *Dark Night* magazine along with a photo shoot for the cover. That should take until mid-afternoon. Then I have you scheduled for a late lunch before heading to the gym. I know you wanted to get in a workout. Tonight you have dinner with the *Thunder* cast."

A relaxed, fun meal with his co-stars was definitely one thing he was looking forward to. Billie had met all of them but there was a part of him that couldn't wait to show her off as his future wife.

Where did that thought come from?

"I'll look around the hotel while you work," Billie said. "I might even get a nap in before tonight. I know how you guys like to party."

It would be a late night but Tyler had already decided not to drink as much as he had with Sam. No need to have a repeat of the other morning. Billie just might slap him if he ended up drunk in her bed a second time with no invitation.

Curtis had stopped looking at his iPad, his brows pinched into a frown. Tyler was beginning to recognize his assistant's expression of worry and panic.

"Curtis? Is everything okay?"

Being new, the younger man would often be concerned about things that didn't need to be worried about. He'd learn eventually. So far he was doing well, considering Tyler had pretty much just thrown him into the role with only Billie to show him the ropes.

"No. Yes. Well...it's just...the magazine thinks they're interviewing both of you. Together. Garrett said something about this being your first interview as a couple. Is that not right?"

Fuck. Billie had stiffened next to Tyler, her fingers curling so tightly around her handbag that the knuckles were white.

She hated surprises. She didn't even like them on her birthday.

As an actress, Billie was fine with the press. She'd done photo shoots and given interviews so Tyler could only assume that her reticence was because they were going to be asked about their impending nuptials.

Curtis's gaze was darting back and forth between Tyler and Billie, his face pale. "I think I was supposed to mention it to you. I'm really sorry."

Before Tyler could respond Billie piped up. "It's fine. It's not like we didn't know this was coming at some point this weekend. Good thing I brought plenty of clothes. I'll just need a few minutes to do my hair when we get to the hotel."

"No problem." Curtis's pale face had turned pink. "I'm really sorry, Billie. I was trying to get everything set up for the convention and I guess this slipped through the cracks."

Billie smiled at the young man and Tyler was once again reminded of how sweet and kind she was. So different than many of the people in Hollywood. No wonder she'd been practically chewed up and spit out by the industry. She was tough but this town was hell on people in general and women in particular. Tyler reached for her hand and gave it a squeeze of gratitude.

"It's really okay," she assured him. "You're learning and there are going to be bumps in the road. This is actually rather minor. You're doing a good job."

"Thanks," Curtis said with an eager smile. "I really like this job."

That made Tyler laugh. "I'd like to hear you say that in about six months after we've racked up tens of thousands of miles in the air and you haven't seen your friends or family in weeks. I actually had an assistant who threw a plate of tacos at my head."

Curtis's eyes had gone wide. "She hit you?"

"She missed." Tyler chuckled at the memory. "And quit immediately. I think she has a nice, calm job now at the DMV. Not everyone is cut out for this life."

"I like it so far. It's so exciting."

"I'm glad you're enjoying yourself, Curtis. I hope it continues."

They arrived at the hotel and luckily there was no welcoming committee of paparazzi waiting for them. The bellman handled the luggage while the three of them went to the front desk where a smiling woman stood behind the counter.

"Mr. Gaylord," she exclaimed, her smile widening. "We're so glad to see you again this year."

Again? He remembered staying here last year but he didn't remember her. He met way too many people to commit all of them to his memory banks.

"Good to be here. Are our rooms ready? We'd like to get unpacked before our next appointment."

"The same suite as last year." The hotel clerk leaned forward to accept his credit card, showing off her ample cleavage. Frankly, Tyler was a leg man. Specifically Billie's legs. "I have your keycards all ready for you. Is there anything I can do to make your stay more...pleasurable? I'm happy to be of service."

One glance over his shoulder told Tyler that his fiancée was finding the exchange with the desk clerk amusing. Her lips twitched and she was clearly trying not to burst into laughter. He was lucky that she wasn't threatened by all the female attention he received from fans.

"I think we have all that we need." He accepted the two key cards and the clerk handed another set to Curtis. "Thank you."

The clerk named Lucy wasn't giving up without a fight. She giggled and fiddled with a strand of her blonde hair. "There are a few new restaurants in the area that you might want to try while you're here. I'd be happy to show you when I get off of work later."

"I'm pretty booked up–" he began but Billie interrupted him.

"That's a great idea," she replied with a gleeful smile. "Except that Tyler and I are going to be in interviews and photo shoots all day. You wouldn't mind showing Curtis, would you? That would be very helpful. Thank you so much. This hotel has amazing service."

Score one for Tyler's fiancée. She was smart and beautiful.

Lucy's eyes went round with surprise and she didn't answer for a moment. "I guess I could do that."

Curtis didn't seem to get what was happening, though. Frowning, he shook his head. "Won't I be with both of you?"

Billie tapped her chin and nodded. "That's right, Curtis. You'll be with us. Looks like we'll have to say no to your very kind offer. Thank you, though. It was very thoughtful."

Lucy looked relieved and a little embarrassed. Curtis still looked confused. And Billie wore an angelic smile.

Tyler held up his keycard. "We need to unpack but thank you again, Lucy. You've been very helpful."

The three of them didn't say much as they rode the elevator to the sixteenth floor. Curtis gave them a few reminders about appointments the next morning but Billie didn't say anything. Tyler was planning to give her some praise for her smooth move down at the check in desk. It couldn't be easy being his intended bride around all these predatory females, yet she never complained.

Their bags had made it to the room ahead of them and Tyler gazed longingly at the huge bed in the suite. He hadn't been sleeping well lately and he would love to crawl under the covers and catch a nap. No such luck. The next three days were jam-packed with work.

Curtis pulled open the drapes so the sun shone in and they could look out over the San Diego skyline. "I'm on floor twelve, room twelve-oh-eight, but if you need anything all you have to do is text me. I'll be back in about an hour so we can head to the photoshoot. Is there anything I can get you before then?"

"Wait." Billie was scowling as she gazed around the opulent suite. "Is this it? Shouldn't there be two bedrooms?"

Curtis looked confused again which was becoming his default expression, the poor bastard. He had no idea that Tyler and Billie were a showmance and there was no reason for him to know. Now he had to be wondering why one of the biggest womanizers in Hollywood had a separate bedroom from the woman he was going to marry.

"Snoring," Tyler said before Billie or Curtis could say anything. "I snore loud enough to wake the dead. Poor girl often has to crawl away into a separate bedroom to get any rest. I should have told you, man. Sorry about that. We usually get a two-bedroom suite so Billie can get away from me if she needs to. When the initial arrangements were made Billie wasn't planning to attend. You didn't do anything wrong."

This might actually be a good thing. He and Billie forced together to act like a newly engaged couple for a long weekend. They could both use the practice.

Wearing a strained smile, Billie nodded in agreement. "Tyler's right. I forgot that the original arrangements were only for him. It's not a big deal. I was just confused for a moment."

Curtis started tapping on his iPad. "I can try to change–"

"No point," Tyler said crisply. "It's convention weekend and there won't be a hotel room to be found. Don't worry about it. If my snoring gets too bad, I'll just bunk out here on the couch. I've slept on much worse on location."

"If you're sure?"

Curtis didn't look sure at all. Billie, however, had recovered her composure and she appeared completely unruffled by the room snafu. She was a terrific actress.

"Quite sure," she replied, grabbing the handle of her suitcase. "I better get started unpacking."

She disappeared into the bedroom and Curtis tugged at his collar, looking uncomfortable.

"Did I screw up? Is she mad?"

"She's not," Tyler assured him. "Billie doesn't sweat the small stuff. Don't worry about a thing."

The assistant seemed to accept the explanation and then headed to his own room, leaving Tyler to deal with Billie. Cautiously he entered the bedroom, unsure as to what mood she'd be in.

"Hey, babe. Thanks for not yelling at Curtis."

Her back was to Tyler and she was hanging up her clothes in the closet.

"It wasn't his fault. He didn't know."

Was she saying that Tyler should have known? That this was his fault? He'd take the blame if that would make this situation better.

To complicate matters, he was warming to the idea of sharing a room and a bed with her. He'd meant it when he said he wouldn't rush her but this certainly might move them along at a quicker pace.

"Then I'm sorry."

Whirling around, she frowned at his apology. "What are you sorry for? Did you make the reservation?"

"No, but I feel like I should have done something."

"It doesn't matter. It is what it is. We'll just have to bunk together. I can sleep out on the sofa."

She could but...

"Billie, it doesn't make any sense for you to sleep on the couch." His arm swept over the bedroom. "The bed is huge. It would fit you, me, and maybe Sam too. We can both use the bed and get a decent night's sleep. We're going to need it this weekend. We've shared a bed before and it wasn't a big production."

"I think Sam should stay in his own room."

Laughing, Tyler walked over to the dresser and twisted open one of the complimentary bottles of water. It turned out convincing a woman to sleep with him was thirsty work. He couldn't remember the last time he'd had to do it. High school, maybe?

"I'll let him know that he's not welcome." Tyler gingerly stepped out onto a limb, hoping it didn't snap out from under him. "We need to get used to this. We're going to be traveling quite a bit and sharing a room isn't going to be optional after the wedding."

"Okay."

Billie turned back to her unpacking and didn't expound on her answer, which immediately had Tyler's warning sirens going off. When she stopped talking was when they had issues.

"Are you upset?" he asked again. "We can talk about this."

"I'm not upset," she said without even a glance at him. "But I hope that at this point you can admit that I was right. More is changing than my last name and you know it. We may have shared a bed in the past but that was then and this is now. It's different."

Tyler couldn't argue the facts. It was different. He was aware of her in a way he hadn't been before.

And he didn't want to go back to what they'd had. He didn't want to be just her friend, but he wasn't sure exactly what he did want. It was probably time to figure it out.

CHAPTER
Twenty~Two

THE INTERVIEW TURNED out to be less of an ordeal than Billie had thought it would be. This certainly wasn't her first interview and it wouldn't be her last, but it was the first as Tyler's fiancée. She'd been dreading intimate questions into their private life but the magazine interviewer seemed much more interested in Tyler's career and their wedding plans.

There were a couple of questions about Billie's own acting career which she answered as vaguely as possible. Her former agent Ina had called Billie right after the engagement was announced but she couldn't see herself going back to someone who had ended their relationship over a set of silicone boobs. A few other agencies had shown some interest but Tyler wanted Billie to sign with his own agent Josh. She liked Josh and had a great deal of respect for him, so in the end that's what she was going to do but it was kind of nice to be courted by people who wanted her. It was so different than the majority of her career, even if it was only because she was marrying Tyler.

Luckily the evening ahead was going to be relaxing and pleasant. Billie had met Tyler's *Thunder* co-stars on several occasions and they were always friendly and fun. Sam Collins was Tyler's closest friend but Mike Watson, Nate Mason, Maxwell Hayes, and more recently Kirby Glenn would be there as well. Much had changed since they'd made the first movie. Nate and Max were married now to amazing women and were deliriously happy. Mike and his wife Amy had added a second child to their family. Meanwhile, Tyler, Sam, and Kirby seemed determined to hold onto their bachelor status. Until now.

Sam hopped up from his chair and beckoned to Billie when she and Tyler entered the private basement of the restaurant through a side entrance. The actor had positioned himself as something of an older brother to Billie and she adored him. Although less than five years older than Tyler, he seemed to be much wiser in the ways of the world and people in general. She wasn't sure what he'd gone through that had made him that way but she was often grateful for his down to earth advice.

"How's my girl?" Sam asked, pulling her into a giant bear hug. "Is that asshole treating you right? Just say the word and I'll kick his ass, darlin'."

Billie had no doubt Sam would do exactly as he said. He'd been known to get into a bar room brawl or two which simply ramped up his reputation with the fans as a total badass action hero.

Kissing Sam's cheek, she laughed at his declaration. "He's been behaving himself but I'll keep that in mind."

"It's like I'm not even standing here," Tyler muttered, getting his own man-hug from Sam and then the rest of the cast. "Some best friend you are."

"I wouldn't be a decent friend if I didn't make sure that you were taking good care of your woman," Sam shot back with a grin. "Now quit your bitching and grab a chair."

The private room had a large round table in the center of the room and a long buffet table against the wall with a parquet dance floor off to the right. Sam had known what he was doing when he chose this restaurant. There were no windows for paparazzi to see through and the double doors to the upstairs public area were closed with a guard on the outside. No one was going to get a photo of tonight's festivities without explicit consent.

As soon as Billie and Tyler were brought drinks by the waitress, Nate clinked the edge of his glass with his spoon and stood up to get everyone's attention.

"Excuse me." He cleared his throat. "Paige and I, well, we have something of an announcement." He looked lovingly down at his pretty, smiling wife, holding her hand in his. "Paige and I are pregnant. That is, she's pregnant and we're expecting. And that's not all. We're expecting...twins!"

The room erupted into a free for all. There were tears, smiles, hugs, laughter, and many congratulations. Nate appeared emotional and misty-eyed while Paige glowed with true happiness. Billie hadn't even known the couple was trying to have a child but she was absolutely thrilled for them. Paige was already a great mother to her college-aged son Jason and Nate was going to be a wonderful father. The twins were lucky as hell to be born into the Mason family.

"I'm just happy to get all of the pregnancy and child-birth done in one go," Paige laughed. "I'm not getting any younger. It will be good to only do this once."

Nate shook his finger at his friend Max. "We're expecting an announcement from you two any day now."

Carrie blushed prettily and tried to hide her face but Max beamed with pride and gave them a naughty wink. "We're working on it. Stay tuned."

Nate slapped Tyler on the back and grinned. "Maybe you two will be next."

Billie wanted a hole in the floor to open up and swallow her. Marriage was stressful enough. She couldn't handle thinking about children right now. Besides, kids weren't a part of the agreement. This wasn't for real. It was a surprise that she needed to remind herself of that these last few days. It was starting to feel like a true engagement. Sort of.

To her utter shock, Tyler wrapped his arm around her shoulders and pulled her close, dropping a kiss on her cheek. "I wouldn't mind having a cute little toddler that looks like Billie."

"He should look like you," she heard herself saying before she could stop the words. "I mean, I bet you were cute as a little boy."

A strange look passed over Tyler's features, so quickly and then gone as if it had never happened. He smiled and tugged at a strand of her long hair. "Naw, I want him or her to look just like you, baby."

There was a series of "awwws" but Sam's expression

was one of playful disgust. "That was the most nauseating thing I've ever heard. The only thing missing was violins playing in the background."

"You're just jealous," Tyler mocked. "Go find yourself a good woman before you turn into a crotchety old man yelling at kids to stay off your lawn."

It was strange to hear Tyler speak of settling down as a happily married man. Only a month ago he'd been a light-hearted playboy.

"Jesus, I'm with Sam on this," Kirby groaned. "I hope all of this love and commitment isn't contagious. I'm rather enjoying my bachelor status."

Kirby was in his early thirties, a few years younger than the other men, and he was playing the field for all he was worth since becoming a star in the *Thunder* movies. The tabloids were full of pictures of him whooping it up in Vegas or closing down the clubs in New York City.

Max shrugged as the wait staff began to load the buffet table down with food. "It gets old eventually. Trust me on this. It's all a party now but soon you'll be so jaded all you'll want to do is have a quiet evening at home."

"I'll take my chances," laughed Kirby. "Damn, the food smells great. I could eat a horse."

"Just make sure that horse has no carbs," Sam said as they all stood to fill their plates. "You're a sex symbol now and that means you have to watch your figure."

The meal passed in a haze of amazing food and laughter. Billie had forgotten just how much fun this group was when they were together. At one point they began doing impressions of other famous people and acting out scenes from their favorite movies. Tyler was such a ham at moments like this, his personality larger than life. Her ribs hurt from laughing so hard.

"Come on, baby," Tyler urged. "Do your Mary Poppins impression. It's great."

That Mary Poppins impression was something that had just been between her and Tyler and she wasn't planning for that to change anytime in the near future.

"No way," she denied. "I'll let you be the center of attention tonight. It looks like your ego needs the applause."

"Ouch," Sam laughed. "Man, she's really got your number, doesn't she? At least she knows what she's getting into by marrying you."

Tyler pretended to preen for the audience. "I've been told I'm a catch."

Rolling his eyes, Max groaned. "It's not too late to run for your life, Billie. We'll hold him back so you can get a head start. You deserve better than this guy. In fact, I have a friend I'd like to introduce you to."

Billie knew good and well this was just Max busting Tyler's balls but her fake fiancé was having none of it. He'd wrapped an arm around her waist and pulled her too close to his warm muscular body. It brought back memories of waking up in the same bed with him and she felt the warmth flood her cheeks.

Forget all about that.

What about the one bed back in the hotel?

She really needed to let her imagination know who was boss.

"Billie doesn't want to meet any of your friends," Tyler said, shaking a finger under his friend's nose. "I make her very happy if you must know."

Max's laser-like gaze swung to Billie and she almost shrunk back in her seat. It was as if he could see through their charade.

Like he knew the truth. That she and Tyler were a sham.

"Does he, Billie? Does Tyler make you happy? Because if he doesn't we'll take him out to the parking lot and teach him a lesson about how to treat a woman."

Damn, these guys were all about their displays of testosterone. It was all about who could "out-masculine" the other one.

Turning, she looked up at Tyler who was gazing down at her as if he was afraid of her answer. He was afraid. For real. He didn't know what she was going to say and it mattered to him. Because she mattered.

"He treats me very well," she finally replied, a lump constricting her throat. "I have no complaints."

Tyler was the one person in her life who had never let her down.

CHAPTER
Twenty~Three

TYLER LOVED his *Thunder* co-stars like brothers. They'd traveled together, partied together, stood up to one asshole director together. They'd even been injured doing stunts they had no business doing together. He'd take a bullet for these guys and he knew they'd do the same.

But he was going to kill them if they didn't shut the fuck up.

"Billie isn't my first girlfriend," Tyler said through gritted teeth in response to yet another piece of advice from Nate, Max, and Mike. The married men in their little group. "I'm not going to do something stupid."

Nate barked with laughter. "You are definitely going to do something stupid. All guys do. It's how you handle that stupidity that's important."

Max nodded. "Just apologize and admit you're wrong. Move on and get to the makeup sex."

Tyler couldn't believe his ears. Did they think their

advice was helpful? He looked to Mike for support. "You don't agree with this, do you? I mean, it's crazy. I'm not admitting something is my fault when it isn't."

"Yes, you will," Mike chuckled. "When your woman isn't happy, trust me when I say the entire household will be fucking miserable. The sooner you man up and admit whatever you did was wrong, the sooner harmony can be restored."

"What if I'm not at fault?" Tyler asked defensively. He could be clueless about a hell of a lot of things but he wasn't a total asshole.

The three husbands just smiled in response.

"When was the last time you and Billie argued about something and it wasn't your fault? At least a little?" Nate asked with a grin. "It takes two to tango. She can't argue with herself. You have to participate, mate."

Nate had a point, although Billie had a stubborn streak a mile wide and that didn't make life any easier for the two of them.

"So that's your big secret to a happy marriage?" Tyler jeered. "Just roll over and play dead? You're a bunch of pussies. Do your wives keep your balls in a jar on the mantle too? Christ, this is pathetic. You're big fucking movie stars. Action heroes. Women practically climbed up the sides of your hotel with their fingernails trying to get at you. Now look what you've become. Whipped. Totally whipped."

"Don't believe your own press, Tyler," Max warned with a shake of his head. "We're not really action heroes. We just play them in a movie."

"I know that," Tyler argued, already tired of the subject. He and Billie were fine. "But what you're advocating is crazy."

Mike scraped a hand through his hair. "You don't get it. We're not saying don't stand up for yourself. Of course you should do that. But when all the arguing is over and you two are just hurt and angry, not talking to one another, be the bigger man and just say you're sorry. I guarantee you she'll apologize as well. We want to make our wives' lives easier, especially with all the crap they go through because we're actors. Why keep arguing about something stupid - and it's always stupid - when you can just make up and go on with things? When you love a woman you want her to be as happy as possible, right? Right?"

Lifting a shoulder casually, Tyler nodded. "Well, yeah. Of course."

Frowning, Nate's gaze raked over Tyler. "You do love her?"

That question was easy.

"I love Billie," Tyler replied firmly, because he did love her.

Was he *in love* with her? That was a whole different discussion. He wasn't even sure he knew what that was.

Max clapped a hand on Tyler's shoulder. "Then always put her first. I didn't and it almost cost me Carrie."

"I'm not as dumb as you are," Tyler shot right back. "Anyone could see that you and Carrie were meant to be together. All you needed was a push."

The three men didn't say a word, simply letting Tyler's own statements sink into his brain.

"This...is my push," Tyler said slowly. "But I don't need one. We're getting married."

"But are you truly committed?" Nate asked worriedly. "Because things are going to start changing here pretty rapidly."

"You sound like Billie."

"We're just trying to help," Max replied. "You don't know a damn thing about love and marriage."

"And you did?"

Max grinned. "We're just trying to save you the lessons we had to learn the hard way."

They were making this out to be a bigger deal than it needed to be. Marriage sure had changed his friends. Now they worried about every little thing.

"I appreciate the thought but Billie and I are just fine. In fact, we're great. So you guys can just relax. I have this all under control."

"Just don't fuck this up," Max warned. "You and Billie are perfect for each other. Hold on to her."

"I intend to."

It was all bravado. Tyler didn't have a handle on this new type of relationship. Things were changing and there wasn't a damn thing he could do about it. He wasn't sure he even wanted to stop it.

But for sure, he intended to hold onto her. Tight.

———

Tyler had been acting strangely for the last hour or so, making Billie wonder what he'd been talking to Nate, Max, and Mike about. The four men had slunk into a quiet corner and huddled up, speaking low so no one else could hear them. From the expressions they had been wearing it had been a serious discussion and hadn't necessarily ended well. Max and Nate looked miffed and Mike had walked away rolling his eyes.

And Tyler? He had excused himself and disappeared outside for about fifteen minutes before coming back to the party, a hell of a lot more subdued than he'd been before. This wasn't the place to quiz him, however, so she let it go for now. If he wanted to talk about it, she'd be waiting.

As always when this group got together the music was turned on and the dancing started. That was the great thing about hanging around with actors. They were so comfortable with their bodies they didn't have many - if any - inhibitions about letting go on the dance floor. Billie loved dancing and she enjoyed it even more with Tyler. His arm would link around her waist, holding her close without making a show about it. It was then that they could just have fun and not worry about all the crap they had to deal with on a daily basis. Movies, roles, the press, and the ever -present wedding plans.

But something different was happening tonight.

She and Tyler were still having fun, gyrating with all the other guests out on the dance floor. They had both worked up a sweat and his skin glistened under the lights, calling her attention to the cords of his neck and the muscles bunching in his arms. There wasn't much space and she was pressed close Tyler, their bodies brushing every time they moved, sending tingles to her fingers and toes. A few months ago, Billie wouldn't have thought she could be this affected by a mere touch from him, but since she'd agreed to marry him all the rules had been flung out the window. Then there was the whole naked in bed thing that she couldn't get out of her head. Tonight wasn't going to help with that.

Holy hades, it is hot in here.

Her dress clung to the damp skin of her back and at some point one of the spaghetti straps had slid off her shoulder slightly but not exposing anything risqué. Tyler's fingers slid under the strap and she almost choked as arousal shot through her system like white lightning. Instead of slipping it back over her shoulder, he played with it while urging her closer to his large frame and insinuating his thigh between her legs as his other hand glided down her spine to land on the swell of her bottom.

The vibration of the music could be felt all the way from her feet to just where his legs met the juncture of her thighs. Her heart beat in time with every thump-thump of the music, both of them melding into a throbbing ache in her lower belly. Their gazes collided and held, neither one of them able to look away as the air crackled dangerously around them. Everyone around them disappeared and it was only the two of them moving in perfect synchronicity.

Billie didn't know which one of them started it but his lips were now on hers, firm and demanding, every inch the conquering male. A tide of sensation ripped through her veins, leaving her panting with its intensity. It was like everything they'd done together had been leading up to this moment of pure awareness and pleasure.

She could feel every nerve under her skin as his rough fingertips brushed her bare flesh, sending a jolt up her spine. A whimper escaped her throat, but luckily he was too busy staking claim to her mouth to notice or hear. His tongue ran along her lower lip and she opened to him, her capitulation a foregone conclusion. He smelled so delicious and she couldn't inhale without getting a lungful of his scent. A heady combination of citrus and musk.

This was far more than the crush she'd had all those years ago. She knew Tyler now, the good and the bad, but she still wanted him with a ferocity that shook her to the core. She hadn't prepared herself for this, and frankly had thought she was above it. That somehow she was the one woman in the world that Tyler Gaylord didn't affect.

She'd been dreaming. She'd always been attracted to him but she'd shut down those feelings, knowing she would only get hurt. Being his friend was far more important than being his lover, although at this moment they were running neck and neck.

Friendship. Home. Billie needed this man so much and for more than a furtive fuck in the limo on the way back to the hotel. He was more important than a few minutes of pleasure and a rush of endorphins. He was her lighthouse in the storm and she wasn't stupid enough to throw it away because her panties were damp and her mouth dry.

Bitter tears stung the backs of her eyes and she placed her palms on his chest, pressing him away when every cell in her body was telling her to pull him closer. As close as two people could be. At first he resisted but then seemed to notice that she wasn't moving to the beat any longer, her feet stationary and his hold on her loosened.

Tyler, don't let me go. Hold me.

"I need to visit the ladies' room."

Billie didn't wait for him to reply, turning on her heel

and practically sprinting out of the room and away from temptation. Because that's what Tyler was - pure sin and seduction.

And if she was brutally honest with herself, she didn't have a prayer of resisting. She was only delaying the inevitable.

CHAPTER
Twenty-Four

EVERYTHING WAS AS FUCKED up as could be. Just when life had started to get back to normal, it turned around and gave Tyler a good swift kick in the balls when he least expected it.

He and Billie had been dancing. Kind of dirty dancing, grinding against each other and it had been hot, sweaty, and sexy as hell. He hadn't been able to stop his hands from roaming up and down her slim curves or from kissing her full lips. A man could only take so much, after all. He'd admitted to himself that he wanted Billie.

Now she knew too.

And apparently wasn't thrilled with the idea. She'd ran from the dance floor like he was a serial killer in one of his movies, brandishing a big fucking knife. They'd managed to get their relationship back on an even keel and he had to go mess it up because of he'd been thinking with his dick again.

Now what? Should he leave her alone or go after her?

Normally he would follow her and find out what was bothering her, but he had the sinking suspicion that the problem was *him*. He was bugging her and he didn't have an answer for that conundrum. Because Tyler wasn't planning on going anywhere that was away from Billie.

Fuck this. I'm going after her.

He was determined that some things were going to stay the same whether his ring was on her finger or not. This was one of them. They were friends, and friends helped one another.

Tyler was halfway to the door she'd exited through when his phone vibrated in his pocket. He didn't receive many calls this late on his personal cell phone unless it was one of his friends on location in a different time zone. Retrieving it from his pocket, he saw that it was his agent Josh. This had to be important.

"Hey, Josh. What's going on?"

And make it fast because I need to find Billie.

"I think you're going to be happy to hear from me. I just got off the phone with Ron Weller. He's willing to meet with you."

A rush of elation welled up inside of Tyler. It had worked. He wanted to kiss Billie and buy her a Porsche. This was the chance he'd been waiting for.

"That's great news. When?"

"He's there at the convention promoting that historical movie he just finished. Both of you have impossible schedules but I found a spot where you can both meet. How does breakfast day after tomorrow sound?"

It sounded like an Oscar winning meal.

"Sounds great, Josh. You really outdid yourself with this one. I can't thank you enough, man."

Josh cleared his throat. "Listen, there is one more thing. Weller wants Billie to be at the meeting too. I guess he wants to see what you're like with your future wife. Is that going to be an issue?"

Tyler certainly hoped not, although Billie's behavior tonight wasn't encouraging.

"No problem," Tyler assured his agent. "This guy takes this *man in love* stuff seriously, huh? Just getting married isn't enough for him."

"You have to know that Ron Weller is a well-known asshole in this business," Josh said dryly. "A pure control freak. I know that this script is everything you want but I can assure you that Weller isn't. Off the set, he's a great guy but when he's working it's like a Jekyll and Hyde thing. He's sucked in some unwitting actors and then made their lives a living hell."

Tyler could handle himself on a set. He was all business too.

"It will be worth it in the end. I wouldn't say that every director I've ever worked with was a teddy bear, Josh. Remember the first *Thunder* film? We were all plotting his demise by the last few weeks of shooting."

But the finished product had been excellent. Sometimes creativity wasn't pretty.

"I remember. I also remember that he was as tired of all of you as you were of him."

"So it was mutual. Where are we meeting Weller?"

"I'll send you the details." Josh paused. "I went way out on a limb to get you this meeting so don't fuck it up."

Tyler didn't plan to.

"Thanks for the confidence vote. I'll call you tomorrow."

Shoving his phone back in his pocket he strode out of the exit, up the short flight of concrete stairs, and straight into an alley behind the restaurant. Billie was leaning against the brick wall and staring up at the sky, but from the stiff set of her shoulders she'd heard him join her.

Tyler glanced around the dirty area replete with an overflowing dumpster and a few dozen cardboard boxes stacked precariously high. Billie was standing way too close and he had a terrible vision of those boxes tumbling down right onto her head.

"You always know the nicest places to hang out, baby girl. What's next on the schedule? A cock fight? Or maybe an underground fight club?"

Her sigh was loud in the silence. "So much for some peace and quiet. Go back inside, Tyler."

Her voice had been thick and a little shaky. He didn't hear her like this much but he recognized it. Contrary to popular belief, he wasn't a complete bonehead.

"Don't think I will, babe. Tell me why you're crying and I'll fix everything and make it all better."

"Because that's what you've always done for me," she whispered softly but loud enough for him to hear. "You can't fix this."

He'd stepped closer and could now see her tear-stained face by the sliver of moonlight. Something clenched tightly at his chest and he had to concentrate to take his next breath. He didn't like it when Billie was unhappy. He felt...powerless and small. As if he failed her in some way. He lifted a hand to wipe the tears away but she jerked away from him as if she expected a slap instead of a tender caress.

What the fuck have I ever done to deserve that reaction?

His heart hurt where she'd shoved a virtual knife. Intellectually he knew that her reaction probably had more to do with her than him but his emotions were a different story. It hurt not to be trusted.

Dropping his arm to his side, he didn't budge an inch from where he was standing, crowding her personal space.

"Try me. I bet I can. Give me a chance."

Straightening, she shook her head, rubbing at her cheeks with the back of her hand.

"Not this time. Just let it go."

He wished he could but that was something he couldn't do. Not again. It felt like lately he'd been letting everything go and it couldn't continue.

"Because the problem is me. You know, babe, I might actually be the one person you should talk to. Seems like the best person to solve an issue with me would be...me."

"It's not you, it's me."

Realizing what she'd said, they both started laughing and the knot in his chest loosened slightly. If they could laugh together, it wasn't all bad.

"God, that was so trite," Billie giggled. "I can't believe I actually said that."

Tyler had to help her believe that not all things had changed.

"You can still talk to me. Who I am as a person hasn't changed."

Except that he kind of had changed since putting that ring on her finger. He felt different. Maybe more like a prospective husband, thinking about Billie and the future. It wasn't unpleasant, just surprising.

Finally she looked up at him, the conflict she was feeling clearly expressed in her eyes. He wanted to pull her into his arms and tell her that he would take care of everything.

Terrified she'd run away again, he didn't move a muscle, simply letting her speak her mind.

"I've changed. That frightens me far more."

Unless she didn't care about him anymore. She might think he was more trouble than he was worth.

"You're still the same stubborn Billie I've known for the last five years."

She placed her hand on his chest right over his heart. "I want to talk to you. I've missed that."

He spread his arms wide. "I've got all night. Let's grab a pizza and hunker down for a slumber party. You talk and I'll listen."

"You have to be up early in the morning," she reminded him with a gentle smile. "You have a big day and it's not a good idea to go into looking like one of the zombies from 'The Walking Dead'."

She was putting him off, trying to delay the conversation. "Nothing is more import–"

Trying to silence him, Billie pressed her fingertips to his lips which he in turn kissed, an action that surprised them both. But it felt right to do it.

"It can wait."

He wrapped his much larger hand around her smaller one, entwining the fingers.

"Tomorrow night. We'll order room service and hang

out. Just the two of us. We'll talk."

"We're supposed to go a party given by that liquor company, remember?"

"I remember, baby girl, I just don't care. Fuck 'em. We'll tell them I'm coming down with a cold. No one wants cootie germs. So promise me. Tomorrow night?"

"Tomorrow night," she promised. "Thank you for not pushing me on this. Now I have some time to sort of gather my thoughts."

Tyler might need some time to figure out his own. If Billie wanted out of the agreement, he didn't know what he would do. He had grown to like the idea of marrying her and being her husband. Dare he say it?

He was looking forward to it.

If he was honest with himself - and it was long past time for that - he needed her for far more than a movie role. Tyler needed Billie. Period.

CHAPTER
Twenty-Five

ANOTHER AWKWARD NIGHT sharing a bed with Tyler. When they'd returned to the hotel suite Billie had quickly taken off her makeup, brushed her teeth, and then slid into bed. All the way to the opposite side as far as she could get from Tyler. She was afraid that in her sleep she'd automatically reach out for his warmth and comfort.

After a fitful night's sleep, she'd slid out of bed as the sun was coming up and straight into the shower as Tyler slept on. She hoped to be put together and in control when she spoke to him next. She needed to tell him what she was feeling because going on like this wasn't an option. He'd challenged her to be "all in" and now that she was going back wasn't going to happen. They could only move forward. Together.

Applying a touch of blush with a big, fluffy brush she grabbed her phone off of the bathroom vanity when it rang, not wanting to wake Tyler. He needed his rest for the day ahead.

"Connie, it's good to hear from you. Is everything okay with Sierra?"

Billie had been working from the assumption that no news was good news.

"Things are really starting to look up for Sierra, Billie, and she has you to thank for that. The attorney filed for divorce along with a temporary order for support until they can go to court."

Pffft. Waste of time.

"Brian's never had a pot to piss in his entire life," Billie scoffed. "He's not going to give Sierra a dime. In fact, I wouldn't be shocked if he sued her for support. She was the one who kept food on the table with her waitressing jobs."

Worthless piece of skin.

"Your sister said something to that affect as well but the attorney said it's standard. Brian has assets he could liqui-date. A truck and a boat."

"That sounds like an excellent idea. I'd pay for the lawyer to get those papers ready."

"I doubt he'd ever sign them," Connie sighed heavily.

The bastard was never going to give Billie's sister a day's peace.

"He doesn't know where she's living, does he?"

"I don't think so. With your money she was able to get a nice one bedroom apartment in a decent neighborhood. Once the divorce is final she can look for a more perma-nent solution. The social worker said it was important right now to be able to move quickly if Brian figured out where she was."

There was something in Connie's tone. Something she wasn't saying out loud.

"The son of a bitch is out of jail, isn't he?"

"Yes," Connie admitted, her voice hesitant. "I think a couple of his buddies bailed him out."

That's just dandy. Shit and fuck.

Brian's mom and dad had washed their hands of him years ago so it certainly wasn't them, nor was it his brother who had once popped Brian right in the solar plexus when he'd verbally ripped into Sierra in front of the family one day. With his nasty temper, he'd pushed away most people in his life so Billie was surprised to hear he even had friends still.

"So how is Sierra staying safe? What if he finds her?"

"She's in another town completely over two hundred miles from here under an assumed name. The social worker arranged it. She also recommended that Sierra change her name officially, and when the divorce is final leave the state."

If Sierra was willing to relocate maybe she could move to California. The guest house was too small but comfortable. In fact...

"Connie, I need to talk to Sierra. I think she should just move out here with me."

If she asked, she knew Tyler would hire security for her sister until Brian was dealt with. The stalker laws were also strict in California due to the number of celebrities.

More silence.

"Connie?" Billie prompted, her heart skipping a beat in panic. "There is something wrong, isn't there?"

"No," Connie finally piped up. "I'm telling the truth here. Things are looking up for Sierra. It's just..."

"Just...?"

"Sierra isn't ready to talk to you, Billie. I told her she should when she got her new cell phone. I told her she needed to call you and thank you for what you've done but she said no. She needs time, honey."

"Time for what?" Billie asked, a bitter taste on her tongue. "She doesn't want to talk to me? That's fine. Let her know the offer is open."

"Honey," Connie said softly. "Don't be like that. Sierra wants to talk to you desperately. I could see it in her eyes, but she's ashamed that you had to bail her out of the mess she's made of her life. She's embarrassed and there's a part of her that isn't quite ready to admit what you've been saying all along. Give her some time."

Shame was something that Billie could understand. She had her share of it. Damn, she and Sierra were a freaking mess.

"Just...just let her know that I want her to come live here with us. We can keep her safe. She doesn't need to admit anything to me and I'll wrestle myself to the ground before I say I told you so. It won't be easy but I'll shut up."

That made Connie laugh. "This I'd like to see. But I will give her the message, honey. You just need to let her get settled in a bit and then I'm sure she'll call you."

"She doesn't have to. The money doesn't come with strings."

Billie hated shit like that. Obligation and guilt. Neither were productive.

"She wants to," Connie said again. "She has a few things

to work out first. She's seeing a counselor and hopefully that will help. She knows she has a lot of work to do. She knows she pushed you and pretty much everyone away."

Billie's eyes welled with tears as she thought of all the times she'd tried to reach out to Sierra only to be rebuffed. Eventually she'd given up. That had been a mistake. "He made her do it. He wanted to isolate her."

She'd been so focused on the call she hadn't heard Tyler come up behind her until his large hand came down on her shoulder, comforting and strong. This time she couldn't stop herself from leaning her cheek against his arm, wanting – no, needing - to soak up his strength. When it came to her family she wasn't the strong person she wanted to be.

"She knows that now, honey. She's getting stronger. You'll hear from her soon. I know it, so don't give up on her, okay? She needs you."

Billie thanked Connie and then placed the phone back down on the vanity as a few stray tears slipped down her cheeks. The last few days had been so full of emotion. It was a good thing they had a jam-packed schedule today. With any luck, she wouldn't have time to dwell on her problems.

"Who was that, baby girl? Want to talk about it?"

It wasn't asked in a pushy way. It was all up to her but she'd long ago decided to be honest with Tyler about her family situation.

"That was my friend Connie back home about my sister Sierra. She's out of the hospital and relocated far from her asshole husband. The attorney has filed for divorce so things are in motion."

Kneeling next to her, he rubbed the backs of his knuckles against her cheek. "That's good news. Is there anything else they need? Anything at all?"

This was why Tyler was so precious to her. He might act like an idiot sometimes but he had a heart the size of the Pacific Ocean. Which was good when she told him what she'd offered.

"Well...I kind of told Connie that Sierra should move out here to California. That we could keep her safe here. I was even thinking she could stay in the guest cottage for awhile."

There was certainly room in the main house but Sierra would probably want some independence.

Cautiously she watched Tyler's expression and breathed a sigh of relief when his eyes lit up and a grin bloomed across his too handsome face.

"Babe, that's a fan-fucking-tastic idea. And I have tons of contacts that can help her get a job. You wouldn't let me help you but will you let me help her?"

Carding her fingers through his sleep-tousled hair she gave him her best smile. "I will let you help her but she's not ready to talk to me yet. Connie said I need to give her time."

His smile dimmed slightly at her reply. "That's fine, I guess. But...she doesn't want to talk to you?"

"The last time we saw each other we didn't end on the best of terms, remember? Brian didn't want her to be in touch with family and I left Wisconsin."

"And you feel guilty about that."

Sometimes Tyler was too perceptive by far. As an actor, he studied people for a living.

"If I hadn't—"

"Don't even go there." Tyler waved away her objections. "You didn't do anything wrong. You can't help someone that doesn't want it."

"That's true but I didn't have to be so goddamn relieved about it. There was a big part of me that was happy when she told me she never wanted to speak to me again unless I was nice to her husband. She gave me the out I was looking for. Her life was messy and I didn't want to deal with it. I'm a terrible person."

Lifting her into his arms, he sat down on the edge of the massive bathtub, placing her on his lap. His hand stroked up and down her spine in a soothing motion. "You're not an awful person. You're human. You were frustrated that you couldn't help your sister and that she wouldn't listen. I've been there too, although the situation wasn't as dire. Tina was dating a real douchebag back in high school and she just wouldn't listen to me no matter what I said. Long story short? She ended up with a broken heart."

Tina was Tyler's older sister by eleven months and that had to have driven him crazy that she wouldn't listen to him.

"Did you say I told you so? Because I think Sierra believes I'm going to say it to her."

Tyler chuckled and pushed a stray strand of hair behind her ear. "Hell yes, I did and let me give you some advice. That's a sure way to fuck up a sibling relationship for awhile. Don't do it."

"I wasn't going to, although I'd want to. But I am happy

that she's getting better even if I don't get to talk to her. I don't want to make this about me."

"I have an idea."

Tyler had that dangerous look on his face. The last time he'd worn it they'd ended up on a road trip to the Grand Canyon because he was bored and in between movies. It was the best vacation they'd ever taken though. The pictures of him riding a donkey were priceless. If she ever had an inkling to retire young she could probably sell them for big money to any of the tabloids worldwide.

Groaning, Billie tried to wriggle off of his lap and run away. "Oh no. An idea. I cringe at the mere thought."

"Just simmer down." His hold on her tightened and his grin turned wicked. "Let's make tonight about more than just talking. Let's make it a celebration too. Celebrate your sister getting better. Hopefully she'll join us out here eventually and we can have a real party."

"You love anything with champagne," Billie teased, her tears long gone. "But I think that's a lovely idea."

When they were like this, it was as if nothing had changed. Billie felt so close to Tyler at this moment. If only she could wrap this up and keep it for those times when she felt lost and alone.

For that time in the future when Tyler moved on and away from her.

CHAPTER
Twenty-Six

LATER THAT MORNING BILLIE, Tyler, and Curtis along with a large bodyguard arrived at the convention center and were led through a crush of costumed attendees that appeared to be having the time of their lives. Their outfits were imaginative and elaborate and Billie couldn't help but be impressed. These people didn't do anything halfway and that was a trait she'd always admired. Tyler had it too.

Lately there were many things she admired about her husband to be. Today it was how his jeans fit. After last night she was hyper-aware of every little thing that made him Tyler. His easy grin. That dimple in his cheek. The way his hair sometimes fell over his forehead, or even how he used his hands when he spoke. The tension between them was high but she was determined to act as casually as possible today. This was business.

"Tell me again why the *Thunder* movies come to these events?" she asked Tyler as they turned a corner and saw a group of superheroes getting their photo taken. "It's not based on a comic book."

Tyler shrugged as a flash from a camera temporarily blinded both of them. "More than comic book movies come to these things. Any type of theme movie or series come here to debut their trailers, especially if the movie has characters that are unique or interesting. Just wait, you're going to love it. It's really fun."

Billie would have described what she was seeing as *organized chaos* but it all seemed to work for the most part. There appeared to be a line for everything. Autographs. Pictures. Panels. Souvenirs. Food and drinks.

The massive security guy ushered them into a small room where Sam, Nate, Max, and Kirby were already waiting. "It will only be a moment and you can go through those doors and out to your panel. If you need anything, please help yourself."

There was a table of snack foods, water, and soda. The bodyguard had disappeared somewhere, leaving them with a chatty and rather hyper young man who appeared to work there.

"Okay, you're going out in just a minute," he said, grinning from ear to ear. "Now are the ladies going to stay back here or would you like them seated in the audience?"

Good question. What was she supposed to do while Tyler was working?

"If it's alright with the ladies they can watch from the wings," Sam stated with authority.

Nate nodded. "Right, I don't want Paige out in the audience without security."

Billie's brows shot up. Why on earth would Paige need security?

Tyler and Max both agreed and the three women were stationed just out of the audience's view behind a curtain as the men filed onstage to the screams and applause of their fans. Carrie's eyes widened and she placed her hands over her ears as the decibel level rose alarmingly.

Paige groaned and leaned close to the other two women so they could hear. "This is why our men strut around and think they're God's gift. Nate is going to be insufferable for a few days until I get his feet back on the ground."

Indeed, the men were giving the fans their best Holly-wood smiles, waving as camera flashes went off in the crowd until the boys had to be blind. If Tyler hadn't been cock of the walk sure of himself before this moment, he certainly would be now. He was eating up the adulation with a giant spoon, although to be fair all the men were.

The panel began and the happy go lucky moderator named Steve opened with a question about the *Thunder* movie being their last - for most of them - and the inter-view was off and running. The hour was halfway over when the moderator asked Tyler about being engaged.

"It seems like the single men of *Thunder* are dropping like flies," Steve laughed. "Was there something in the water during the last shoot? Since you wrapped filming, Nate and Max have both married and Tyler, you're engaged. Of all of you, I have to say I never thought I'd be talking about you as a potential bridegroom. What happened?"

"That was a shitty question," Carrie whispered, her nose wrinkled in disgust.

Yes, it was but Billie had been expecting it.

Tyler's gaze swept the audience before turning back to Steve. "Billie is the most amazing woman in the world. It was that simple."

A chorus of *awws* was almost drowned out by boos that were just as loud. The crowd was split as to whether Tyler's engagement was a good thing. Now Billie understood why Nate didn't want Paige in the audience.

However, Tyler's declaration had been quite sweet and he was totally selling it to the crowd. He held up his hands, his smile wiped away, and shook his head.

"Hey, that's not nice. Billie is a wonderful woman."

"I love you, Tyler! Marry me!" yelled a fan from the back of the room. A cacophony of other women joined in exhorting all the men to dump their women and marry them. Soon Steve had to quiet the crowd again with a threat that he'd clear the hall if it continued.

"Feel the love," Paige said sarcastically. "Jesus, I hope we don't get shanked at this convention."

"I think I'm going to stick to the bodyguard," Billie replied, eyeing the restless crowd, over half of them female. They looked riled up about losing their men to marriage.

When the noise quieted down, Steve continued. "Correct me if I'm wrong, but you've known Billie Oliver for many years. When did you realize you were in love?"

Rubbing his chin, Tyler pretended to think about the answer. Or maybe he was thinking up a quick lie. Because he didn't love her. Not that kind, anyway.

"I'm not sure when the exact moment was but it kind of just snuck up on me, and now she's the most important thing in my life. I couldn't survive a day without her."

He was so convincing Billie almost believed it. And she knew what the deal truly was. But damn if he didn't have a lovesick expression on his pretty face and his eyes had gone all puppy dog. He really should win an Oscar.

"That is so sweet," Carrie said. "You and Tyler are such a cute couple."

"Thank you, but Tyler's the cute one."

Paige chuckled. "I think that's debatable."

The panel went on for awhile longer, both Nate and Max getting to wax poetic about their own wives, much to the chagrin of the ladies in the audience. Some fantasies had clearly been shattered today. Eventually the discussion circled back around to the movie and some of the men saying goodbye to their characters. When the panel was complete the burly security guard magically appeared again and escorted them to the autograph signing area.

Paige immediately took charge. "I don't know about you but I can't imagine sitting here for the next three hours watching Nate sign his name over and over until his fingers are numb. How about we go get some lunch and then walk around a little bit? These costumes are incredible."

"I could eat," Billie piped up, her stomach growling its approval. Breakfast seemed a long time ago.

"Me too," Carrie said, elbowing her brand-new husband. "We're out of here, Hamlet. See you back in the room."

"Wait," Tyler said, catching Billie's arm. "You're just abandoning me here at the mercy of this crowd?"

He was smiling so he wasn't really upset. Once he started interacting with his fans he would have forgotten she was there anyway.

"Absolutely," Billie replied, keeping her features solemn. "I'm throwing you to the wolves. Curtis will protect you."

The younger man who had been keeping a low profile this whole time smiled, his chest puffing up with importance.

"Heartless woman." Tyler's arm wrapped around her waist. "Then I want some sugar before you leave."

He was laying it on a bit thick, but then after last night she wasn't all that opposed to getting another kiss. After all, that was what she'd been thinking about all morning. How it had felt to be in Tyler's arms. Dinah's voice echoed in her head.

Enjoy it.

Bending his head, Tyler captured her lips with his own. The kiss was lingering and possessive but not overtly so in light of the audience they had - friends, security, volunteers, and a few hundred fans in line for an autograph. It was only when they broke the kiss that she heard the catcalls from the crowd who approved the display.

"This is definitely going to end up on Instagram or YouTube," Billie said in a scolding tone.

"Let them be jealous." Tyler's blue eyes had deepened to almost black. "I'll miss you."

Her entire body shook as if she'd touched a live wire.

After last night, their relationship had experienced a tectonic shift and now he wasn't bothering to mask the simmering desire in his gaze. If panties truly could turn into dust and disappear with just a look, her undies would have been history.

"I'll miss you too."

How she managed to casually walk away she didn't know but she did, not allowing herself even a glance over her shoulder even though she could feel his eyes on her ass.

"Holy shit," Paige marveled as they melded into the crowd, the bodyguard discreetly trailing behind them a few feet. "The air vibrates with sexual tension whenever you two are within a foot of each other. I think I need a cigarette and I don't even smoke."

"Chocolate," Billie stated firmly. "We need chocolate and lots of it."

She didn't smoke or drink. She only had one vice left. Sugar.

———

Normally Tyler was all about work. He could lose himself in it with a single-mindedness that amazed his coworkers. Today, however, he found himself thinking about Billie when he should have been concentrating on the hundreds of fans that had lined up since early in the morning to get his autograph and a selfie. Anyone who went to that much trouble and aggravation to meet him deserved his whole-hearted attention.

Buckling down, he worked through the line one by one. The volunteers kept it moving, making sure that each fan didn't take more than their share of time. The encounter followed a simple routine. He gave them a big smile, said hello, and asked them their name. Then he'd sign whatever they put in front of him and finally he'd ask if they wanted a picture, all the while trying to chat with them. He would ask various questions such as which *Thunder* movie was their favorite or what other booths and panels they'd visited so far. Sometimes they'd have a great costume on and he'd compliment it. His goal was to make the meeting memorable for the fan. This was their time with him even though it was short.

In between people, he turned to Curtis who had been hovering in the background handing him fresh Sharpies in different colors like a well-trained pit crew at Daytona and asked him to grab some water bottles for the guys. The convention center was warm and Tyler was working up a sweat. When he turned back, he wasn't expecting to see two ample breasts at eye level but there they were.

Their owner was leaning on the table, her hands braced on either side of him, and she was way too fucking close. She might be attractive but she was in his personal space. As surreptitiously as possible, he slid his chair back a few inches to put some distance between them.

"Hi, what's your name?"

Her long honey blonde hair fell over her shoulder and she gave him a coy smile.

Ah, I've been here before.

"Amber."

"Nice to meet you, Amber. What would you like me to sign today?"

She leaned forward a little farther, her breasts even more prominent, and then pulled a black Sharpie from her back pocket.

"Me."

Shit.

I've been here before too.

There were always one or two female fans every year that wanted him to sign their breasts or their ass cheek. And he always did it much to the delight of everyone around him as they snapped pictures or took short videos. The women received the attention and admiration they were looking for and he made a fan happy. A win-win.

But that was all before he was an engaged man. Now it just seemed wrong to be that close to another woman's boobs even if it was only business. He was beginning to panic when Max tapped him on the arm and pulled him aside.

"Just take the pen and hold it toward the end near you," Max directed. "Keep your hand and arm away from her body and tell her to keep still. You can do this. It might be easier if you stand up."

God bless Max. That was exactly what Tyler did, managing to sign his name across Amber's ample bosom without touching her even once. Then they took a selfie with her tank top pulled down showing off the signature before a volunteer hustled her away and the next person took her place.

"Thanks, man," Tyler whispered to Max. "I didn't know

what to do there for a minute. This married man stuff is more complicated than I thought."

"Rule of thumb," Max laughed. "If you even think for a moment you shouldn't be doing it, then for the love of God, don't do it."

Billie had been right. As always. Things really had changed.

CHAPTER
Twenty~Seven

TYLER'S CHEEKS hurt from all the smiling he'd done today. He needed a hot shower and a cold beer, plus a quiet evening with Billie. It was their celebration dinner and he had planned what he hoped would be a wonderful evening. Low key, and most of all, private. After last night, he wanted some quality time with Miss Billie Oliver.

To be bold and honest? He wanted to take her to bed.

They'd been dancing around it all day. This morning the tension had been thick enough to cut with a knife, and Billie had been sweetly blushing whenever he gave her more than a casual look. He hadn't been able to hide his desire and he hadn't even tried. It was there, real and strong, and it simply wouldn't be denied any longer. The more he thought about it the more he was shocked that they hadn't ended up in bed together before now. It was the logical progression of what was admittedly the best relationship he'd ever had with a woman.

"Tyler, did you get the message from Josh?" Curtis

asked as the three of them entered the hotel elevator ready to get some rest. Billie had her nose in the evening paper getting her daily fix of current events. She had this thing about reading actual newspapers instead of on her phone. "The meeting is going to be in Weller's suite at seven tomorrow morning. Is that okay?"

It was but even if it hadn't been Tyler would have moved heaven and earth to be there. This was his shot at something more, at being taken seriously as an actor like Max, Nate, and Mike. They did plays on the stage and were heralded by the critics as great actors of their generation. Tyler, on the other hand, was lauded for his abs or his smile. Eventually he wasn't going to be so pretty anymore and if he wanted any sort of career he had to take action. This movie was the perfect move.

"It's fine," Tyler assured his slightly jumpy assistant. This was Curtis's first convention and he'd run himself ragged worrying about the crowds, the temperature, the security, and a few more things that Tyler wasn't even aware of. The poor kid was going to have a heart attack at an early age at this rate. Tyler had told him to relax and that all conventions were like this but he wasn't sure Curtis believed him. "You're off for the evening so go have some fun. Don't worry about me and Billie until tomorrow morning."

"What about—"

"Nothing you need to do," Tyler interrupted smoothly, patting the younger man on the shoulder. "You're officially off duty. Thanks, by the way, for taking care of that other thing for me. I appreciate it."

Curtis gave Billie a sideways glance but she was

immersed in the newspaper she was carrying. "Glad to help. I hope it was what you had in mind."

"I'm sure it will be better than anything I could have done myself."

The elevator stopped at Curtis' floor and he exited, leaving Billie and Tyler alone. She was still engrossed in her paper and he didn't want to disturb her. It would be more fun when she walked into the suite if she was taken completely by surprise. Despite his fatigue, Tyler was already almost bouncing up and down with excitement and he didn't want her to notice.

Sighing heavily, Billie slapped the paper against her thigh. "What is wrong with people? Why can't we all just respect each other and treat others as we'd like to be treated? What happened to the golden rule? When did people become so sick and twisted?"

With an almost silent whoosh, the elevator doors opened and he and Billie stepped out.

"Are you mad about a particular story in the paper or just all the news in general?"

"In general."

"It's usually something with an animal or a child that puts you in this mood. Why do you put yourself through that every day? Stop reading the paper."

She gave him a scandalized look. "It's important to be informed. What if something really important happened in the world?"

"If it's that important someone would tell me about it."

They reached the hotel room door but Tyler didn't unlock it immediately.

"It's not the same," she argued. "I didn't have the

greatest education so I make sure that I know what's going on in the world."

"What is going on in the world?"

"Chaos."

"That's nothing new. I bet you Martha Washington said exactly the same thing in 1776. Now, I know you love your daily news fix but can you turn your attention to me, please? I have a surprise for you."

Tucking the paper into her handbag, he was rewarded with one of Billie's smiles.

"I guess I can do that. What kind of surprise? Is it a pony? I've always wanted a pony."

That was a running joke between them, although he was pretty sure Billie had never wanted an actual fucking pony. If for one moment he thought she had he would have purchased one years ago.

"Yes, that's exactly what it is. I had Curtis go out and buy a fucking Shetland pony and bring it up through the lobby of a five-star hotel and into the most expensive suite in the joint. I hope you like shoveling horse manure because it's been up here alone with nothing but food all day long."

Billie doubled over with laughter, holding her stomach as her cheeks went quite red. Damn, he loved making her laugh. Billie was beautiful all the time but like this...she was devastating. Watching her, something shifted in his gut and he had to stop himself from reaching out and pulling her body against his and covering every inch of her skin in kisses.

"I swear I would pay to see that," she said, hiccupping and coughing through her gales of laughter. "A pony in

Tyler Gaylord's hotel suite. I bet if I put a bug in Sam's ear–"

"That's enough," he growled, knowing where she was going with this. Sam Collins loved to pull practical jokes and he was definitely not above putting a goddamn horse in Tyler's hotel room. Shit, he was shocked that Sam hadn't already done it. "Don't give that asshole any ideas. He has plenty of his own."

Pushing open the door he stepped aside so Billie could enter. Her eyes went wide and he thought he could see tears glistening there. Curtis had done a hell of a job. Tyler made a mental note to give the young man a bonus.

The dining area of the suite had been completely transformed. White tablecloth. Red roses in crystal vases. A chilling bottle of sparkling white grape juice - since Billie didn't drink. Candles were lit everywhere and the air was filled with the soft sounds of some romantic song he couldn't remember the name of.

But she hadn't said anything or even moved from where she was standing. Did she hate it? Was it too obvious? He hadn't had to romance a woman in years so he was rusty as fuck.

"It's for our celebration," he said softly. "I thought we would do it up right."

Tentatively she stepped farther into the room, not saying a word until her gaze landed on the other surprise. A Monopoly game. Curtis had also made a trip to the nearest toy store.

"Where did you get this?" Billie asked, her lips turning up at the corners. "You know I love this game."

"I do." He made a big production of sighing and acting

put upon. "I thought you might like to play and kick my ass."

Wrinkling her nose, she ran her fingertips over the box and he desperately wished that was his own skin. "I don't win all the time."

"You win *most* of the time."

"I do, don't I? But it's not because I'm some great Monopoly player. It's because you have the attention span of a toddler and you get fidgety and start making mistakes."

That was true. When they played as a team against his friends, the two of them always slaughtered the competition.

Then she did the one thing he hadn't expected. She tapped the box twice. Their signal that all was okay. She liked what he'd done.

Billie leaned down and took a deep whiff of one of the roses, but he wanted to bury his nose in her hair and inhale her delicious scent. "Candlelight and board games. You really did think this through. I love it."

"Curtis did all the work," he had to admit. It was only fair.

"It was your plan, and you were kind of busy today. I think I can cut you some slack. Signing all those auto-graphs today. I heard you even signed a set of world-class knockers too. That must have been fun."

Damn. How quickly had that made social media?

He could feel the heat rising in his cheeks and he opened his mouth to explain but she was already shaking her head. "I was just busting your balls a little bit. I know you didn't do anything wrong."

"I assume there was video," he said, relieved she wasn't mad. He'd tried to be...delicate. Professional.

"More than one," she confirmed with a smirk, checking the chilling bottle. "You did good. You managed to fulfill her request without touching her once. I think she was disappointed, though."

Amber had been a bit miffed when she'd walked off but honestly what had she thought was going to happen? That he was going to sign her boobs and fall instantly and madly in love? Kirby might do that but Tyler was too damn old.

"I'm not worried about that girl. I was worried about your reaction."

"If you wanted to be with that girl then that's where you'd be. Not here." She wiped off the chilled bottle with a small towel draped over the ice bucket and then handed it to him. "Can you open this? I think we should make a toast."

He was happy to do that. As usual Billie was practical and no nonsense. "What are we drinking to?"

She held up the champagne flutes. "To being a team. No...to being a family."

Soon they'd be husband and wife but he and Billie already had a bond that went beyond friendship. But her saying it meant more than just words. She wasn't running from this and him anymore. He could see it in her eyes. She was here and she was committed.

"I'll drink to that." The cork popped out and he poured two glasses of the sparkling juice, handing one to Billie. They clinked glasses. Twice. "Here's to you, me, and family. We're a team, Billie. I'll always be there for you no matter what."

"I'll always be there for you," Billie echoed taking a sip of the golden liquid. "This is pretty good for grape juice."

"Hey, this is the best sparkling grape juice money can buy," Tyler laughed. "I spared no expense for my best girl."

"Your only girl."

That didn't bother him in the least. Billie was all he needed.

CHAPTER
Twenty~Eight

THEIR CELEBRATION HAD ALL the earmarks of a seduction. Gaylord-style. Roses. Fake champagne. Candlelight and soft music. An amazing dinner. The only thing out of place was the Monopoly game, but then he wasn't a Lothario in the traditional sense. He didn't need to try very hard.

A few days ago Billie might have called him out on his surprise but tonight she felt no such urge. This heat that had been shimmering between them was pushing them together, slowly but surely. She could kick and scream, fight it until she was exhausted but deep down that wasn't what she wanted. She'd crossed over last night into a scary no-man's land but turning back was impossible. Something inside of her had been awakened after his kiss and pretending they were just buddies wasn't something she could do anymore.

They were a couple now, and she wanted to see what being Tyler's woman would be like.

She didn't however want to make it too easy for him. Knowing Tyler as she did, he appreciated things more when he had to work for them at least a little bit. She wanted to draw this seduction out and enjoy it as much as possible.

She stood from her chair at the dining table and went to retrieve the Monopoly box, holding it up for his inspection.

"How about a game while we eat our dessert?"

The chef had prepared a decadent chocolate cake to go with the chateaubriand and the garlic twice baked potatoes and asparagus with Hollandaise sauce. Every bite had melted in her mouth and made her taste buds dance.

"You want to play, babe?" His blue twinkled and he seemed to be in a playful mood. "We can do that."

Tyler pushed the dishes aside while Billie set up the game. It started the usual way but tonight it was more difficult to focus. She was distracted by his deep chuckle and his hands when he moved his token around the board. She'd never noticed before but he had a small scar on his thumb and a patch of freckles behind his elbow. Every single thing about him had become fascinating, making it tough to function in the real world.

As usual, Tyler bought every single thing he landed on while she was more cautious with her cash. When she landed on Boardwalk she easily had the money to purchase the property. Three turns later she landed on Park Place and she was off to the races. Tyler didn't stand a chance as she began building a hotel empire. Thirty minutes later he surrendered his yellow properties to pay for rent and she began building there too with hotels on all three spaces.

"I'm screwed," he groaned as he palmed the dice for his turn. His token was about to go through some dangerous territory and one wrong roll could almost wipe him out. "You're a shark when you get the lead, baby. Have a little mercy."

"Cry to your mama. Come on, roll the dice."

Shaking his head and laughing, Tyler tossed down the two dice and they skittered across the board, stopping right by the Community Chest cards. He'd rolled a ten.

"Shit," he muttered under his breath. "I'm fucked."

Indeed, Tyler was in a sticky situation. He'd landed on Park Place and owed her big. Clearly he didn't have enough cash - again - to pay. Billie was eyeing his two red properties. If he gave her those, she could build more hotels. But that would still be letting him off easy.

He held up two one hundred dollar bills. "This is all I have."

"That is not all you have." She tapped his property cards. "You've got some valuable real estate."

Rubbing his chin, he appeared to be delaying, hoping for a reprieve. "If I hand over those properties I might as well just fold my tent and go home. It will be all but done."

"You don't know that for sure. You could make a big comeback."

He eyed the board and then her mountain of cash. "Just how do you think I would manage that? Steal your money when you're not looking?"

Ha. Like that would happen. She was always watching him, especially tonight.

"How about...?" Billie considered his situation and

wanted to be merciful. "Both of your red properties and I'll let you keep your cash."

"How about," Tyler countered immediately, "I give you one red property, one hundred dollars, and...the shirt off of my back."

Wait. What? Tyler was offering his *shirt*? For real? She hadn't seen that coming. Honestly she thought he'd be much more subtle about his seduction but now he was basically offering to strip for her.

When she really thought about it, a traditional seduction simply didn't make sense. They had too much history as friends. But there was something more when she looked into Tyler's eyes.

He was nervous.

Tyler Gaylord - sex god and movie star - was afraid of being rejected. For good reason too, because she'd been hot and cold since the day she'd agreed to this crazy engagement. He thought she might say no so he'd thrown out a goofy offer so if she turned him down he could play it off like it was part of the game.

So Billie had two choices. Refuse his shirt and demand both properties. They'd go to bed together but still very separate, the sexual tension still building between them. She wouldn't have to deal with the reality of this relationship for at least another day and could sit back and pretend nothing had changed. Or she could throw caution to the wind. Something that did not come naturally to her. Her entire life she'd needed to always think ahead, be careful, strategic. Living wild and free was something other people did, but not her. Frankly, she didn't know if she had the courage. Once she said yes, nothing would ever be the same.

Too late. It's not the same now.

If she'd learned anything in her life it was that she had to move forward. Looking back over her shoulder and pining for what might have been wasn't the answer. There could be no room for doubts.

She stuck out her hand and wiggled her fingers in a come-hither motion. "Hand it over then."

Before I change my mind.

Tyler didn't move at first but then a slow smile crossed his gorgeous face and his blue eyes darkened with...desire? Lust? The pupils were blown wide.

Tugging the cotton t-shirt over his head, he placed the garment in her outstretched hand. His scent hit her immediately as she tossed it casually over her shoulder. Her mouth went dry at the display of manly attributes before her. His chest was wide, his stomach flat, and the skin golden from the California sun. There was just a sprinkling of hair around his pectorals and then lower on his abdomen, a treasure trail that disappeared under the waistband of his jeans. Her fingers itched to reach out and explore it, find out if it was as silky as it looked.

Her palms began to sweat and she had to concentrate on her lips and tongue to be able to speak. "You still owe me a red property and a hundred bucks."

Chuckling, he retrieved the rent but didn't set it on the table, instead holding it out so she had to reach for it, their fingers brushing.

Billie wouldn't have been surprised if sparks had actually flown from their flesh where they touched. Her hand visibly trembling, she shoved the card and the money to the side as her stomach tumbled and twisted in her middle. The chocolate cake suddenly seemed like a bad idea. Tyler would have to be blind not to see her turmoil and she wasn't in the habit of disguising her emotions with him anyway.

Tyler held out the dice. "Your turn."

This time she held out her hand, palm up so he could dump the dice into it. Distracted, they played a few more turns but the next time Tyler landed on one of her properties with a hotel he only had fifty dollars.

At this point, the sexual tension was sky high and the temperature in the room felt like it was a hundred degrees. She was hot and bothered, and all she wanted to do was open the window and hang her head out to get a lungful of fresh air. She'd had to set his shirt aside because whenever she inhaled she was getting a hit of Tyler that made her head swim.

"Looks like I'm busted," he said, holding his lone fifty dollar bill. "Unless you're willing to make a deal."

"I'm listening," she said, her voice coming out like a frog's croak.

Just take the pants off, dammit.

Billie hadn't had sex in almost a year and now she was acting like some sex-starved female, panting after a hot guy. The intimate act had never been all that important to her, frankly. She'd enjoyed it but she hadn't screamed anyone's name when she orgasmed or felt the earth move under the bed. Sex was good and nice, and she liked the closeness. Not once in her life had she fantasized about ripping off a man's jeans and kissing whatever she bared.

Not once. Until tonight.

Now it was all she could think about. She'd seen Tyler in various states of undress many times over the last five years and it had never affected her the way just seeing him without a shirt did now. He wasn't a modest man and he'd done partial nudity in his movies but this would be different. Tonight he would be all hers.

Leaning forward, his lips hovered mere inches from hers. She could feel his warm breath against her cheek and she reached out, running her fingertips over his stubbled jaw.

"Perhaps we can work out a deal that will be mutually beneficial."

Tyler's voice dripped sex and the promise of pleasure to come.

Enjoy it.

Dinah's words echoed in Billie's head and for maybe the first time in her life she tossed away all of her inhibitions and grabbed the brass ring.

"It's going to cost you," she said, her own tone breathless and needy. He couldn't have failed to notice her own arousal. Her cheeks were hot and her hand had wandered down his neck to his chest where it had splayed out over his heart, feeling it thud strongly under her palm.

"I'm ready to pay the price. Are you?"

Yes. A million times yes.

CHAPTER

Twenty-Nine

TYLER HAD BEEN HALF-AROUSED PRETTY MUCH every single minute since last night's kiss but the moment Billie had intimated that she'd make love with him he'd gone from half-mast to full-on ramrod hard in a flash. Heat flooded his veins and his heart thudded painfully against his ribcage.

He was fucking nervous. This was Billie, and for the first time in recent memory, sex was going to mean something. This wasn't some passing physical attraction where they'd both get their freak on and then go their separate ways in the morning, never to lay eyes on each other again. This was more and she was everything he'd ever wanted.

Whoa. What the hell was that about?

He'd felt a momentary twinge of fear, like a noose tightening around his neck but then he'd thought about Billie and how it was all better when she was around. She truly was everything he'd ever wanted in a woman, and she was going to be his wife. The noose had slipped from his neck and wrapped painfully around his heart, squeezing to the point he could barely take a breath.

The relationship that had started out as fake and manufactured had morphed into something far different and more wonderful. This was what was supposed to happen all along. He and Billie were meant to make love.

What that meant down the road he didn't ponder. This was big enough and he wasn't quite ready to deal with the implications of making his best friend his lover. She'd said they would change and she'd been right. More than he'd ever imagined. He simply hadn't thought it would be so good.

Lifting her from her seat, he set her on the table, insinuating himself between her thighs as his lips descended, capturing hers in a soul-destroying kiss. Her mouth was like velvet and he couldn't get enough, his thirst for her unquenchable. She tasted like chocolate and sin as she returned his kiss with equal fervor. His hand cupped the back of her head, his fingers tangling in her long hair, the strands wrapping around his fingers.

A mewling sound escaped her lips as a groan was torn from his own throat. This encounter was going entirely too quickly. Billie deserved far more than a quick coupling on the dining room table like animals. She needed gentle wooing, soft kisses, tender caresses, but his inner beast was growling and roaring, exhorting him to claim and conquer.

Pushing the neckline of her blouse aside, he trailed wet kisses over her jaw and down her neck to the spot where her pulse beat madly under his lips. He nipped at the sensitive flesh of her shoulder, feeling her tremble in his arms. The exposed portion of her bra wasn't plain white cotton but it wasn't black lace either. In true Billie fashion, it was a pale, delicate pink with lace edging along the cups. Not able to help himself, he ran his tongue along that lace, wringing a gasp from her full rosy lips.

"Do you like that, baby?" he asked, his face buried in the valley between her breasts, inhaling the delectable combination of coconut and vanilla. Breathing in her heady scent, he marveled that Billie didn't need sexy lingerie or expensive perfumes to turn him on. All he needed was her. "Do you want more?"

She made a sweet sound in her throat but no words came, instead nodding her head as her fingers trailed up his spine. Her eyes were glazed and unfocused, the pupils blown wide with arousal. If he had any doubts that she was as affected by him as he was of her, they were gone completely. Her hair was mussed by his hands, her clothes askew. She looked wanton and wanting, giving him a look he was sure was as old as time. His cock ached with need but tonight of all nights he wouldn't be giving into its demand so easily. He wanted to make this evening special for Billie.

Mostly he didn't want her to have any regrets in the morning.

Scooping her into his arms bridal style he carried her into the bedroom section of the suite, laying her on the bed before pulling down the covers to expose the snowy white sheet underneath. Her green eyes glowing, Billie reclined on the pillows and held out her arms to him.

The wave of emotion that rolled over him was so strong he almost fell to his knees.

"Come to bed with me, Tyler."

———

Tyler didn't join Billie on the bed right away. To her breathless delight, he stripped off the rest of his clothes first, starting with those faded but sinfully wonderful blue jeans and ending with the black boxers and white cotton socks. Crawling over her, she allowed herself the luxury to truly study him, something she hadn't ever allowed herself to do before.

Too good to be true. That's the only way she could sum him up in mere words. The alphabet hadn't yet been invented that did his male beauty justice and at the moment she couldn't form real words or sentences anyway. Tyler was an athletic man and would have been whether he was an actor or not. Consequently, his body was all muscles, flat in some places and curved or ridged in others. That treasure trail she'd spied earlier during the game called to her and she could see that it ended at the base of his impressive cock, hard and long against his stomach.

She wasn't even aware she'd reached out until her fingertips were tracing the purple veins under the soft skin. Teasing the underside, she was rewarded with a ragged moan sounding from somewhere deep inside of Tyler and his enjoyment of her exploration made her even bolder. Sitting up, she replaced her fingers with her tongue delighting in the gasps and moans her ministrations wrought from this man she'd thought she'd known so well.

But here in this intimate moment, just the two of them,

Billie was aware that this was a part of him she'd never seen. The vulnerable male hungry for pleasure. Greedy for...her. Her need was just as urgent for him and she realized that he too was seeing a part of her that she'd never shown before. This was more than stripping off clothes. They were removing the masks of civilization that they wore for the real world and allowing their instincts to take control.

So far her instincts were telling her to make him sweat. Swallow every inch of him that she could and give him pleasure that he wouldn't forget for a long time, if ever. Her head bobbed up and down as his fingers wound into her hair, guiding her where he needed her the most. Her hands didn't rest either, running up and down his powerful thighs and over his perfect glutes, honed from hours running and in the gym.

"Baby, if you don't stop this is going to be over before it even starts, and there are a hell of a lotta things I want to do to you."

It was only then that she remembered that she was still fully dressed and he was totally nude. She'd take him all the way to completion and not regret it but it might be even more fun to allow him to make love to her too.

Pulling off of him with a pop, she reached for the top button on her blouse but his fingers brushed hers away. "This is my job and I intend to enjoy every minute of it."

Billie couldn't say for sure whether Tyler enjoyed it but she did. Each touch of his hand burned her skin and sent sensation skittering through her body all the way to her toes. Arousal built in her abdomen as her blouse and then her jeans were tossed away, leaving her in nothing but her panties and bra. The way Tyler was looking at her...with such naked lust had her own pulse racing in return.

Surprisingly gentle for such a powerful man, he pinched the fasteners of her bra together and it fell away, revealing her already tight nipples. Tracing around one with a fingertip, he dipped his head low and captured the other in his warm, wet mouth. With a moan of pleasure, she threw her head back as he suckled at the tight bud, worrying it slightly with his teeth before moving to do the same to its neglected twin.

Instinctively her hips lifted and he didn't hesitate to take the hint, his hand gliding down her body and straight to her center, wet and ready for him. Pressing two fingers inside of her, she gasped as he found a particularly sensitive spot, rubbing it until all the oxygen was forced from her lungs and she found herself begging for...what? Not less but more. Much more.

His deep chuckle rumbled in his chest and his thumb grazed her clit, back and forth, over and over until she thought she would go quite mad with need. He kept her on the edge, not letting her go over but not letting her come down either. She hovered on the precipice, her eyes tightly closed and the world spinning on its axis so fast she was sure it would fly off into the universe somewhere and collide with the sun, exploding into a billion little pieces that would glitter in the inky night sky.

"Say my name, baby," he ground out, his lips close to her ear.

"Tyler."

She did say it, softly, lovingly, caressingly, but then she said it again louder the second time as the bubble that had been building in her belly burst and the pleasure flooded through every cell in her body, almost painful in its intensity.

Before she could even catch her breath she felt Tyler pushing at her entrance, his large cock stretching the tight walls. It had been a long time since she'd been filled so thoroughly and completely, if ever. He possessed her in every way, mind, body and soul.

And her heart. She couldn't deny that. He'd snuck in when she wasn't paying attention and he'd become her world.

Forcing her lids open, Billie gazed up at the man who had - like the movie star he was - taken center stage in her life. His intense blue eyes were dark with passion and a muscle jumped in his jaw as he held as still as possible to allow her to grow accustomed to his invasion. Running her fingers down his muscled back, she anchored her hands on his perfect ass and began to roll her hips. Just a little at first and then more, quickly gathering confidence as an expression of bliss crossed Tyler's face.

He dropped his forehead so it was resting on hers as he snapped his own hips back and then forward, sending rushes of pleasure straight to her sensitive clit. "That's it, baby. Damn, you are tight. I'm barely holding on here."

With every stroke his groin rubbed against her, pushing her toward another release. Unlike so many of the men she'd known in the past, Tyler wasn't all about himself. To her surprise and delight he gritted his teeth and held back, urging her to come for him a second time as he made love to her slowly and gently, as if she was rare piece of china that could shatter if not held and touched just right.

Their gazes locked, he leisurely thrust in and out as if they had all day, his cock rubbing that sweet spot inside of her until she was once again on the edge of a cliff, ready to fall over. Her nails sunk into the flesh of his back as liquid heat flowed through her veins, the fire they created almost consuming her in its wicked flames.

"Tyler."

His fingers had moved between their bodies and he barely had to touch her at all before she exploded, her orgasm even stronger than the first. Waves battered at the walls of her senses and she had to clutch at his shoulders, holding on for dear life as she allowed the pleasure to take control, content to let it rule her if only for a few moments. Tyler found his release right after and she watched fascinated as he threw his head back, showing off the cords of his neck. With a groan of pure male satisfaction, he said her name and then buried his face into her neck, his breath warming her skin.

They stayed just like that for what seemed like forever but then he eventually rolled off of her, wrapping his arm around her waist and taking her with him and tucking her into his side. She rested her head on his chest and listened to his galloping heart as it gradually slowed down to a strong and steady thump. His fingers played with strands of her hair as the sweat cooled on their bodies. At some point, Tyler pulled up the sheet to cover them before pressing a chaste kiss to her forehead.

So many facets to this man. A sexy seducer one moment, a gentle lover the next. Then to confuse her even more, a tender protector afterward, holding her close and keeping her warm and safe. Who was the real Tyler

Gaylord? If it was all three of these men, plus the loyal friend that she'd known for so long she would surely be lost. He'd own every single piece of her heart and she'd never get it back. He could have all of her, she'd completely surrendered.

The crush she'd had on him seemed so long ago and far away. It paled in comparison to the overwhelming emotions that had taken over her very being. This was far more than she'd ever expected to feel for anyone, and she couldn't deny the truth.

Billie was falling in love with Tyler.

CHAPTER
Thirty

BILLIE RELAXED UNDER THE HOT, steamy spray of water, closing her eyes and letting it cascade down her front, soothing her body and mind. She was surprisingly at peace after crossing over the friendship boundary and into a sexual relationship with Tyler. At first when she'd realized she was falling for him she'd been panicked and worried, unsure as to how she was supposed to act after such a life-altering realization.

But as she'd lain in his arms afterward a peace had come over as he'd whispered funny things in her ear and stroked her long hair. Without saying a word, Tyler had shown her that he didn't regret what they'd done one little bit. It felt natural and right, and not a bit strange or awkward as she'd expected it to. It was simply an extension to the already solid bond between them. Whatever the future held they would deal with it together as a team. Tyler might not be in love with her but she was the closest thing he'd ever had to a real relationship with a woman.

He was certainly more than she'd ever had, whether friend, family, or lover.

She and Tyler had stayed up for hours, talking and making love. They'd made plans for Hawaii and even talked about the wedding and honeymoon. If he was feeling freaked out or suffocated, he hadn't displayed it. After weeks of feeling out of place with him and not sure how to act, they were back in sync. She felt completely comfortable with him again.

Billie had her best friend back. She had also acquired a passionate lover along the way which was quite pleasurable. Making love with someone she trusted so totally had been a revelation and she'd been able to just...be herself. With Tyler she never had to pretend to be something or someone she wasn't. She was enough.

Rinsing the conditioner from her hair, Billie heard the bathroom door open. She'd left Tyler asleep in their bed but apparently her knight in shining armor was awake and looking for her. The shower doors were completely fogged so she couldn't see anything but his outline. Hopefully it was him and not a serial killer.

"Close the door," she scolded, wiping the water from her eyes. "You're letting out all the heat and steam."

"Of course I am. It's roasting in this bathroom. Are you trying to poach yourself? And save me some hot water. We have a big meeting in less than an hour."

They did and Billie was nervous about it. This role was something Tyler desperately wanted and the entire reason they'd become engaged. The director obviously wanted to see them together. Perhaps he was suspicious of the timing of their relationship?

"That's why I woke up early. I'll be done here in a minute and the shower will be all yours."

The shower door immediately swung open and Tyler stood there in all his glory. Buck naked and hard as a rock. Had he woken like that or had he gotten hard thinking about taking a shower with her?

Did it matter? Nope.

Stepping into the tiled cubicle, he closed the door behind him and then pulled her into his arms, sandwiching his hard cock between them.

"You weren't there when I woke up. Don't do that again."

Bossy too, but she kind of liked the fact that he'd missed her in bed. She wouldn't push back on that.

"I needed a shower," she said instead, sighing with pleasure when his lips found a sensitive spot behind her ear while his hands gave her bottom cheeks a playful squeeze. "I'm done, really. I should go and get ready. We don't have a lot of time this morning."

Lifting his head, Tyler gave her his best sinful smile. "We have time. This won't take long."

She didn't know what he was talking about but then he dropped to his knees and pushed her up against the tiled wall, propping her thigh on his shoulder. His fingers came up and began to trace along her folds, just brushing her clit lightly like butterfly wings on the petals of a flower. Gasping, her head dropped back and she gave herself over to the pleasure. So fucking good.

Tyler was right. This wasn't going to take long.

His tongue joined his fingers and unlike last night when he'd drawn their activities out as long as possible, prolonging her arousal, this time he went in for the kill. Pressing two fingers into her tight, wet channel, he swirled his mad-skilled tongue around and around her clit, then swiped at it with the flat of his tongue before starting the pattern all over again. Within minutes she was a trembling, shaking mess and would have fallen to the wet floor if he hadn't been holding her up. Her knees were jelly, her heart was pounding, and a pleasurable heat was sweeping over her body. She only needed a push and she'd go over.

He didn't make her wait. Closing his mouth over the little button he sucked hard, sending her straight into the stars. She screamed his name and the sound echoed off the bathroom walls, sounding loud to her oversensitized nerves.

Before she could even finish her climax he had her lifted so her legs were around his waist and her back pressed hard against the slippery tiles. Thrusting up, he entered her in one stroke and they both cried out at the exquisite sensation of his cock fully sheathed inside of her. This was no languorous coupling of last night. This morning Tyler rode her hard and fast, barely allowing her to catch her breath. They were like animals going at each other, never getting their fill.

She felt her orgasm building in her lower belly again as she pressed kisses along his jaw and neck, anywhere she could reach. With every stroke he pushed them both higher, and she clawed at the already scratched and bruised flesh of his back.

"You like that, don't you, baby? You want my cock."

She'd learned something about Tyler last night. He

liked the dirty talk. A whole lot. She had to admit it was kind of a turn-on so she tried to give it back to him too.

"I love it. Fuck me harder, Tyler. Give it to me."

She didn't think it was possible but he did just that, thrusting into her harder and rubbing those sensitive areas every...single...time...like an expert marksman.

"You bet I'm going to give it to you, baby. This cock is just for you."

Of all the crazy dirty talk, it was his declaration of exclusivity that sent her over the edge. His proclamation that his cock was only for her was apparently just what her libido needed and she was off to the races. Toes curled, she screamed as her climax hit her unexpectedly, sending her spiraling into the clouds. Tyler was right behind her and he thrust into her twice more before going completely still, his chest rising and falling rapidly.

Even when he finally lowered her legs to the floor, he still held her up and thank goodness for that because she was still a quivering mess. Grabbing onto the metal bar in the shower cubicle she took several deep breaths, a big smile blooming on her face. Tyler too seemed to take his time recovering but she could see the happiness she felt reflected in his expression.

Billie was so happy that she couldn't control what happened next. Out of the blue she started to giggle, and then to make matters worse Tyler joined in, making her laugh all the harder. Her stomach hurt and she held her hand over her abdomen as she wiped tears of happiness from her eyes.

"What are you laughing about?" she asked him, reaching up to trace that perfect jaw with her fingertips.

He shrugged and chuckled, pulling her in for a long kiss that almost singed her lips off.

"I don't know. You were laughing so I started laughing. What were you laughing about?"

She didn't even think about lying, not with him. "I'm not really sure, actually. I'm just so happy."

His hands cupped her face and his heart was in his eyes. "Me too. Billie, I–"

She placed her fingers over his mouth. "You don't have to. Never think that you have to. This is enough."

It was more than she'd ever had.

He kissed her fingers and then pulled them gently away. "No, it's not. You deserve the words. Billie, I think I'm falling in love with you. I've never been in love so I'm not sure what it's supposed to feel like but I think this might be it."

She was dizzy all over again but she forced herself to not look away. This moment was way too important.

"I think I'm falling in love with you too," she said. "It's scarier than hell, isn't it?"

His expression relaxed into a grin. "It is but I'm glad I'm not out here alone."

Linking her hands around the back of his neck, she pulled him down for another kiss.

"I think you knew I was out on that limb with you. I think you knew I always have been."

"It's going to be good, babe," he said earnestly. "I promise I'm going to do all I can to make you happy."

Did he not see it? Did it not show?

"I already am."

CHAPTER
Thirty-One

AFTER MAKING a pact to bathe together every single day, Tyler and Billie dressed and headed to the director Ron Weller's suite just two floors up for a breakfast meeting. It was only one of the most important meetings of Tyler's life. Certainly not *the* most important but it was in the top five. He was happy to have Billie holding his hand the entire way. Just having her next to him made him more relaxed and confident. If this guy couldn't see how much he adored Billie then he needed to get his eyes checked.

"Are you ready?" she whispered as they stood in front of the director's hotel suite door. Tyler's agent Josh was supposedly already there according to his last text.

"As ready as I'll ever be. Let's do this."

The door swung open and Josh stood on the other side, looking less than his usual happy self. His shoulders were tense and his lips were pressed together until they were almost invisible. Not a good sign. They entered into a living/dining room area dominated by a sectional sofa on one side and a large dining table on the other. Both looked out onto the San Diego skyline. It was the exact same view that Tyler's room had only the suite was configured differently.

Ron Weller, the current hot shot director after his Oscar award-winning movie just months before, stood from the table and held out his hand. Weller was about Tyler's age but he looked ten years older, his skin tanned and weathered from the sun. Tyler had read that Weller liked to sail when he wasn't working on movies.

"It's nice to meet you again, Tyler. When was the last time? Was it Cannes?"

The butthole knew it wasn't Cannes.

"Actually I think it was at the *Vanity Fair* party after the Oscars a few years ago."

Weller nodded as if he remembered it well. "Yes, that's right. I didn't see you this year."

"I was working," Tyler replied, not bothering to go into details. Weller didn't give a shit about some big budget popcorn movie with car chases and Hollywood bad boys. Sliding his arm around Billie's waist, he pulled her close and dropped a kiss on the top of her head. "I'd like you to meet my fiancée, Ron. This is Billie Oliver. You may have seen her work in–"

"*Lace Angels*," the director interrupted, shaking her hand. "Fabulous film, Miss Oliver, and you were especially good. The scene where you confront your mother was incredibly powerful."

Tyler hadn't thought about that movie in three years

but now that he knew about Billie's past it was no wonder she'd been so good in that film. She'd had the emotional baggage to work with the script. Kind of like Tyler himself.

"Thank you, Mr. Weller, and please call me Billie."

"And you must call me Ron." He swept his arm toward the table. "Please come sit down and have some breakfast. We can talk about your interest in my upcoming film."

Tyler, Billie, and Josh settled at the large table and quickly placed a few items on their plates. Honestly, Tyler was too nervous to eat but he wasn't going to let Weller see that. He'd known industry assholes like this guy for years. Never show fear. Never show that you give a shit. Leave them no ammunition.

And smile the entire time like you had the world by the balls.

Weller refilled his coffee cup before opening the conversation. "I was surprised to hear about your interest in playing Zak, Tyler. He's a far cry from your usual characters."

Billie stiffened beside Tyler so he placed his hand on her thigh to let her know it was all just fine. He'd expected a fencing match. Weller wouldn't be persuaded easily but his financial backers were a different story. Two of them were sitting at the table with them. Gray-haired and not good-looking enough for Hollywood, they practically reeked of cash.

Now these guys cared about who Weller cast in the movie because they wanted a hefty return on their investment. Tyler was a proven box office draw and could hit all the important demographics. Weller wanted art after fulfilling his studio contract with that historical movie. These boys wanted money.

Before replying to Ron, Tyler decided to play one of his aces. Leaning forward he offered his hand to one of the backers. "I'm Tyler Gaylord, I don't think we've met before."

The golden boy smile and charm always paid off and this time was no exception. The two men shook Tyler's hand and told him what fans they were. It appeared to be sincere, too.

But that didn't mean they wanted him for this movie, though. Their opinion remained to be seen. Tyler finally turned to Weller to answer his query.

"I feel very close to Zak, Ron. I think I understand where he's coming from and I'd like to give him a voice, bring him to life."

The man's brow quirked and a cynical smile played on his lips. "You haven't even seen the script."

"I've read the book. Unless you're going completely off with the story, I know that I can embody this character and bring him to the masses. Show them his pain and his joy, but mostly his passion, what makes him tick."

"My movies aren't for the masses."

Except for the last one he'd directed but he'd already made it clear it was about the money. The guy thought he created visual masterpieces. He'd compared himself to Picasso in one interview. Tyler would concede that Weller was good, but he was no Spielberg or Scorsese.

"I understand Zak." He wasn't going to argue the merits of box office success with Weller. "I know how he feels and what motivates him."

The director shrugged. "A lot of actors do."

This time it was Josh who spoke before Tyler. "But those actors aren't willing to work for scale on this picture. Tyler is that excited about this character. He's willing to waive his usual twenty million asking price."

The two finance men straightened up in their chairs. Yep, he had their attention. They were practically openly salivating. The older of the two men began typing something into his phone. "What about points on the back end?"

"He's willing to waive those too."

The money-men were almost in a frenzy, red-cheeked and tapping madly into their cell phones. Tyler had done exactly what he'd set out to do this morning. Make a goddamn impression.

Weller, on the other hand, wasn't happy. His eyes had narrowed to silver-blue slits. "What do you want in return?"

Normally Josh did all of this and Tyler only heard about it later but it looked like they were going to negotiate right here and now.

"Top billing," Tyler said before Josh could reply for him. "A push from the studio for awards season. Executive producer credit."

Weller was already shaking his head. "Absolutely not."

"Which was the deal-breaker?" Josh asked. "Billing? Awards? Or the credit?"

"The credit," Weller bit out. "He's an actor, not a producer."

"His resume says differently." Josh held up his hands in a stop motion. "This meeting isn't about negotiating. This is about both of you meeting and talking about Tyler's interest in this film. If he's not what you want, we'll be leaving. He has a big day ahead of him meeting with thousands of fans."

Whoa, Josh wasn't bluffing either. He was fully prepared to walk out without a backward glance. As much as Tyler wanted this role, he knew it was the right thing to do. He'd take Weller's snide remarks about his acting and background, but he wouldn't be knocked around in negotiations when he was willing to give up monetary gain for artistic credibility. His stance wasn't exactly unprecedented, either. Big box office stars often took lousy money to make more "serious" films, but they usually received something in return.

The younger money man was openly sweating. "There's no reason to walk out of here. This is just a friendly discussion."

Like how hunters and deer were best buddies.

Weller's attention suddenly swung to Billie, his gaze laser-like in its focus. "What do you think of all of this? Do you think your fiancé would make a good Zak?"

Her fingers tightened in Tyler's and she turned to look at him with such love and adoration in her expression that he almost choked on his own spit. He'd waited his whole goddamn life for a woman to look at him like that. He'd waited five years too long. She'd been a few feet away the entire time. He'd been a blind idiot.

"No," she said softly, her lips curling up into a smile as everyone in the room but Tyler gasped in shock. He knew what she was going to say, just as he knew what she was going to have for breakfast or what movie she wanted to watch. "He wouldn't be a *good* Zak. I think he'd make an *amazing* Zak. He's without a doubt the most nurturing and protective man I've ever known in my life."

Chest puffed up with pride, Tyler couldn't stop himself from leaning down to brush her lips with his. He wanted to stand up and brag, *"That's my woman. Isn't she the most wonderful in the world?"*

But of course he didn't because she'd be mortified if he did. Instead he put every ounce of emotion he could into his touch, holding her hand as if his life depended on it.

Weller was staring at them oddly as if he didn't quite understand what he was witnessing. Tyler couldn't blame the man; after all, few people were going to believe that he'd been tamed by Billie Oliver but it was the truth. He was down for the count and he was happy about it. No way did he want to go back to his old life.

The director's expression was stormy but he did something Tyler didn't expect. He reached behind him and picked up a binder on the end table.

"Here is a copy of the script. Why don't you take a look at it and see if you're still interested after you read it? If you are, we can let the business people negotiate." Weller leaned forward. "If you do decide to do this movie, I think it only fair to warn you. I don't put up with any shenanigans on my set. Come ready to work and to dig deep or don't come at all."

Weller stood and that seemed to be the end of the meeting. The three of them stood as well and headed for the door, the script tucked under Tyler's arm. No one said a word until they were in the elevator and it was Josh who broke the silence first.

"I'm not sure what just happened in there but I think

you have the part. God help you, Tyler, because that guy is a total asshole. He's going to make every day of production a living hell for you."

As long as Tyler was playing Zak he didn't give a shit. Weller could kiss his ass.

CHAPTER
Thirty-Two

IT HAD BEEN a long day at the convention but Billie and Tyler were finally back in their hotel room. The minute they'd walked in the door she'd made a beeline for the bathroom, stripping off her clothes and soaking in the jacuzzi tub. After making a short phone call to his publicist, Tyler came in to join her.

Reclining back on his chest, she ran her toes down his calf. Even his feet were sexy. It wasn't fair. "Can I ask you a question?"

"You know you can, babe, but why do I get the feeling that it's going to be one that I'm not going to like?"

She wasn't sure whether he was going to like the question or not. Tyler didn't like explaining his motivations and reasonings. He made decisions and when she second-guessed them he could get impatient and frustrated. That didn't mean he didn't listen to her concerns. He did and sometimes he even changed his mind. But the questioning process wasn't always the easiest for him.

"Ron Weller is a douchebag."

Chuckling, Tyler bent his head and pressed a kiss to her shoulder. "True, but that's not a question, babe."

"It's the first part of the question." Sitting up, she twisted around so she could see his expression. "This guy is a total asshole. Everyone could see it. Why do you want this role so badly knowing you'll have to deal with him day in and day out? There are other movies that can get you an award, Tyler. Other films where you can grow and stretch your abilities. What's so special about this one?"

At first, she didn't think he was going to answer her. His body language began to close up and his gaze shifted away as if he was hiding something. She almost turned back and gave up when he spoke.

"I understand Zak because I was him. Not all of his life, of course, but I understand what shaped him."

Billie had read the book the movie was based on and she couldn't think of a character further from Tyler than Zak.

"You're going to have to help me here. How are you like Zak?"

His mouth quirked up into a half smile. "I was just like him. I was the geeky, ugly kid in school with braces on my teeth, wearing thick glasses. I was bullied and teased pretty much every day of school until my sophomore year of high school."

There was absolutely no way Tyler was telling the truth. She'd seen a picture of him as a one year old baby and he'd been definitely cute.

"Your mother showed me photos of you so I know that's not true."

"Mom showed you a baby picture, but she didn't show you any photos of my awkward adolescent years. She only showed you what I allow her to show. I begged her years ago to put the bad ones under lock and key. I was the chunky, nerdy kid in school, babe."

Now that Billie thought about it, Tyler was right. She'd seen baby and toddler pictures and then some from his high school years. Nothing in between. How had she not noticed?

Her gaze couldn't help but run up and down the beautiful man before her. "What happened? Obviously you aren't...I mean...now..."

Tyler ran his fingers down a few stray strands of her hair that had escaped the hair tie.

"I grew six inches the summer between freshman and sophomore year in addition to getting contacts and also having my braces removed. Suddenly I wasn't heavy anymore. I grew another three inches before Christmas. My mom was beside herself trying to keep me in clothes that year. By June I was six foot one and hitting the gym every day."

It was hard to imagine him different than he was now. "But you couldn't have been ugly–"

"Baby," he laughed at her consternation. "Trust me. I was a homely kid. I grew into my nose and ears. Mom said she should have known I'd be tall because I also had big feet as a kid. I didn't look like this."

"You're gorgeous now."

"Thank you," he replied huskily, capturing her lips with his and taking her breath away. "It was a long time ago but I've never forgotten. Zak had the same issue. He'd been bullied in school but later in life he found his true love in Rebecca. Kind of how I found you."

Her chest didn't feel large enough to hold her heart. What was it about this man that could turn her into mush with a look or a simple statement?

"You romantic fool," she teased. "Just don't try to prove your love and devotion the way Zak did. He went a little too far."

"Zak didn't want to live in a world without Rebecca," Tyler said, shaking his head. "Jumping in front of that bullet was the only way."

"But then she had to live without him," Billie pointed out. "Plus, she had the guilt of knowing he'd saved her life. That's a heavy burden for anyone to carry. So don't do it. Now if you want to sacrifice the remote or the last cookie, I'm fine with it."

"I'll always give you the last cookie. Unless it's chocolate chip. Then it's survival of the fittest, baby."

She poked him in the chest. "Just stay away from my oatmeal scotchies and we'll be fine."

Wrapping his hand around her pointer finger he raised it to his lips. "So are you okay being with the geeky kid?"

Hell yes.

"Haven't you heard? Geeks rule the world now. Of course I'm okay."

"I kind of got the feeling that your school years weren't all that great either."

They had that in common and she'd never realized. He'd understood because he'd experienced it too.

"They weren't but we were teased because we were poor."

"It's the same thing but what matters is who we become."

She opened her mouth but quickly closed it. Perhaps that wasn't the thing to say.

"Spit it out, Wilhemina. You know you want to."

Sighing, she rolled her eyes. "It's just...it kind of explains you. I mean, you've always enjoyed the attention of attractive women but this sort of puts it into perspective."

A grin split his face. "You think that I lack self-esteem and I need women telling me I'm hot? Honestly, I like it when they do but I don't need it. At least I don't think I do. Maybe early in my career I was hungry for validation but shit, I hope I'm past all that by now. I want to be known for other things than how my jeans fit."

"And that means this movie," she finished for him. "I get that you think you can play Zak because you understand his pain but you could also play so many other parts that would be just as amazing. You don't have to work with this douche. Find another script."

His fingers tenderly brushed her cheek. "I'm going to tell you a secret, something I don't say to many people. Hell, I think you may be the only one, actually. I'm not that great of an actor. I'm decent but I'm not in the same league as Nate or Max. They're great actors, theatre trained and all that. I'd love to be like them someday but I may never be that good. I'm not sure about Hamlet or Richard the Third but I know I can be Zak."

Did he honestly believe that? "You've been reading too many of your reviews. You're a wonderful actor and I know that you can dig way down deep and do great characters' roles. You have it in you."

"Maybe now." He seemed to have trouble putting his thoughts into words. "Let's face it, six weeks ago I'd never even been in love. Just how deep do you think I am?"

"Give yourself some credit. See yourself through my eyes. You're as deep as the ocean. I wouldn't be with a guy who was pretty but superficial. You just pretend to be that way, but it's not who you really are."

He pulled her closer to his chest, pressing a kiss onto the corner of her mouth. "You're good for my ego. If there were only some way I could thank you for believing in me. Some physical action that would demonstrate my adoration and devotion."

This was the Tyler Gaylord she knew and loved. "You are a big goof. Take me to bed and make me forget my own name."

"Yes, ma'am."

Life was good and Billie was happy. She had everything she'd ever wanted.

CHAPTER
Thirty-Three

BILLIE SLIPPED on her sunglasses and stretched out onto the lounge chair, her bikini-clad body capturing all of Tyler's attention. Even against the gorgeous Hawaiian backdrop, she was the most beautiful thing there and he wasn't too proud to say that she'd kept him in a state of perpetual arousal since they'd arrived three days ago. Because of the warm temperatures and the isolated nature of the beach house he'd rented, she mostly wore teeny-tiny swimsuits or the occasional sundress. Happy to be in each other's company, they had yet to venture out to see other human beings.

They'd had perfect weather so far, sunny and warm, with slightly cooler nights. The home sat right on a private beach and when they weren't swimming, snorkeling, or sunning themselves, they were inside the elaborate master bedroom making love. It was the best vacation he'd ever been on and - as lovely as the island was - Billie was the reason.

Putting down her book she turned toward him, sliding her glasses down far enough that he could see her eyes. "So? How's the script? Is it any good? Books are always better than the movie."

Tyler didn't disagree and this script was no different. "It's good. They've had to cut a lot of the childhood scenes and I think it makes his motivation weaker. On the other hand, I won't have to compete with a little kid for the Oscar or a Golden Globe."

"Never work with children or animals," Billie giggled. "But you're going to break that rule if you do this movie."

"*When* I do this movie," he corrected. "I think Josh can get the deal done."

They were still wrangling about the producer credit. The money men didn't care. This was all Weller being an asshole. He didn't like anyone else to get any credit, formal or informal. After his Oscar win he'd spent the next several interviews trashing everyone he'd worked with, bragging that he'd been the savior of the film. But Hollywood didn't care if he was a jerk, they only cared if he made movies that sold tickets.

"I still think you're insane to work with Ron Weller. He'll make every day of that nine week shoot a misery."

"No doubt but I think he underestimates how crappy I can make his life, too. We've seen how he works now so I can be prepared. My public relations machine is a hundred times more powerful than his. He'll come out looking like the smaller man."

"That won't be hard considering he is the smaller man. When I talked to Josh this morning he said that because Weller is interested in you for the movie he's getting several more offers for these more serious films. Are you going to take a look at those?"

"You talked to Josh today?" Tyler didn't remember her being on the phone but then he'd fallen asleep in a hammock on the front porch after breakfast. They'd been up most of the night doing debauched things to each other. "What did he call you about?"

"He's sending some scripts to the house and would like me to look them over when we get home. It seems that being your fiancée is a big boon to my career. Go figure."

He'd been thinking about that and more. "I had a thought that maybe we should work together. I can talk to Josh about putting the word out. We can actively look for a project for the both of us. If you wanted to, that is. I know you have your own career."

Sitting up, Billie looked more excited than he'd expected. He'd thought she might not want to have her acting career more entangled with him than she already did.

"I think that's a great idea. We could do a romantic comedy. Like Spencer and Tracy."

He smirked at the idea, not sure the public was ready for him to tell jokes for an hour and a half. "Hmmm...or maybe an action movie. Like Pacino and DeNiro."

"As long as I get to be DeNiro." She nudged his leg with her toes. "You'd be great in a romantic comedy. You have great timing and you're genuinely funny."

He gave her his best sad puppy face. "Yeah, but I'm not trying to be funny. People just naturally laugh at me."

She threw back her head and laughed for real, her green eyes sparkling with delight. How had he not noticed how incredibly beautiful she was? How sweet and smart? How kind and caring? How had he not whisked her away and married her before now?

Marriage. Not the fake kind that they were planning but the real fucking deal. He'd been thinking about it more and more and he'd come to a conclusion. He needed to talk to Billie about this whole mess he'd dragged her into. He wanted to cancel the showmance for good and this time propose for real. Like on one knee, begging if he needed to. He didn't want her to ever think for one single minute that he'd married her for a movie role.

Billie was the one.

And now that he was sure, he couldn't wait until the autumn and a big fancy wedding. When she was in the shower yesterday he done some research online regarding getting married in Las Vegas. It was easier than he'd imagined. If she wanted the big to-do he'd bite the bullet and wait, but if she didn't? Vegas, baby.

"I know why they laugh at you," Billie said, pushing up her sunglasses and putting her nose back into her book. "You're a big goof, remember?"

"But I'm your big goof."

He'd be content with that. For now.

————

Billie was having the most amazingly erotic dream. She was lying on the sandy beach, water tickling her toes with every pull of the tide. The sun beat down on her nude body but suddenly she felt a shadow fall over her, blocking her from the warming rays. Opening her eyes, she blinked a few times as a figure came into focus. Tyler, as naked as she was, hovering over her with that look on his face. The hungry one that made arousal stir inside of her at the very thought of someone wanting her so fiercely.

He fell to his knees on the sand and began kissing her, their mouths fused together and their tongues dueling for supremacy. Tyler's hands were everywhere at once it seemed, leaving a trail of fire in their wake. Billie moaned his name as his lips trailed lower, down over her breasts, tickling her belly, then finally brushing her clit with the flat of his tongue.

Jolting awake as if she'd been stabbed with a cattle prod, she moaned Tyler's name as her eyes focused more clearly on the ceiling above her. She was lying in bed and that naughty boy was kneeling between her legs, his face pressed up against her most intimate parts. What a lovely way to wake up in paradise.

His skilled tongue did devilishly evil things to her swollen button and it didn't take long until he had her legs trembling and her head thrashing back and forth. The little shit was keeping her on the edge deliberately and she would have none of that dominant control bull. At least not this morning. Maybe they could play that game tonight. Right now she wanted an orgasm and Tyler had taken her to the brink.

Curling her fingers into his scalp, she gave his hair a tug to let him know her patience had waned. She felt his chuckle against her sensitized flesh as his mouth closed over her clit, giving it flicks with his tongue until she plunged over the edge. Given barely any time to enjoy the bliss, Tyler flipped her over onto her belly and pulled her up to her knees. His fingers flexed on her hips and he leaned forward, his lips close to her ear and his warm breath caressing her shoulder.

"Brace yourself, babe. We're doing this fast and hard."

It was her own fault, really. She'd teased Tyler the night before when they'd been fucking in the kitchen, her on the counter with her legs over his shoulders, that she wasn't made of glass and she wouldn't break. Apparently he'd taken those words to heart because he thrust into the hilt in one go, sending a shockwave through her already overwrought nervous system.

Already starting her climb, she braced herself with her hands planted on the mattress to withstand his hard thrusts, each one stimulating her g-spot and sending her arousal spiraling upwards. Tyler had one hand tangled in her long hair and the other anchored onto her bottom, giving him the control he needed. There was something so incredibly hot and sexy about this. He was taking her as if he couldn't help himself and she loved every single second of it. She was probably going to be sore afterward but it would be totally worth it.

"Yes," she hissed as his cock ran over a particularly sensitive area. "Fuck me harder."

Their breaths ragged and labored they crossed the finish line together when Tyler reached around and rubbed her clit, his dexterous fingers finding just the right rhythm to make her scream with ecstasy. Eventually they fell back to the mattress, their bodies covered in sweat and happy, satisfied smiles on their faces. They had nothing better to do all day than stay in bed if that's what they wanted to do.

Rolling over, Billie nuzzled Tyler's chest, pressing a chaste kiss just where his heart beat below, his skin salty on her lips. "I love you."

She didn't feel the need to dress up her declaration in fancy words or complicated adjectives. The words weren't the important part. It was the emotion behind them.

"I love you too, baby girl. More than you can possibly imagine."

Looking up, she searched in his expression for any form of fear or regret.

"Are you okay with that? You didn't plan on this."

"Neither did you but here we are. And it's great. I thought I was happy before but this is so much better. You make everything in my life better."

Tyler wasn't the talkative type either, preferring actions to make his point, so his words of love meant all the more to her and she tucked them away in a corner of her heart for safekeeping. No matter what happened in the future, no one could take them from her today.

They dozed off, cuddled together in the luxurious bedroom, Billie tucked into the space under Tyler's chin where she fit perfectly. She'd been dreaming of fluffy clouds and sunshine when a buzzing sound made her open one eye, groaning at being awoken so abruptly. Tyler had rolled over and was holding her phone up in front of her.

"It's yours."

Squinting to see the screen, her heart stopped momentarily when she saw who it was. Connie. Hopefully with good news about Sierra. Could divorces be arranged that quickly?

Placing the phone to her ear, she sat up in bed. "Hi, Connie. How is everything? Is Sierra recovering well?"

Connie didn't beat around the bush. "You need to get Sierra out of Wisconsin, Billie. That asshole found her and she'd be six feet under if her neighbors hadn't stepped in. He's in jail now because he violated the restraining order but I don't know how long they can keep him. The social worker moved Sierra but I think he'll just find her again." Billie could hear the tears in her old friend's voice. "Please get her out of here so she can be safe."

Billie would have gone a long time ago but Sierra had been adamant that her sister stay out of her life. She didn't want Billie's interference.

Glancing at Tyler who was wearing an expression of concern, Billie responded the only way she could. Sierra might not want Billie in her life but she needed her. Paradise was going to have to wait for another time.

"Tell me where she is. I'm on my way."

CHAPTER
Thirty-Four

"YOU DIDN'T HAVE to come with me," Billie said for the twentieth time since the phone call from her friend. "You could have stayed in Hawaii and taken the rest of your vacation."

Tyler wasn't quite sure what to say to his woman as they settled into the rental car at the Madison, Wisconsin airport. The little town where Sierra was hiding was only about an hour away. Connie had given them the address and he'd easily programmed it into the GPS.

Sure he *could* have stayed in Hawaii all by himself, soaking up sun and drinking rum drinks but why the hell *would* he? The woman he loved needed him and he didn't want her dealing with this alone. Of course he was going to go to Wisconsin. He was a self-absorbed son of a bitch, that was true, but he wasn't an asshole.

"Why would I stay in Hawaii when you aren't there? I'm happy to be here, babe, helping you."

Shoving her purse down on the floor, she folded her

hands primly on her lap. "I was just saying that you could have stayed."

Blowing out a frustrated breath, Tyler pulled out onto the freeway. "No, what you were saying is that you think I'm too shallow to want to deal with anything that isn't fun. You're not trusting me again with the good and the bad. You think I only want the good."

She was studying her hands as if she'd never seen the before. "I do trust you."

"Good. Then know that we're there for each other no matter what. Do you think I don't know how difficult this is for you? You're going to see your sister for the first time in years and that has to be a big goddamn deal. I'm not letting you do this alone. We'll go together to get her and take her back home with us. We're a team, right?"

They always had been but even more so now. He'd never felt this crazy bond with another human being and damn if it didn't feel like the best thing ever.

"A team," she repeated softly. "Then I think I should warn this team that Connie said that Sierra still isn't convinced that she should come to California."

"Then we'll convince her," Tyler said firmly. He couldn't let the sister of the woman he loved be in danger any longer. If he had to hire a team of bodyguards he would keep her safe.

The drive was easy and the weather cooperated, staying sunny and fairly warm despite the forecast for rain. The GPS guided them to what looked like a fairly new apartment complex, all the buildings painted blue with white trim. Well-maintained and cheery, there was row upon row of buildings but it only took a few minutes to find the one they were looking for. Her apartment was on the second floor overlooking a little pond with flowers planted on the sidewalk leading up to it.

"Are you ready?" he asked as Billie gathered her things, but he knew the answer without her having to tell him. Her face was pale and her lips trembled visibly. She was terrified and he wasn't sure how to make everything okay for her. This wasn't in his control. He couldn't drop a bunch of money or use his fame to fix it all.

"As ready as I'll ever be. Let's go try and convince my estranged sister to pick up her life and move to a completely new state with me. This should be easy."

There was sarcasm in Billie's tone which was a good sign. She still had her sense of humor although he could feel the tension in her body as they climbed the stairs side by side. She was - rightfully - nervous.

Connie was supposed to have warned Sierra that they were coming so Tyler hoped he didn't scare the young woman by knocking but they had no other choice. There was a flurry of activity behind the door, although he couldn't tell exactly what is was—hopefully not a gun—and then a muffled voice spoke.

"Who is it?"

Clearing her throat, Billie leaned close to the door so she didn't have to speak loudly.

"It's Billie and Tyler. Can you please let us in?"

The door didn't open right away and for a moment Tyler thought that maybe Sierra was going to refuse to do it, but then he heard the locks being disengaged, one after the other. Good, she'd had decent locks on the door. That was something at least. When she swung it open, he wasn't sure what to expect. A woman who looked just like Billie? They were twins but not identical. Sierra's hair wasn't as dark and her nose was slightly different. There was definitely a strong resemblance, but Sierra had her own brand of beauty. It was there clearly in her delicate features despite the faded bruises on her cheek and eye. Shorter than Billie by about two inches, Sierra looked like a strong wind might blow her away. The t-shirt she was wearing had short sleeves that showed off more cuts and bruises on her way too thin arms. Even the shorts she was wearing hung off her frame as if made for someone ten pounds heavier.

"I guess you should come in," Sierra said, stepping back and allowing them to enter. The apartment was decorated in a sparse fashion with only the basics. A couch and a chair in the living room along with a small television on a table. There were no personal effects at all, nothing that told him about the personality of the person that lived there. Sierra must have left all of it behind when she escaped. That made Tyler want to take her shopping and replace every bit of it with brand-new. He'd have to wait, though, because this abode was simply a temporary stop off on the road to a better life.

Sierra moved past them and sat down on the edge of the chair, elbows on her knees and her head hanging down so her curtain of dark hair hung across her face. Tyler couldn't see her expression but the tension in the air was so thick even he wanted to tug at the collar of his white button-down shirt. Several years of unspoken words hung in the air between these two women.

"Connie called me." Billie perched on the far end of the

couch as far away from her sister as she could. Trying to be the buffer between them, Tyler sat on the couch as well but closer to Sierra. "She believes you'd be safer coming with me and Tyler to California and I think she's right. We can't let Brian find you again and there's no way he'd think you left the state."

"I'm fine. You didn't need to come here." Sierra was still staring down at the floor, not looking up to speak.

Billie's lips tightened and she let out a frustrated breath. "You're not fine. The social worker is worried about your safety. We can get you out of here right now and make sure he doesn't get to you."

"I appreciate you wanting to help but I'm not your problem."

Throwing her hands in the air, Billie stood. "You're my family. That makes your problems my problems."

Jerking her head up, Sierra's face was wet with tears. "I can take care of myself."

Her purse falling to the floor, Billie stepped closer to her sister. "I'm sure you can but you need a little help to get back on your feet. I can give you that." Billie's eyes flashed with what looked like anger. "Or is it that you'll take help from everyone but me? Because I could have sworn you told me that you hated me for trying to break you and Brian up and that you didn't want me around anymore. So I left you alone like you asked me to. I've felt guilty every single day for leaving but frankly you never gave me a choice. You cut me out of your life with a dull knife."

Every cell in Tyler's body screamed to intervene, pull Billie into his arms and soothe her anger and hurt. Tears were falling on her face now as well and he had to fight his instinct to wipe them away. Those were cleansing tears of anger and hurt and his baby girl had been holding them in far too long. He loved her and he'd lay down his life for her but at this moment she and her sister had to say a few truths to one another. They were both hurting.

"Of course I said that," Sierra yelled, more tears gushing from her swollen eyes. "Brian didn't want you around and every time after you visited me he used to get so..."

Dashing at her cheeks with the back of her hand Billie growled, her teeth bared. "He beat you, didn't he? After I left he'd beat you. That useless, fucking waste of goddamn skin. Every time I came to see you I begged you to leave with me but you never would. If I ever see his lazy fucking ass again I'll beat the shit out of him with my bare fucking hands."

That was a lot of dirty words out of his woman's mouth but she'd had a good reason. Tyler felt the same way about this Brian guy and he hadn't even met him, but he was already thinking of ways to ruin the man's life.

The two women seemed to have run out of things to say, which was a surprise to Tyler because it appeared they had a hell of a lot more to talk about, especially after that little tidbit of information. Billie simply stood there waiting for Sierra to respond but the young woman didn't say anything. Her body shook as she sat in the chair whether from anger, fear or something else, Tyler wasn't sure.

"Are you going to say anything?" Billie asked after several long moments passed. "Anything at all?"

And just like that, Sierra's lips tightened. Exactly like

Billie's had a few minutes ago. They were sisters and if Sierra had some other things in common with Billie then she was stubborn as hell. This standoff could last for hours...days, even. Tyler had many faults and lack of patience was one of them. They could argue in California.

"Sierra," he finally said, his gaze flicking back and forth between the two women. "Would you like some help packing your things?"

It was time to take control of the situation because this was getting them exactly nowhere. There was a plane to catch and he wasn't leaving Sierra here. He'd remembered how his mother had taught him to be assumptive when he wanted something. He'd used it with Billie quite a bit so he'd give it a shot with Sierra. From this moment on he was simply going to act as if it had all been decided and she was going with them. Case closed.

"I don't have much," Sierra admitted, her expression guarded and he didn't expect anything less. She'd seen him for the first time about ten minutes ago. He had the distinct feeling that she trusted few people. Especially men.

Flicking a glance at his watch, he gave her what he hoped was his best reassuring smile.

"Why don't we get those things packed up then? We need to get back in the air as soon as possible."

He didn't know why Sierra didn't argue with him. Perhaps deep down she really wanted to go but didn't want to admit it. Or maybe she was too exhausted to fight about it. It didn't matter at the moment because she stood and walked into the bedroom, leaving him behind with Billie.

Scooting across the couch cushion, he wrapped an arm around her, dropping a kiss on her cheek. "It's going to be okay."

"She hates me," Billie said, her voice thick with tears. He longed to be able to take away her emotional pain but he didn't have a clue as to how. All he could do was try to help in the few obvious ways he could see. "And I hate myself. I never should have left."

They'd had this conversation before but it looked like they might need to have it a few more times. "She doesn't hate you, baby. And if you had stayed what do you think would have happened? Do you think Sierra would have left him any earlier? Do you think you could have somehow magically changed the situation? She told you she never wanted to see you again so you left and tried to make a better life for yourself. You don't have to apologize for that."

Wringing her hands together, Billie rubbed at her wet cheeks. "I would have been there when all this happened."

Tyler wasn't the type to carry a handkerchief so he did the best he could with his fingertips, wiping up her tears and pushing back the strands of hair that clung to her damp skin. "Okay, let's say that you stayed. You didn't get to see Sierra but you stayed. Would you have been in any position to help when she decided to get out? At least we can take her away from here."

"Probably not," Billie conceded, taking a shuddering breath. "I'd probably be at the same dead end job or one just like it. But let's face it, Tyler, I'm not the one helping Sierra. You are. It was your money that paid for the divorce and the new life. It's your money that's bringing her back to California."

"Don't you ever say anything like that ever again," he replied, warning clear in his tone. "We're together and that means that everything I have is yours. Even if we weren't together, I think you've earned that money over the years putting up with my shit. Don't think I don't know that you could have walked away from me and my antics a long time ago. Your friendship has kept me grounded and made sure I didn't become just another Hollywood statistic."

A smile curled on those full, pink lips. "You have been a handful at times."

"There you go. Now let's get your sister and get out of here."

CHAPTER
Thirty~Five

AFTER ZIPPING through several time zones east and now a few more going west, Billie was understandably passed out in her chair, seatbelt buckled. In deference to the delicate situation with Sierra and wanting to make the best time to Wisconsin and then home, Tyler had chartered a jet for their travels and he was glad that he had. After all the crap she'd been through, Sierra shouldn't have to withstand the stares of onlookers regarding her bruises. It also gave them the privacy they needed. The last thing he wanted was for Sierra to get dragged into his life and end up on the cover of some trash tabloid.

Taking her out of that apartment had truly been sad. She'd come out of the bedroom dressed in a plain white blouse and a pair of what looked like new jeans that didn't fit her very well, just like the earlier outfit. It was then that it hit him that she was probably wearing donated clothes and he'd practically slapped his forehead in shame. She'd walked out of her old life with only the clothes on her back. Damn, she was brave as hell, just like his Billie. Courage ran in the family. As soon as she was rested and the bruises faded, they'd take her shopping and buy her all new things. He couldn't fix all the hurt and pain between these sisters but it was a small action he could take that might make her feel better about herself.

With Billie asleep, Tyler slipped out of his seat and went to the back of the airplane where Sierra was sitting and reading a magazine. A cup of coffee sat in front of her barely touched and growing cold.

He sat across from her and waited until she looked up. "Can we talk for a moment?"

Folding the magazine closed, she shrugged. "I suppose so."

The charm offensive had been at the apartment but now he wanted to be honest. "First of all, I don't think we've actually been introduced. I'm–"

"I know who you are," Sierra interrupted, her expression solemn, giving nothing away as to her emotions underneath. "You're the big movie star Tyler Gaylord. You're marrying my sister. I saw it on television."

"Yes, I am," he easily agreed. "That makes us family too. I want to be sure you know that you have more than just Billie to help you, Sierra. You have me and I'll do anything to make sure that you get a chance at a new life."

"Thank you," she said quietly, but nothing else. She wasn't much of a talker.

"When we get to Los Angeles we're going to go to my home. You're welcome to stay as long as you like. Forever, if you want. There's a guest cottage behind the main house that you could stay in if you like your privacy. Billie used to live there." Tyler grinned at the memories. "That's how we met actually. I was her landlord."

Sierra lips turned up at the corners slightly. Progress. Almost a smile.

"I can help you get a job eventually. I have a lot of contacts and friends. It shouldn't be too difficult."

That little smile fell and her features took on a worried, almost scared look. "I need to find work right away. I'm a good waitress and I work hard."

Taking a chance, Tyler reached out and placed his hand over her much smaller one. It trembled but she didn't pull it away. A small victory. "I bet you are. Billie's a hard worker too so I bet it runs in the family. But let's not worry about that for a few days, okay? You need to get settled and heal a little bit."

Her fingers flew up to her still discolored cheek. "He was really angry this time. Normally he'd only hit me where the bruises wouldn't show."

Tyler was definitely going to kill this guy. Slowly and painfully. The fucker had put that much thought into his beatings.

As sorry as Tyler felt for Sierra - and he did feel sorry for her - he had something he needed to say.

"Sierra, I know that you and Billie have a few issues to work out. And damn, I know you've had a rough life. Billie told me about how you two grew up and I'm real sorry all that happened to you. But I need you to understand that I love Billie more than anything in the world and it's my job to protect her. I understand there are things that I can't keep from hurting her but there's one thing I won't allow you to do. I won't let you hurt her."

Tears welled up in Sierra's eyes and she nodded. "I'm not mad at Billie and I don't blame her. Not at all. This is my stupid mistake." She shoulders shook as the sobs came harder. "I'm just so ashamed. Look at what a fucking mess I've made of my life."

He moved to comfort her but suddenly Billie was there, inching him over so she could embrace her sister.

"You don't have anything to be ashamed of," Billie said, pulling her bruised sister into a careful hug. "Brian's the asshole here."

Sierra shook her head, more tears baptizing her pale cheeks. "I should have left but I just couldn't. I was afraid. I was afraid of so many things. He convinced me that I was worthless and that I couldn't stand on my own two feet. Then when you left he said that even my own sister didn't want me and that he was all I had in the world. If I left him bad things would happen."

That little son of bitch. He'd done quite the mind fuck on Sierra.

Billie's nose wrinkled in distaste. "He's the worthless one, and you did finally leave. You're going to be fine and we're going to get you a new life. He can fucking go to hell. You didn't deserve any of it. No one does."

Sierra turned to Tyler. "And I won't hurt her. I promise."

Whipping her head around, Billie gave him a dirty look. "Just what did you say to my sister?"

Shit, he'd better watch himself. They were going to gang up on him and it was two against one.

"It's fine," Sierra assured her sister. "He was being protective, that's all. He wanted to be sure that I wasn't going to try and blame you."

Billie's lips turned down. "I should have–"

"Gone and built a great life for yourself," finished Sierra. "Staying wouldn't have helped me. The social worker and the therapist have helped me understand that I had to help myself. I had to want to get away more than I was afraid to leave. And that last time he beat me it happened. As I lay on the kitchen floor I thought to myself that this was it. I was going to die this time and I realized that I didn't want to die. I wanted to live and get away from him."

A few tears slipped down Tyler's cheeks and he quickly wiped them away. At this rate, they were going to drown over dry land. He didn't cry much either but if any event warranted a few tears it was this one. His beautiful girl finally had her sister back. She'd never complained but she'd been in a great deal of pain losing Sierra. Now they could heal.

"I'm glad you're here," Billie said simply, giving her sister another hug. "We're a family again. I've missed this so much."

"Hey, I'm part of this family too," Tyler complained playful, trying to lighten the atmosphere. "When do I get a hug?"

Both women grinned and Billie launched herself at him, wrapping her arms around his neck and placing a big kiss on his lips. Sierra was much more restrained but at least she was wearing a smile. It was the first one he'd seen.

CHAPTER
Thirty-Six

BILLIE LED the way to the guest room in the main house. Although Sierra could move into the guest cottage at a later time, they wanted her as close as possible while she was recovering. It also made Billie feel more secure to have her sister just down the hall. Frankly she didn't think Brian could scrape together the gas money to get to Hollywood but just in case, they'd keep Sierra close until they were sure he'd received the message.

Brian needed to stay the hell away.

"This will be your room." Billie set the grocery bag of clothes and small toiletries on the long dresser. It had been painfully sad to see her sister's life encompassed in one plastic sack. Billie hadn't had much more when she'd left Wisconsin but at least she'd left on her own terms. "You've got the run of the house including the workout room, the sauna, and the pool in the back. You might want to stay out of Tyler's office though, not because he doesn't want anyone in there or anything, but because it's kind of a mess. If he sees you in there he might put you to work looking for whatever he's lost."

Her attempt at humor failed spectacularly. Sierra simply nodded as she stood in the middle of the room, her gaze darting here and there but never stopping for long.

"There's an ensuite bathroom over here," Billie continued, desperately trying to get her sister to speak. Say anything, even if it was only to yell and scream. Tyler had pulled Billie aside as they'd loaded into the limo after the plane touched down and asked her to give Sierra some space. Her sister had never been outside of Wisconsin until today so the transition from living in fear all the time to being safe was probably going to be a bumpy one.

Despite his goofy behavior sometimes, he could be wise. Especially in situations that he could see from the outside. Clearly she was too close to all of it to be unbiased. She just wanted her sister back.

Sierra still hadn't said anything and Billie was tired and cranky from all the traveling. Reining in her patience, she tried one more time.

"I'm going downstairs to the kitchen to fix us some dinner. Is there anything special you want? Curtis, Tyler's assistant, said we're fully stocked with food. You can come down and keep me company while I cook."

"I think—I think I'll lie down."

The rejection felt like a slap in the face but Billie had to steel herself for more. Sierra was going through some serious stuff, had been through hell, and this wasn't about Billie's feelings. Frankly they weren't that important right now. What was vital was keeping Sierra safe and getting her set up in a new life. Billie's hurt feelings were going to have to take a back seat.

"That sounds like a good idea," she said instead. "Come down in a little while to have some dinner."

Tyler was already in the kitchen rummaging around through the cabinets. "What do you think we should have for dinner, babe? I was thinking something carb heavy."

Because Sierra desperately needed to put on some weight. She'd noticed it too.

"How about spaghetti and meat sauce?" Billie suggested. "If Curtis bought everything I put on the list we should have all that we need to make it."

Rolling his eyes, Tyler retrieved a package of dried spaghetti noodles from the pantry. "Of course he got every-thing on the list. Can you imagine a world where Curtis forgot something?"

"No," she said, sputtering with laughter. "He's turned out to be pretty efficient, hasn't he? I thought he did a good job in San Diego. Other than that mix-up with our hotel rooms."

"Really? I kind of liked that mix-up."

Honestly? So had she.

"I bet you put him up to it." She placed the frying pan on the stove and dumped in the hamburger.

Tyler waggled his brows suggestively. "I wish I'd thought of it. I really do need to give the kid a raise."

The meat sizzled in the pan as Tyler sprinkled salt into the boiling water for the spaghetti.

Billie began chopping up some fresh garlic, her mind still upstairs with her sister. "Do you think we should have her checked out by a doctor? I mean, she just got out of the hospital."

"I think you should let your sister be an adult and make those decisions. Don't treat her like she's a child. She needs to feel like she has control of at least a few things in her life. Take the lead from her."

"I know, I know," Billie replied, setting the garlic aside and working on the basil. "I just want her to be okay."

Tyler came up behind her and pulled her back into his front, his arms wrapped around her, more comforting than sexual. "She will be. We'll make sure of it. But think of it from her standpoint—we just dragged her to a home and state she's never known. There's going to be some adjustment there. Be patient. I know you want to help her. I do too. We're going to have to take things slowly."

Turning in his arms, she looped her arms around his neck as his lips descended on hers. It had been far too many hours since he'd kissed her like this. This was about so much more than just fucking. This was love and being there for one another.

The sound of a clearing throat had them jumping away from one another. Sierra stood there quietly just sort of watching them and Tyler was actually blushing bright red. It wasn't something she saw often and it was damn cute on him.

It was kind of embarrassing being caught out by her sister, like two teenagers necking on the couch but Billie was determined to play it off as if it was no big deal. She was an actress, after all.

"Hungry?" she asked brightly. "Dinner will be ready in about twenty minutes or so."

"It smells good," Sierra replied, sliding onto one of the island stools. "This kitchen is nice."

That was an understatement. The kitchen was gourmet with nothing but high end finishes. Even the pots and pans were copper and cost a small fortune. Tyler had hired a designer to pick everything out while he was on location shooting a *Thunder* movie.

"You know, I really need to check some things in my office." Tyler began backing toward the living room. "You know that stuff we talked about? I better do that now."

He ducked out, leaving Billie and Sierra alone.

"He didn't have anything he needed to do, did he?" Sierra asked. "He just wanted us to have time to talk."

"He did," Billie confirmed. "But we don't have to. You're probably talked out."

Throwing all the ingredients into a pot for the sauce, Billie turned her attention to the garlic butter for the bread.

"I want to but I don't know what to say."

"Say whatever you want."

Folding her hands on the granite countertop, Sierra was silent for a long moment as if gathering her scattered thoughts.

"First I want to say thank you for coming to get me. I know that you didn't have to."

It was probably better not to say too much and simply let Sierra do most of the talking.

"I wanted to but you're welcome."

"I also wanted to say I'm sorry about the last time I saw you. I know that I hurt you and didn't mean to."

"Yes, you did," Billie replied quickly. If they were going

to talk then they needed to be honest. "You knew what you were doing."

Sierra sighed, her cheeks red. "Alright, yes. I knew what I was doing. Brian had me so twisted around I actually thought you were trying to tear me away from the one person who loved me. The day you came to tell me you were leaving and wanted me to go with you I was angry with you. So I said those awful things."

"That you hated me."

"I never hated you but I was angry and conflicted. Looking back, I think I was so furious because there was a part of me that wanted to go with you but I was scared. At that point, I was scared of everything and you weren't scared of anything. I've always admired that about you."

Sierra didn't have a clue. "I was scared all the time. I was terrified when I left thinking that I might be making a huge mistake."

Glancing around the kitchen appreciatively, her sister smiled. "Looks like you did the right thing. You have a good life with Tyler. He's not much like the characters he plays in the movies but then I guess he wouldn't be. He's an actor, after all. He seems to adore you so hold onto him. Take it from me, a good man isn't easy to find."

Sierra was too young to be that cynical and Billie wanted to kick Brian in the balls over and over again. "You'll find the right man someday."

Snorting, Sierra shook her head. "I'm done with men. Apparently I have the worst judgment of the male species ever. No, I'll just be a doting auntie to your kids. I'll be happy with that."

Billie blushed at the mention of children. It had been

something she was thinking about lately. She'd love to have a little boy that looked just like Tyler.

"You might change your mind."

"I doubt it." Her smile fell and her expression turned haunted. "I was so scared all the time and it just became normal for me. That's how every day was and I didn't think it could ever be any different. I worried all the time about what might set Brian off. Did I clean the dishes right? What if he didn't like what I was wearing? There was always something, although in the beginning it wasn't all that bad. It got much worse after you left. I think he thought that he'd succeeded in separating us so now he had free reign."

"What set him off that last time?" Billie heard herself asking, although she wasn't sure she wanted to hear the reason. It was only going to make her more furiously angry at Brian.

"Toward the end he didn't need much of a reason. He'd drank his way through my tiny paycheck and he was mad that we were broke and he couldn't buy more booze. That's was all the excuse he needed."

"I'm sorry that happened to you."

It was such a lame statement but Sierra didn't seem to think so. She smiled and reached across the island, patting Billie's hand. "I've been talking to a therapist and trying to figure out how I ended up in that situation. I've come to the conclusion that I wanted attention so badly that I took any that I could get. At first Brian treated me really well and he was always telling me how pretty I was. I fell so hard and even when I knew that I'd been fooled I just couldn't admit it. Not to you or to myself. I was so ashamed."

"You have nothing to be ashamed of. It's Brian who should feel that way."

"Well, he doesn't," Sierra shot back with another snort. "He thinks it's all my fault."

"Brian is a fucking idiot and karma is going to catch up with him before long. He's going to fuck with the wrong person someday. Sadly, neither of us will be around to see it."

"I really am sorry, sis," Sierra said again. "You have no idea how much."

Billie shook her head. "You don't have anything to be sorry for. We start new from today and put the past behind us."

"I can do that if you can."

For the first time in years, she heard hope in her sister's tone and Billie was happy to be a part of it. Maybe they could be a real family along with Tyler. A new beginning for all of them.

CHAPTER
Thirty-Seven

A WEEK later Sierra was looking immeasurably better. Her pale skin was now tinged with a little California sun and the bruises and cuts had faded. Yesterday Billie and Tyler had dragged her out of the house to get some new clothes which had been a battle royale. Sierra didn't want to be any trouble but then she'd never seen Tyler in full-on balls to the wall mode. A force of nature, he wouldn't be denied the fun of buying her a whole new wardrobe.

Today Billie and Sierra were finishing up a spa day of pampering - mani-pedi, massages, and for Sierra a brand-new hairstyle - and then they were meeting Tyler for a casual late lunch at a local restaurant. He'd sent Billie a cryptic message while they were getting their toes painted. The lunch was a celebration of some kind.

"Do you know what we're celebrating?" Sierra asked as they entered the trendy bistro.

"I have no idea but maybe your divorce came through."

Now that Sierra was living in their home, Tyler and his team of attorneys had become actively involved in her situation, including the divorce and the criminal charges against her worm of a husband. Sierra was also continuing therapy to help her transition to a new normal.

"That would be cause for celebration but I just know that Brian is going to drag it out as long as possible."

"Little prick," Billie muttered as they joined Tyler at an out of the way table. The proprietor was a fan and always gave them a table that couldn't be seen from the door or the front window.

"Damn, woman. I hope you're not talking about me," he said with a grin. "I haven't screwed anything up since at least yesterday."

Tyler hadn't messed up in weeks. In fact, he'd been so wonderful she could barely keep from cuddling up on his lap and kissing him, regardless of where they were or who they were around.

"I wasn't talking about you," Billie replied sweetly, giving him a simple peck on the cheek. "I was talking about Brian."

"That makes sense." Tyler grinned and rubbed his hands together. "Do you ladies know why we're here today?"

Sierra gave Billie some side eye and smiled. Her sense of humor was slowly returning and she liked to tease Tyler best of all. "To eat lunch?"

Billie shook her head, well into the spirit of the game. It wasn't fair that they kind of ganged up on him but if anything, he encouraged it. He said it was nice to see them bond as sisters again.

"To show off how gorgeous we look after our morning at the spa?" Billie guessed.

"That goes without saying, babe. But there is something else. Something big. Actually, two something bigs."

Looking like a little boy with a huge secret, Tyler was practically vibrating in his chair. If they didn't get him to speak quickly he was going to bounce out of the restaurant like Tigger in the Hundred Acre Wood.

"So tell us," Billie urged, rolling her eyes. "Just say it."

"It's just I still can't quite believe it." Tyler threw up his hands but didn't get a chance to go on as the waitress approached their table. The sisters had to wait for the news until after they ordered and the server disappeared into the back kitchen.

"Okay, she's gone. Spill it, pretty boy."

"I got the movie."

Such a simple sentence but Billie wasn't sure she'd heard it correctly. Had it really happened?

"Can you say that again?"

He was wearing the most gleeful smile and it looked damn sexy on him.

"I got the movie. I'm playing Zak."

Throwing her arms around his neck, Billie no longer worried about who might be watching. "That's the most amazing news. I'm so proud of you."

Although she wasn't a fan of Weller, this was what Tyler wanted. If he wanted it, she wanted it for him.

"Congratulations, Tyler," Sierra said. "I'm not sure who Zak is but it sounds like you're happy about the role."

"It's a great opportunity," Tyler replied. "The director is a jerk but the role is juicy and very different than anything

I've done before. I'm hoping to show I can stretch as an actor. But that actually isn't the biggest news. Remember I said I have two surprises to celebrate."

"Spill," Billie urged with a giggle. "You're keeping us on the edge here."

"That wasn't the only news Josh had. Turns out there's another role that needs someone to fill it."

"Josh is Tyler's agent," Billie explained to Sierra who seemed to be watching all of this with amusement. She'd get used to all this movie obsession in time.

"He's your agent too," Tyler said, dropping a kiss to her forehead. After their clinch in the kitchen, he'd been quite circumspect when it came to affection in front of Sierra. "And the role is for you, baby. Do you remember that Lilliana Dowling took the co-starring role in Sam's new movie? Well, she was in a car accident in Nice and broke her leg in two places. She's going to be fine but she needs surgery and several months to recover and rehab. Sam immediately told the producers and the director that he wants you to take the role."

Any movie Sam Collins starred in was probably going to be a huge hit and this one was no exception. A murder mystery with light moments and some romance, she'd heard about the script the last time she'd talked to Sam. He must have remembered how much she'd loved the concept. She'd read the book the script was based on and it was fantastic.

But it was still hard to believe. Her - Billie Oliver - co-starring with Sam Collins in a major motion picture? It hadn't been that long ago that she'd been dumped by her last agent because she wouldn't get breast implants.

"Sam wants me?"

Tyler nodded, looking more excited for her than he had been for himself. "Josh said the part is yours if you want it. You won't make what they were paying Lilliana but the money is still good. You can get this movie under your belt and still be done in time for the wedding. Any post-production work can be done after while I'm working on the Zak film."

"That's...amazing."

It was still hard to wrap her mind around it. She'd been sure her career was going nowhere and then out of the blue...this.

Tyler was frowning at her, not understanding why she wasn't jubilant. "You want it, don't you?"

Did she want it? Glancing at her sister sitting across the table, Billie had to put her first. This wasn't the best time to be flying off to some location for months, leaving her sister behind to grapple with a divorce and a new life.

Tyler's gaze followed Billie's and his expression relaxed immediately. "I guess I had three pieces of news. I miscounted. After talking to Josh and Sam, the production company had planned to hire an assistant for you for the run of the shoot. Sam told them Sierra was your assistant so they're hiring her too. You both will be together for the duration of filming."

Eyes wide, Sierra looked at Billie then Tyler, then back to Billie. "Are you serious? I've never done that kind of work before."

Tyler gave her a wink. "I think Billie won't make you do anything too tough. It's mostly keeping her on sched-ule. Look at it this way, you'll get to order her around.

That is, if she takes the role. Billie, you haven't said much."

"I'm stunned," she confessed, laughing at herself. "Completely blindsided but in a good way. I'm still in disbelief."

"Believe it. You're a good actress and Sam knows that. He wouldn't ask you to do anything if he didn't think you could do it. He's way too protective of his movies to work with just anyone. He wants you."

And Billie wanted to do it. She could do it, and working with Sam would be a dream. The only thing better would be working with Tyler.

"I want it." She turned to Sierra who was regarding them with a combination of awe and amusement. "Please come with me. I'm going to need all the help I can get."

"If you're sure...?"

"Very sure."

Sierra's eye lit up with happiness. "Then of course I will. I'd love to."

Billie was going to make a movie with Sam. She was going to be the co-star. It was a dream come true. She'd worked hard but Hollywood was also about luck and timing.

"Where are they shooting and when do we need to be there?"

Chuckling, Tyler sat back in his chair as the waitress slid their entrees in front of them.

"The twenty-first in Paris."

Sierra's mouth fell open and Billie couldn't stop the huge smile that spread across her face.

"Paris? In less than three weeks?"

They had a boatload of work to do before they could leave. For Paris.

Life was darn near perfect.

Untitled

———

The next two weeks were a whirlwind of packing and preparations. Billie had contacted their wedding planner and finally set a date for the second week in October along with a myriad of other decisions that she and Tyler had finally sat down and made. They'd decided on colors - an autumn palate - and even a location - an orchard in Colorado that they had rented out for the entire weekend. Now that those major decisions were made the others would easily fall into place. Billie might even look for a wedding dress while in Paris.

There were travel arrangements to make as well and Curtis stepped in to help with that. He was guiding Sierra through the process and filling her in on his duties, although Billie had assured her sister she wasn't nearly as needy as Tyler. She could stay on time and didn't need anyone to remind her of appointments. The only snag they'd hit was that Sierra didn't have a passport. They'd expedited its processing and it had shown up yesterday, much to their relief.

"What does Curtis have you doing now?" Billie asked as she entered Tyler's office. "This isn't some sort of hazing ritual, is it?"

Curtis and Sierra had their hands full of scripts, all rejected at some point in the last year for one reason or another by Tyler. At Josh's bidding, they had kept them for awhile in case the project came up again but eventually they would be shredded.

Laughing, Curtis dropped the stack of scripts onto the back credenza. "I promise I'm taking good care of your sister. We're just trying to get a handle on all this office clutter and rotating out the oldest scripts and storing the newer ones."

"Curtis says I'm a natural at this," Sierra said, elbowing her mentor. The two were getting along great, much to Billie's relief. It was also helping Sierra to feel more normal; at least that's how she'd described it. She didn't want to sit around contemplating the wreck of her life all day. She needed to be busy and she was excited to see Paris.

Sierra retrieved a folder from the desk and held it out to Billie. "We were catching up with the filing and I think this belongs to you. You can take it or we can file it, whatever you want."

Accepting the folder, Billie flipped it open. "I doubt that it belongs to–"

This wasn't Billie's file. This was a file *about* Billie. About her past. It was Tyler's.

He'd known about her life all along. Wow, he was a great actor because she never would have suspected that he wasn't surprised when she told him. He ought to win that Oscar he coveted. He was that good.

Snapping it shut, she held it to her chest. That place where her heart was currently breaking into a thousand pieces. He'd talked about trust so many times but in the end he hadn't trusted her. How long had he had this? Since she'd moved in? Since he'd needed her to be his wife?

"It is mine. I'll take care of it."

Without another word, she turned on her heel and headed for the bedroom. Tyler was at a meeting and she'd have some time - uninterrupted - to look through this.

Then figure out what in the hell she was supposed to do now.

CHAPTER
Thirty-Eight

WORN OUT AND NOW DRY-EYED, Billie shoved socks and underwear into her suitcase along with the rest of the clothes she'd already packed. She'd be gone for quite awhile filming the movie but she wouldn't need a wide array of wardrobe choices since she'd be working most of the time. The thought of being on a movie set again was the only thing getting her through the day.

Billie was a good actress but she couldn't pretend that everything was fine. Not with Tyler. He'd see right through her little act. So it was with a heavy heart that she changed her and Sierra's flight reservation to Paris from day after tomorrow to tonight. She needed to put some distance between herself and Tyler so she could get her head on straight. She needed to do something about her heart as well because it was currently lying in about a dozen pieces on the ground.

After reading the dossier that Tyler had collected on her, Billie had literally been sick to her stomach. Although there was nothing in there incriminating, and she'd told him the important highlights, it was still a horrible realization that he'd had her *investigated*. He'd dug into her past while all the while smiling to her face as if nothing was going on behind the curtain.

Nothing to see here, folks, except a private detective digging for dirt.

Tyler had lied to her. That was the most hurtful part of all of this, although his casual use of the word *trust* was a close second. He kept saying she wasn't trusting him but all along he hadn't trusted her. All he would have had to do was ask and she would have told him whatever he wanted to know. But he'd never asked. Not once.

The timing of all of this was disturbing as well. How old was the folder? He never cleaned his desk so it could have been five years old or five months old. She could have understood Tyler doing a background check on his new tenant when she first moved in. That made complete sense, although it was vastly more extensive than a credit and criminal history check.

But when she'd started to tell him about her family he could have said he already knew and saved her the less than pleasant trip down memory lane. Instead she'd spilled her guts and he'd acted all surprised, comforting her and telling her it was all okay. Clearly it wasn't if he'd cared enough to hire someone to dig into her life.

The worst alternative was that he'd had her investigated when he'd decided to marry her for the movie role. That really blew the whole trust lecture he'd given her out of the water. Once again...all he'd needed to do was ask. He should have known that she'd never let him get dragged into some unsavory incident from her past. That lack of trust again.

She was hurt and betrayed and she wanted to crawl away and lick her wounds, whining about how life wasn't fair. Figure out what the hell she was going to do about all of this because one thing hadn't changed.

She loved Tyler. But she sure as hell didn't like him right now. In fact, she was beginning to wonder if she even knew him. She couldn't live with a man that lied and went behind her back and she didn't want to have a husband that - when the chips were down - ultimately didn't trust her.

All she wanted was a little time and space to figure out how she was supposed to feel about this. Was she overreacting? Should she just let it go? Was this a deal breaker? Trust was pretty important in a relationship, maybe the most important thing besides love.

———

Tyler bounded up the long staircase and into the bedroom, hoping to find Billie. He'd looked on the back patio, the living room, the library, and the kitchen. He'd been gone most of the day with meetings and then a session with his trainer and he missed her. A few hours of quality time sounded like the perfect way to spend an evening. Maybe he could talk her into seeing a movie or going out to dinner.

He found her packing, a suitcase open on the bed. She was preparing early so she must be excited. She wasn't leaving until day after tomorrow. Tyler wasn't happy to see her go but he was thrilled that she had this opportunity. Finally the public was going to get to see what he'd known for a long time. Billie had talent and working with Sam was an amazing opportunity.

She didn't know it but he'd already talked to Sam about visiting the set in a few weeks once she was settled into the routine of production. There was no way Tyler could go months without seeing her. He could prepare for the role of Zak in Paris as well as Los Angeles.

"Hey, babe. How about we go see a movie tonight? I'll buy the popcorn."

To his surprise Billie didn't turn toward him, instead continuing to place items in her suitcase. A student of body language, however, he noticed the almost imperceptible tightening of her shoulders when he'd spoken.

"Can't," she replied, concentrating on shoving shoes into the empty crevices of the bag. "I have a plane to catch. The car is picking me and Sierra up in about thirty minutes."

Tyler was almost positive he'd been gone a few hours, not a few days. Had the studio made changes to the schedule at the last minute?

"Did Sam call? Are they starting to shoot early?"

This time she did stop what she was doing and looked at him, but her expression wasn't happy. On the contrary, she looked like she'd lost her best friend.

But Tyler was standing right in front of her so it couldn't be that.

"No, I'm leaving early. I can't stay here right now. I talked to Sierra and she's good with going tonight."

A knot of fear was beginning to build in his chest as he

studied her almost emotionless features. This wasn't the Billie he had seen just this morning. Something had definitely changed. "Why can't you stay here?"

Reaching for something in her suitcase, she pulled out a file folder and held it out. "Curtis and Sierra cleaned your desk today and found this."

That knot of fear was like an anvil as his heart fell to his feet. He had a terrible, awful, horrifying feeling that he knew which file that was.

Why the fuck didn't I burn it? Throw it away at least.

Somehow his trembling fingers grasped the folder and he was able to open it to see the contents.

Fuck.

"I can explain."

There was desperation in his tone but then he was desperate. He needed her to believe that this wasn't his doing.

Perching on the edge of the mattress, Billie folded her hands on her lap. "I'm listening."

He sat down next to her, the folder still in his hand. "I didn't do this."

"Are you saying Curtis did it?"

This was awful. Truly terrible. He didn't like the way Billie was looking at him, with no emotion. She should be yelling at him, slinging a few lamps at his head. Anything but this...coldness.

"No," he replied quickly. "Listen, Garrett did this when we got engaged. I'll fire him right now if you want me to."

"Why would I want you to fire Garrett? He was doing his job."

Tyler felt some small relief. Was she beginning to understand?

"Then you know that I didn't do this?"

"That's what you just said."

He placed the file on the bed, not wanting to even hold it any longer. It represented something so shady and dirty, a part of this crazy business that he hated.

"So you don't have to leave tonight."

Standing, she moved away from him to the window and stared out, looking at the pool and the patio. "So when I told you...you already knew? Why did you pretend that you didn't?"

Shooting to his feet, he went to pull her into his arms but she held her hands up and shook her head. Clearly this was far from being resolved. She thought he'd been playing a game with her.

"I didn't know. Garrett gave this to me before but I didn't read it. I opened it, saw what was in it, and closed it. I never looked through it, Billie. I knew if there was anything important you would tell me yourself. You have to believe me."

She walked over to the bed and picked the file up, holding it in front of his face. "You didn't read it? You didn't look through it?"

He shook his head, panic surfacing and making it almost impossible to breathe. "I swear I didn't. I didn't need to."

Opening the file, she paged through it until she found whatever it was she was looking for.

"You didn't want to know that my mother drank herself to death and ended up running her car into a tree? That's such a great little story." She tossed the paper to the floor and pulled out another one. "Here's a great find. My mother was arrested for prostitution but the charges were dropped. Really, Tyler, you should give Garrett a bonus for that one. Fuck, even I didn't know that and she was my mother. There were so many things I learned about myself. It was like the world's most horrifying storybook except that it was about my life."

No tears, just condemnation. Sick to his stomach, he reached out for her but she slapped his hand away.

"I didn't read it, and I don't care about all of that."

He was definitely going to fire Garrett. No matter how the man had saved Nate's career he was possibly blowing the best thing in Tyler's life all because he was a cynical bastard.

His voice came out like a croak as he tried to speak through the lump in his throat. That Garrett and some greasy private investigator knew things about Billie's mother that even she didn't know was...disgusting.

That made Tyler pretty horrible too. He didn't get to come out of this unscathed.

A lone tear slipped down her cheek and Tyler was relieved to see her show some emotion. She'd been far too calm and he'd feared the worst.

"If you didn't care, then why did you keep it? Why didn't you put it down the shredder next to your desk?"

CHAPTER
Thirty~Nine

EVERY SECOND FELT like an hour as Billie waited for the man she loved to reply to her tearful question. Torn apart and heartbroken, she stood there silently, giving him every opportunity to explain himself. So far it hadn't been as appallingly bad as she'd feared. If she believed him - and she wanted to - he hadn't known when she'd told him and he hadn't instigated the background investigation.

It made things...slightly better.

But the big sticking point for her was if he didn't care, then why didn't he get rid of the file? Or give it to her? It made no sense to keep it. Obviously he hadn't planned on showing it to her because he'd had it for awhile and hadn't done that.

He'd kept it close at hand. As if he were planning to open and read it. Someday. Eventually. Maybe when he was alone and she was in Paris? There'd be no danger of her walking in on him then.

"Why, Tyler?" she asked again when he didn't answer.

His own anguish was written clearly in every line of his face. He looked gray and older today and not much like the sex symbol he was. "Why did you keep it?"

Scraping his fingers through his hair, he was clearly struggling to find the words.

"I didn't want you to find it," he admitted, groaning as he did. "I knew you'd be upset that Garrett had you investigated."

"So you kept it on your desk?" That didn't make sense. "You should have known I would eventually find it. Or that Curtis would."

Tyler wasn't that stupid no matter how he pretended to act for the public.

"I didn't plan on leaving it there. I had it in my hand and you walked into the office so I shoved it under the pile of scripts. I intended to do something about it but I forgot."

This might be worse.

"You forgot?" Billie echoed. Hurt, disappointment, and anger all warred for dominance but somehow she managed to sound as if she didn't want to smack his face and then walk away. He'd dealt her a sickening blow and she didn't know how to begin to heal from it. "You forgot a disgusting intrusion into my privacy? You just tossed the file down on the desk and forgot all about it? I find that hard to believe because if the roles had been reversed I don't think I would have done that, Tyler. It would have bugged me every single day until I told you the truth."

"If I could do it all over again, I would do things differently." He sounded frustrated that she wasn't just dropping the whole thing. Well, fuck him. "I love you, Billie, more than I thought I could ever love someone. I made a mistake. Are you going to let that ruin what we have?"

"I won't let you turn this around on me as if I've done something to be sorry for. I didn't do this. You did. I'm just calling you on your bullshit."

He swore under his breath. "This isn't bullshit. I fucked up, okay? I should have destroyed the file but I didn't. I should have told you that Garrett had you investigated but I didn't. And maybe I should have even given you the file. But I didn't. And Jesus, I am sorry. I am so sorry but I can't go back and change the past. I can only go forward. Are you going to hate me forever for this?"

Typical. He was all drama but she wouldn't be side-tracked by his display of emotion. She wanted to be very clear about how she felt about this.

"I don't hate you. Far from it. I love you, Tyler, and that's why this hurts so much." She choked as a fresh spate of tears burned the back of her eyes. "Because there's a part of me that thinks that maybe...just maybe...you kept that file because there was a part of *you* that wondered what was in it. You wondered if I was good enough. Perhaps in the back of your mind you knew that eventually you'd open it and see what was inside, but you didn't want to admit it to yourself. You might have read it the night before our wedding or maybe before. Or you could have waited until we got back from our honeymoon or when I told you I was pregnant with our first child. I'm not sure what your motivation was but if you're brutally honest with yourself I don't think you know either. You kept that file for a reason."

This. When it came down to it, this was what she was hurt and disappointed about.

"I'm not upset that Garrett had me investigated. I'm upset that you kept the file and moreover you kept its existence a secret from me. And frankly, I don't know what to do with that pain and hurt. Tell me how I'm supposed to feel and I'll do it because I'm at a loss. You kept talking about how I didn't trust you, Tyler, but the fact is you didn't trust me."

Dropping down onto the mattress, she buried her face in her hands and let the tears fall. Finally giving in to the wave of hurt and anger that had been building since she'd opened that file earlier today. Just a few hours and yet it felt like a lifetime ago.

"Baby girl..."

His soft voice normally made her feel comforted but it didn't this time. Instead she started crying harder, her shoulder shaking with the force of her misery. This day that had started with such promise had all gone to hell. The bed sagged and then she was pulled into Tyler's strong arms. For a moment she allowed herself to luxuriate in his strength, but then she remembered that nothing was resolved. He hadn't yet answered her questions to any level of satisfaction.

"No," she said firmly, pushing at his shoulder until his arms dropped away. He looked as miserable as she felt. At least he wasn't pretending this wasn't a big deal anymore. "You haven't answered me."

"I love you and I trust you."

Rubbing at an aching temple, she wished she had a time machine and could fly back before she ever knew that damn file existed. "That's not an answer. Why did you keep the folder? Because I have trouble believing you forgot it."

"I don't know."

That she believed. What he would admit to himself consciously was far different than the little voice in the back of his head. That niggling doubt about her past.

"And that's why I'm leaving tonight. I need some space from this to figure out how to deal with the hurt."

"I've hurt you," he said after a long silence. "And I know I have some making up to do, but I think you should stay here. We can talk about this and I can figure out a way to fix things."

Fix things.

She took a deep breath and wiped at her wet cheeks. "That makes us even because I don't know what I'm supposed to do now. Are we supposed to fight? Scream and yell? Am I supposed to surrender and let it go? Tell me, Tyler, what am I supposed to do?"

She was frozen with indecision. The only option she'd even contemplated was leaving early for Paris, going somewhere she could hopefully think clearly. She couldn't do that with Tyler dogging her heels twenty-four-seven.

And he would do that. It was his nature not to drop it until it was resolved. In his favor.

"I don't know that either," he answered bleakly, his shoulders hunched. "I'm just terrified that if you walk out that door you won't come back."

"I live here, Tyler. I have to come back."

"You know what I mean."

She did but she didn't want to contemplate it. "I want

to believe that we can move past this but right now I need some space. I'm asking you to give me that. Will you?"

Tyler wanted to say no. She could see it in his eyes and expression. When he didn't reply right away she could only surmise that he was weighing his options, wondering what would happen if he said no.

She was going to leave anyway. But she'd let him come to that conclusion on his own. Her cell buzzed with a text from the car service. They were outside the gate. It was time to go.

"The car is here for us," Billie said even though Tyler hadn't given his answer yet. At this point, it didn't matter. She needed time and space and she was going to take it. "We need to go. I'll text you when we get to Paris."

"So you're still going?"

Zipping up her suitcase, she sighed with barely concealed impatience. "I am. I told you I needed time to think about what we should do. I'm hurt, disappointed, and angry and I need to be able to process all those emotions. If I stay what would we talk about? Because I'm not ready to make nice right now and that's what you want me to do, isn't it? You want me to forgive and forget? Well, I'm not ready to do that. Maybe I will be in a few days or a few weeks."

"I said I was sorry, babe."

Billie pressed the button on her phone to let the car service in the gate. "I know you are and I appreciate that, but Tyler, this isn't about you. I know that most of the time our relationship is all about you, or your career, or what movie you're making, or what magazine you're being interviewed by, and I usually don't mind. But this time it's about me. Can you allow that? Just this once can it be about me?"

His mouth fell open in shock at her words. He probably was gobsmacked that she'd said them out loud. They didn't talk about the fact that the world revolved around him and his career but today she couldn't keep quiet.

"Yes," he said quietly, his expression almost ashamed. "I can do that."

"I'm not trying to make you feel guilty," she sighed. "I just need you to back off for a little while. That's all."

"I'm afraid I'm going to lose you."

"If you don't give me some space that is definitely going to happen."

Billie couldn't say it any more plainly than that. It wasn't an ultimatum. It was just the truth. If he couldn't give her this she didn't see how they were going to make any sort of long term relationship work.

Tyler picked up her suitcase and carried it down the stairs, neither of them saying a word. There wasn't much left to say. She was talked out.

Sierra was waiting at the bottom of the stairs with her own suitcase, newly purchased and filled with a new wardrobe. She and Billie had gone shopping and Tyler had tagged along, egging them on to buy even more than they'd planned. Tears sprang to her eyes as she recalled his boundless generosity. How could that same man hold onto that vile folder?

Curtis was standing by Sierra looking uncomfortable, but that wasn't far from his usual expression so Billie wasn't too concerned. Tyler could tell his assistant as much or as little as he wanted after she left.

Sierra wore a nervous smile. It was only her second time in an airplane. She was going to be spoiled flying first class. "Are you ready, sis?"

"I am." Billie reached for Tyler and gave him a hug. Although his body was stiffer than normal she found herself pulled closer, his lips pressed to hers for a long time. When he lifted his head she could have sworn she saw triumph there. Did he think that just because she was angry that she still didn't love his stupid ass? "We need to get going or we'll miss our flight. It might take a long time to get through security."

The boys carried the bags down to the car and helped the driver load them into the trunk. Sierra slid into the backseat first and then Billie, her chest tight with the tears she was holding in. She had to go but this was harder than she'd thought it would be.

Being with Tyler was difficult but being without him was just as tough. How ironic. Love could really suck sometimes.

"Call me the minute the plane touches down," Tyler commanded. "Does Sam know you're coming early?"

"I didn't call him. I was too busy changing flights and hotel reservations."

"I'll call him," Tyler assured her. "Both of you have a safe flight. I'll see you soon."

That last sentence sounded like a promise...or a threat.

"I love you," she told him. Because she did. "Thank you for giving me this time."

His fingertips brushed her lips, sending a tingle up her spine.

"I didn't give it to you. You took it. And I love you too."

With that he stepped back and closed the car door so the driver could pull away from the house. A few tears escaped down Billie's cheeks and she scrambled for a tissue from her handbag only to have Sierra press one into her hand.

"It'll be okay. He loves you."

The way Billie felt at this moment she wasn't sure anything would ever be okay again.

CHAPTER
Forty

"IS SHE OKAY? That's all I want to know."

Tyler growled in frustration as he tried to pry information out of his best friend Sam. He wanted to know more
than that but he'd take what he could get. Billie had only
communicated in the barest form since leaving for Paris,
texting when she landed and then every morning to let
him know things were fine.

Fine.

That's it. That's all he knew. Was she still angry? Was
she thinking about ending their relationship? Was she
ready to talk?

He had zero answers and less patience. He'd used it all
up in the last ten days and he had no more to give. Sam
was going to have to do some fucking talking.

"She's fine. She's busy working. You know how the first
few weeks of shooting are. Once she settles in a bit more
I'm sure she'll call you."

Tyler's teeth snapped together. "I know she's fine. She's

told me that, although that's all she's said. I want to know if she needs anything. How's shooting going? Is Sierra doing well?"

"Sierra is fantastic. She's damn smart and learning the movie business quickly. She helps us run our lines and I think we have another actress on our hands, my friend. She's good. Really good. We need to be looking for an opportunity for her."

That was excellent to hear and frankly Tyler wasn't surprised that Sierra had talent. With all that she'd been through in her life she would have a deep well of emotion to draw on.

"And Billie?" Tyler persisted. "How is she doing?"

"She's a terrific actress and this part is tailor made for her. The director is happy and we're on time and on budget which makes the producers and the studio happy. It's a great set and we're humming along here. Are you still planning to come out to Paris?"

That was the hundred-thousand dollar question. He didn't know if he was welcome.

"Eventually," he replied, not wanting to give away the feelings of fear and doubt that had plagued him since Billie had walked out of the door. "She asked for space so I guess I need to give it to her."

He'd told Sam everything and while his friend had been sympathetic he had also been painfully blunt. He was quite adamant that Tyler had fucked up. Big. He also felt that Tyler needed to dig down deep inside and see if perhaps he had indeed kept that file for a reason. Such as maybe he was thinking about looking in it.

So far Tyler had avoided that much introspection,

frankly terrified of what he might find. Billie's last speech about everything revolving around him had hit home and hit hard. Was he really that much of an egomaniac? He was beginning to think that perhaps he was. Whether out of habit or arrogance, he wasn't sure.

"No better cure for the blues than work," Sam replied. "Get your ass in the gym or learn to crochet. Don't sit around brooding while she makes this movie."

"Do you know how to crochet?"

Tyler couldn't picture his alpha male friend with a ball of yarn. Like a cat.

"As a matter of fact, I do. My grandma taught me when I was a kid. I'm not that good but I could make you a scarf. If you think you're too manly to crochet, pick something else but for the love of God do not sit around and feel sorry for yourself. This entire situation is your doing and you only have yourself to blame."

"I know that," Tyler said, exasperated with his friend. Maybe he shouldn't have called him after all. Nothing good was coming from this conversation. "Give me a fucking break."

Apparently that was the one request not to make of Sam because he growled into the phone so loudly Tyler had to pull it away from his ear.

"No wonder Billie left. You're sitting there in your goddamn mansion in the Hollywood Hills acting like none of this is your fault. Like this happened peripherally around you but you yourself weren't involved in any way and you're the victim here. Let me tell you a few home truths and listen to me carefully. Billie, and Sierra too, are the victims here. Their private life was exposed to some sleazy investigator who could have sold that shit to a tabloid instead of giving it to Garrett. In fact, that could still happen because I bet they kept a copy. They might be waiting for your wedding day or some shit like that. And it won't be you that's humiliated, it will be those two women who didn't do anything wrong except become a part of your life."

Tyler didn't have to listen to this shit. "You don't under–"

"Fuck you," Sam bit out, his tone short and hard as if his patience was long gone. "You're fucking spoiled. Billie has orbited around you for five goddamn years, always putting you first even at the expense of her own career. She's done everything you asked of her, even this crazy engagement to get that stupid role that isn't even worth it. And now you won't take responsibility for the shitty action of keeping that file. When are you going to fucking admit that you kept it because you were curious? Because anyone with a lick of sense would think that. You're just lucky that Billie doesn't *want* to believe it. She wants you to convince her that she's wrong. So you sit there like a king in a castle and blame everyone else but yourself. You want Billie back? You want to fix this? Then for once in your self-centered, self-absorbed life put her first when it really counts. Not with shopping or a new car or even her rent. That's just money. But in this life-altering shit? Put her first. That's how a husband acts. Once you do that, it will all be different."

Tyler wasn't going to let anyone speak to him like that, not even Sam whom he respected more than anyone but his parents. "What the fuck do you know about being a husband? About loving someone? You're divorced."

"Maybe if I'd taken my own advice back then I wouldn't be. Now they need me back on the set but even if they didn't I'm tired of talking to you. Don't call me until you've changed your fucking attitude."

Tyler didn't need a dial tone to know that Sam had hung up.

That's just dandy with me. I don't need that shit. I've been good to Billie.

He wasn't like Sierra's soon to be ex, Brian. That guy was a loser.

Of course, it didn't say too much about Tyler that he was comparing himself to the absolute dregs of males. He did treat Billie better but that was still a terribly low bar to clear.

Had it all been his way? Was he playing the victim even now?

Running his gaze around his opulent living room, he shuddered at what it had become these last few weeks. A gilded cage.

Sam's idea of not sitting around was a good one. Tyler needed to get out of these four walls and a run in the canyon was the perfect way to clear his head and really think about what his friend had said. Because one thing was for sure, if Sam was right, Tyler had some major groveling to do.

CHAPTER
Forty~One

BILLIE STRETCHED out on the sofa in the small flat that overlooked the Seine that the studio had rented for her and Sierra. Not fancy but it was clean and comfortable with two small bedrooms, a living room, bathroom, and a kitchen even smaller than the one she'd had in Tyler's cottage. None of that mattered, however, as the best part of their little Parisian home wasn't its space or amenities. It was the location in the sixteenth district on the west side of the city. The quiet streets were lined with shops and charming cafes that looked just like what she'd imagined they would. This particular district had a population of Americans so she and Sierra could easily communicate with the waiters and shopkeepers.

"What time is my call tomorrow?" she asked Sierra who was sipping on a small glass of red wine. She, too, had her feet up after a long day on the set.

"Six and can I say that I never realized that the studios work the actors and actresses quite this hard. You all make it look so glamorous when in reality they're working you to death behind the scenes. This will be your seventh day in a row of working more than fourteen hours. Yesterday you worked eighteen."

"But I have two days off after tomorrow." Billie shrugged. It was the nature of the movie business. "You have to admit there is lots of downtime. I can usually get in a nap. The low budget indie films that I've done in the past all filmed fast. Very fast. We worked incredibly long hours and I was busy for most of that time. We'd do several scenes in one day and we'd be finished in a few weeks. This is new for me too."

"Sam says we're on schedule so I guess that's good." Sierra took another sip of her wine. "You'll be able to get back to Tyler on time."

It was funny how Billie and her sister had picked up their sibling relationship so easily after the years of estrangement. Until Sierra had met Brian they'd been close, sharing secrets and talking over their issues and problems.

"Is there something you want to say? Because if there is you should just say it. You've never been one to beat around the bush to spare my delicate feelings," Billie said with a laugh. She'd been receiving some serious looks from Sierra, not just at this moment but all week.

"Fine, then I will. What is going on with you two? Are you together? Are you apart? Or you on a break? If a reporter stops me on the street and asks me about you what should I tell them?"

"To mind their own business and call my publicist," Billie shot back, then remembered that her publicist was Garrett whom she wasn't speaking to at the moment.

Mental note. Ask Sam if he'd recommend his publicist.

"Funny. I'm being serious here."

"So am I."

Swinging her legs down from the ottoman, Sierra faced her sister. "If you're not ready to talk about it, that's fine."

It wasn't that. It was that there wasn't anything new to say.

"I feel like it's all we've talked about and I'm exhausted from it. I don't know what I should do. If you were me, what would you do?"

At her wit's end, Billie still didn't have a clue as to how she was supposed to handle a situation like this. She loved Tyler, she wanted to be with him, but he'd hurt her. There was no denying that. Maybe it was simply going to take time.

"I don't think you want my opinion."

Sierra had been careful the past few weeks to be sympathetic but non-committal as to how Billie should have reacted when she found the file.

"I do," Billie pressed. "This affects you too. That folder contains your past as well."

Sierra smiled sweetly. "Except that no cares about my past. You're the one in the spotlight."

"Still...it had to be a shock to read some of that. I know it was for me."

Her smile vanished and a far more sober expression took its place. "In a way. I knew Mom had a lot of issues so it wasn't a shock. I'd say it was more of a surprise. Sort of a milder form of shock. I hope she's resting in peace now. I think she was a very unhappy woman."

That Sierra could be so forgiving of their mother's

behavior amazed Billie. "So you've made your peace with her?"

"You haven't? It might be time." Sierra stood and walked over to the windows, staring out at the starry night sky. "She was sick and she did the best she could. That's what we're all trying to do in this world."

"She made a lot of mistakes."

"So have I," Sierra replied softly. "Maybe this world would be a little kinder if we stopped judging people so harshly and cut them just a little bit of slack. We don't know what led to her alcoholism but I do know that it destroyed her life. I don't remember one day where she was happy, do you? Think about that because we shouldn't hate her. We should feel sorry for her."

"You're a better person than I am."

"No," Sierra said, shaking her head. "I'm just beaten up by life, just like she was. Mom wasn't strong enough to fight her demons and for a long time I thought I wasn't either. What are your demons?"

No one had ever asked that. Not directly, anyway.

"I don't know," Billie said. "Tyler says I lack trust."

Sierra nodded in agreement. "We both do. That's an effect of our childhood."

"You didn't say what yours was," Billie reminded her sister. "Only that you didn't think you could fight it."

"My demon is that I never feel good enough so I expect the worst treatment from people."

"That doesn't mean it's my demon too."

"I didn't say it was. I was only answering your question."

"I mean...I don't think I have a self-esteem problem."

Billie wasn't sure she liked where this conversation was going. "I don't think Tyler's too good for me."

"Good. Because he's not."

"In many ways he's lucky to have me."

Sierra picked up her wine glass and took a sip. "I agree."

"So it's not that I don't think I'm good enough."

"Okay."

Billie had had enough. "Just say it. You know you want to."

Shaking her head, Sierra placed her glass in the sink. "I'll ask you a question instead. Is Tyler a good man?"

"Of course he is. I wouldn't be with someone who wasn't. He truly cares about people and he always tries his best. He'd give you the shirt off of his back if you needed it."

"Then I think you can work this out." Turning toward the bedrooms, Sierra paused. "I'm going to bed. We have a big day tomorrow. You probably should too after you make your phone call. Goodnight."

Phone call? Billie wasn't planning to make–

Wait. Yes, she was.

Tyler Gaylord was a good man. Literally the best Billie had ever known. If he kept that stupid folder then she was simply going to have to get over it, because he wasn't the type to hurt her on purpose.

Just as Sierra had said...sometimes people make mistakes and we need to give them a break. We need to be kinder.

I need to forgive and move on. He's not perfect even if I sometimes think he is.

Grabbing her phone from her purse, she dialed his number and waited for him to pick up but it eventually went to voicemail. Unsure what to say, she ended the call. If he saw that he'd missed a call maybe he'd call her back. Although that begged the question why he'd missed the call at all. His phone was practically glued to his hand at all times. He'd answered every text she'd sent him since arriving in Paris within seconds.

Had he grown tired of waiting for her? Was Tyler done? Maybe she'd waited too long.

CHAPTER
Forty-Two

BILLIE TOSSED her silent cell phone onto the table between her and Sam. They were having a bite of lunch between takes and she was regaling him with her telephonic tale of woe. So far Tyler hadn't answered his phone, which either meant he was lying dead in a ditch somewhere or he wasn't picking up her calls on purpose.

"He didn't answer. Again. He hates me."

"He doesn't hate you." Sam serenely took another bite of his grilled chicken. "He loves you."

Pointing to the phone lying on the table, Billie shook her head. "Recent evidence contradicts your statement."

Reaching across the table, Sam picked up her untouched fork and held it up. "If I tell you a secret will you eat your lunch?"

Ears perked, Billie sighed and accepted the utensil. "It better be a good secret."

"The chicken is not that bad. Now eat your lunch and I'll tell you."

The chicken was good and so were the sliced potatoes with cheese and some sort of cream sauce. She patted her full stomach and pushed her plate away.

"I'm awaiting my secret."

Sam had finished his lunch as well and he wiped his hands on a paper napkin before setting his fork on the plate. "I talked to Tyler two nights ago."

And? Had he said he was giving up on Billie?

"That's a secret? That's a lousy secret."

"You're a tough audience." Sam perused the dessert offerings on the table next to them. "How about we share a slice of chocolate cake?"

Sam needed to focus on the task at hand, not scarfing down sweets.

"Are you out of your mind? I'm an actress on a movie set. I can't be eating stuff like that. You shouldn't be either."

Shrugging, Sam reached around behind him and snagged a plate of cake from the table. "I have a fast metabolism. Now where was I? Right, talking to Tyler. He and I had a long chat a couple of days ago. Very enlightening. For him, I think. Not so much for me."

"I swear I am going to stab you with my fork," Billie said between gritted teeth while Sam took a bite of the cake as if he didn't have a care in the world. "Talk."

"As I was saying, Tyler and I had a very interesting conversation where I sat him down and told him a few home truths. You might say I laid some wisdom on his ass. My guess is that he's not answering because he's off thinking about what I said. He'll surface soon and hopefully be a little wiser than when he left."

She would have loved to have been a fly on the wall for that conversation.

"What sort of wisdom did you helpfully impart?"

"The kind where I told him he's a spoiled asshole that only thinks about himself. I told him that he needed to put you first for once."

Now wait...that wasn't entirely fair.

"He does put me first. He's very generous."

Chuckling, Sam pushed the plate into the middle of the table, urging her to help him eat the fudge slab. "Funny, he said the same thing, but I pointed out that throwing money around doesn't count. That made him shut the hell up. I think he's out pondering the choices he's made in life. It's a positive thing for a man to do that every now and then. It can only do our friend Tyler some good."

"He's a good man, and you should know that."

"It's lovely to hear you defending him. Have you told him that?"

"I'm trying but he won't answer his phone."

"Then send him a text. He can read it when he gets back to his messages." He tapped the plate. "Now have some dessert."

Why the hell not? She picked up her fork and shook it at Sam.

"You're an evil man, Sam Collins. Diabolical and scary."

Giving her a wink, he laughed loud enough that heads whipped around to see who was so amused. "You bet I am. Now just relax. Tyler loves you, you love him. You're both going to live happily ever after in the make-believe land of Hollywood and have gorgeous babies. Have some faith."

Faith and trust. She could do this. She wouldn't allow them to be her demons anymore.

Picking up her phone, she tapped out a text to Tyler.

I love you and I want us to work this out. I know we can. Call me and let's put this behind us.

———

Tyler jumped into a taxi, needing a change of clothes, a decent meal, and a shower. He'd spent the last twenty hours either sitting on a plane or sitting in an airport waiting to get on a plane.

But he was finally in Paris.

Curtis had done the best he could to obtain a last-minute ticket to the City of Lights but it still required a change of planes in New York with an ungodly long layover. The poor young assistant hadn't quite understood Tyler's mania to get to Billie but to his credit he'd asked very few questions, simply hopping onto his laptop and doing the best he could.

Sitting back into the seat, he tried to slow his racing heart as he turned his cell phone back on after the flight. He was nervous as hell, hoping Billie wouldn't be upset about him showing up here without calling or checking with her. But what he desperately needed to say simply couldn't be done through an impersonal telephone. He wanted her to see her face when he said it. She knew him so well, better than anyone. She'd know he was sincere and telling the truth.

Sam's hard words hadn't gone over very well - in fact, Tyler had been cursing his best friend for quite awhile after the phone call - but they'd done the trick just as the older man had known they would. They'd been food for thought - the kind that was healthy for you but didn't necessarily taste all that good. Tyler had left the conversation with much to think about and he wasn't happy with what he saw.

He was a man that was used to being catered to, praised, and cosseted from life's harsh realities. He'd fooled himself into thinking that he was there for Billie when he threw his money around. He'd found it far simpler to buy her things than to put himself out there. He'd ignored her past - who she really was - for five years. He'd told himself it was out of respect but he knew now that it was because it was *easier* for him. Everything in his life was about what was easier or more fun. Billie had been right when she'd said that she'd been the grownup in their relationship.

It had to change. Right now. He was going to be the man that Billie deserved and needed. He was going to think about someone other than himself.

But the first thing he was going to do was apologize for holding onto the file. That was a huge mistake and he had been wrong to do it. There had been no malicious intent but he hadn't thought about Billie's feelings. As usual, it had been all about him.

Then he was going to get on his knees and beg her to marry him. For real.

His phone beeped and buzzed as several hours of messages loaded. The first text he noticed was from Billie. She'd called a few times but hadn't left any message so he'd simply pushed forward with his plan, knowing they could talk when he arrived in Paris. Opening the text, his heart pushed against his ribs and it hurt to breathe.

She still loved him and she wanted to talk. Put all of this mess behind them. He could do that. In fact, he could do one better. Within minutes he would be pulling up in front of her flat.

Damn, she hated surprises but hopefully she'd make an exception this one time.

CHAPTER
Forty~Three

BILLIE WAS dead asleep when a thumping noise woke her abruptly. Pulse fluttering, she sat straight up in bed, startled by the unknown sound in an abode she wasn't quite yet comfortable in. There was an alley cat that hung out on the front stoop; perhaps it had knocked over a trash can or a box?

She froze waiting for the sound again and jumped when she did, the pounding coming from her own front door. One quick glance at the bedside table had her cursing their late-night visitor. Only drunks and fools knocked on a door at two in the morning and she couldn't wait to tell them that. Their new friend probably wanted the tenant that had lived here before them.

Billie was wearing one of Tyler's old t-shirts so she dragged on a pair of old blue jeans that had been carelessly discarded on the floor before padding out to the living room, only to see Sierra already at the door smiling at their door knocker.

Tyler.

So it was a fool.

Because he didn't look drunk. He did, however, look awful as if he hadn't slept in days. Eyes red-rimmed, skin on the pale side, even his hair looked like it had been combed with his thumbs.

And he'd never looked more handsome and wonderful in his whole life. Billie had to curb the urge to throw herself into his arms the minute she saw him, she was so incredibly happy to see him. Now she understood why he hadn't answered her text. He'd been on an airplane.

"Tyler."

His gaze traveled over Sierra's shoulder to where Billie was standing, his smile growing wider.

"Baby girl."

Hopefully in fifty or so years Billie would be used to the wave of emotion that came over her when he called her by that name and in that special timbre. But for now, she almost melted into a puddle of goo, her knees turning to water. How had she ever thought she could walk away from him? She could be mad and hurt and want her space, but she would always come back.

And her sister? Sierra was smiling, her gaze darting between Billie and Tyler. "I can see I am totally not needed here. Nice to see you, Tyler. I guess I'll see you in the morning."

Bless sisters. Billie would thank her later. Sierra brushed by on the way to her bedroom and elbowed Billie. "Go get 'em, sis."

The door to Sierra's room clicked closed leaving Tyler and Billie alone. Pleating the cotton of his t-shirt between her fingers, she shifted on her feet, feeling suddenly a little shy under his intense scrutiny.

"I sent you a text but now I know why you didn't answer."

Tyler nodded, dragging his suitcase from a spot behind him and placing it against a wall.

"I was on a plane. Actually, I was on a couple of planes. Curtis couldn't get me a direct flight to Paris so I had to fly to New York first and then wait for what seemed like days to get on the next plane."

Billie wasn't sure what else to say so she didn't say anything at all. There were so many things she wanted to tell him but she didn't know where to start. The better plan was to let Tyler speak. He'd flown thousands of miles to do just that.

"Can I get something to drink?" he asked, shoving his hands into the pockets of his jeans. "I'm kind of thirsty."

"Of course," she said, relieved to have something to do. "Are you hungry? We have leftover coq au vin from dinner."

"I could eat."

That meant that he was starving but didn't want to make a big deal out of it. She warmed up the chicken dish and poured him a glass of white wine to go with it. He ate his late dinner at the kitchen table while she sat across from him, neither of them speaking much except to remark on the weather forecast and her schedule on set. Eventually he finished and placed his fork on the edge of the plate, dabbing the napkin against those well-shaped lips that drove so many women crazy.

"I have a few things to say, babe. Will you hear me out?"

Nodding because she wasn't sure her voice was working, she tried to appear as composed as possible despite her stomach doing backflips in her abdomen. It was as if her entire life and future happiness was riding on this one conversation, which was ridiculous but she couldn't stop thinking it.

"First of all, I want to say that I'm sorry for keeping the file. I should have given it to you that day that Garrett brought it over. I've thought a lot about why I didn't and I guess I didn't want you to be upset about your past. You hadn't told me about it yet and from your silence I knew that there was so much that hurt, although I didn't know why. Maybe I thought I could shield you from it? It sounds stupid when I say it out loud but I swear I had no malevolent intention with it. As for why I kept it? I've given that a hell of a lot of thought too."

Her entire body was like a stretched rubber band, stretched to the point that she could snap back with no damage done or snap and break. It all depended on what his next words were.

"I did wonder what was in that file," he said, but then held up his hands in surrender. "But not because of some morbid fascination or because I thought that an incident in your past would come out and hit the tabloids. I think we both have to admit that if anything ever hits the gossip rags it's going to be something from those first wild years I had in Hollywood. I'm not that proud of my behavior and there could be photographic evidence."

Luckily Instagram and Snapchat wasn't a "thing" back then.

"I think if there were photos or video we would know by now," Billie said.

"I fervently hope so. Now as to why I kept it..." His voice trailed off and she thought she might explode from waiting. "I think I loved you even then and I just wanted to know every detail about you. I'd always respected your decision not to speak much about your life although it frustrated me to know so little, but once we were engaged I wanted to know everything. I wanted that part of you that you kept hidden away - all the things you never told me - except for Sierra. I couldn't help but wonder if there was more and yes, I was curious. I knew reading it was wrong so I shoved it away, hid it among my scripts. I will openly admit that I don't know if I would have broken down and looked or not. I'd like to think that I would have stayed strong because I did eventually forget all about it. Once I had you, for real, that's all I really needed."

That...wasn't so horrible. Human nature and all. He had every right to be curious about the woman he was falling in love with. It wasn't his fault that she didn't talk about her childhood but that she knew so much about his. Except that he'd been ugly. She hadn't known that. They had their whole lives to learn all the small stuff.

It didn't matter. Billie knew all that was truly important. Tyler would never hurt her on purpose. Ever. Somehow she'd allowed herself to forget that immutable fact.

"I understand," Billie finally replied, realizing there had

been a long span of silence when he'd finished speaking. "I think there was a part of me that was looking for a reason to run. This scares me, Tyler. Fear of happiness is a demon I have to conquer. Whenever things are going well I always look for the other shoe to drop because in the past it always did."

She'd come to a few conclusions as well after her talk with Sierra and that was one of them. The second was that not talking to Tyler wasn't solving their issues. It only prolonged them.

"Baby," Tyler said in that voice that dampened panties all over the world. "I have more to say but I need to hold you. Can we go into your room perhaps?"

Privacy. A good idea. Not that Billie thought Sierra had her ear pressed to the wall between her bedroom and the living room...Billie was sure her sister didn't but once they finished talking both she and Tyler were going to be exhausted. It would be easier if they could just fall asleep where they lay.

"Sure. Grab your suitcase."

Doing as she suggested, he followed her into a bedroom down the hall. The small lamp next to the bed was already switched on from when she was so rudely woken and it bathed the corner of the room in a golden glow. Lying against the headboard, pillows propping her up, Billie patted the mattress next to her. "Come join me."

It had been far too long since she'd felt his arms around her and he didn't disappoint, his hunger just as strong as her own. As if by mutual agreement their lips met in a ferocious kiss so hot she could feel her bones melting along with her heart, their bodies pressing even closer together.

His hands stroked down her spine leaving a heated trail in their wake and arousing every nerve ending in her flesh. So good. Tyler could excite her with only a few kisses and it wasn't fair at all. His lips trailed over her jaw to her ear, nipping at the lobe until she was giggling and pushing at his chest, but not really wanting him to stop.

"We're supposed to be talking."

Those skillful lips slid down her throat and his chuckle sent vibrations straight down to her toes. "I'd rather make love. I think you would too. We can talk later."

True, and besides, thinking was becoming more difficult with every touch of Tyler's fingertips and every kiss from that talented mouth. Somehow her t-shirt had rode up, exposing the skin of her belly as his warm hands slid up her ribcage to cup her breasts. His thumbs teased the tips until she was squirming underneath him and he was tugging the offending piece of cotton over her head and tossing it to the side.

Cool air ran over her hard nipples, puckering them even more tightly but Tyler had already moved on to the button of her jeans, popping it open with practiced ease. With her help he pushed her blue jeans down her thighs and off, tossing them heedlessly over his shoulder. Luckily the room was small and she wouldn't have any trouble finding them in the morning.

Clothed only in a strip of lace panties, Billie could feel the heat of Tyler's gaze as he sat back on his heels and studied her from head to toe as if this was the first time he'd seen her almost naked. There was love in those soft blue eyes. She'd seen him look at her like that before but there was something more there this time. A reverence she'd never thought to see or have directed at her. Billie was sure she was looking at him the very same way.

"I've missed you so much." Tyler's voice was rough and dark and incredibly sexy. "I need you."

She needed him too. Right now.

CHAPTER
Forty~Four

TYLER'S REUNION with the woman he loved had gone better than he ever could have imagined. This was it. She was the love of his life and she'd forgiven him for being a huge idiot and hurting her, although he hadn't meant to. Now all he could think about was how wonderful their life together was going to be.

Okay, he was also thinking about all the sex they were going to have, especially the sex they were going to have right this very minute. Just as soon as he could strip off these clothes. His shirt came off easily but his pants were a trifle more stubborn and took a few extra tugs, much to Billie's delight. She giggled as he hopped on one foot, finally tossing away the denim blue jeans and his boxers.

He didn't have a modest bone in his body so he stood in front of her naked and proud, enjoying the way her gaze roamed over him possessively. He definitely belonged to her and her alone and although a few months ago that thought would have scared the shit out of him, it didn't now in the least. He couldn't think of one other woman he wanted or that could even hold a candle to his Billie.

"Like what you see, baby?"

Instead of smiling, she frowned and shook her head. "I'm not sure. I think you need to move a little closer."

So she wanted to play games? He could do that.

He took a step forward and placed a knee on the mattress. "How's this? Close enough?"

Shaking her head, his dark-haired vixen gave him a coy smile as his own hand wrapped around his cock, stroking the already hard and ready flesh. "I think you need to be a little closer."

Kneeling on the bed about a foot away from her, he continued his lazy strokes up and down his cock. To his delight, Billie licked her lips as if she couldn't wait to get a taste. If he had his way she wouldn't have to wait.

"Is this close enough?"

Reaching out a hand, Billie hesitated and then pulled it back. "Seeing is good but it would be more helpful to be able to make a closer...inspection."

Chuckling and grinning, he spread his arms wide. "If it will help, I'll cooperate. Just one thing I would ask of you, babe."

Looking up at him from under her lashes, her fingers hovered inches from his cock. "What's that?"

"Be gentle with me," he whispered and then gave her a playful wink. "I'm new at this."

Laughter bubbled from her full, pink lips. "Tyler Gaylord, that is possibly the biggest lie I've ever heard you tell. I'm surprised lightning didn't strike you just now."

"I thought we were role playing, babe."

"Role playing?" She rolled her eyes as her fingers wrapped around his cock, drawing a ragged moan from deep in his chest. "You're a great actor but I think a virgin might be a stretch."

There was no more talking as Billie leaned forward and took the head into her mouth, swirling her tongue around until he wanted to cry out as the pleasure flew through his veins. All laughter had ceased and it was serious indeed as his fingers tangled in her long, silky tresses, pulling her closer as he slid even farther into the warm cavern of her mouth.

Fucking paradise.

His lids were like lead but he forced himself to keep his eyes open, not wanting to miss a second of watching her bob up and down, her tongue fluttering at all his sensitive areas and then tracing the veins just to make him even more crazy with lust. He had to mentally cool down by thinking about glaciers and skiing just so he wouldn't throw her onto her back and impale her with one gigantic stroke.

His balls were pulled up tight against his body and if she kept going this was going to come to an abrupt end. He wanted it to last.

Reluctantly he pulled away and she mewled in disappointment, pressing a butterfly kiss onto his belly, her breath warm against the sensitive flesh, and then trailing upward until their lips met again. It was hot and sweet and Tyler was flummoxed as to how he had survived over a week without her. If he had his way they wouldn't ever be apart. It wouldn't be easy with their careers but he was determined to make it work.

Pushing her gently back onto the mattress, he held her hands at her sides so he could play and explore uninterrupted. If she touched him he might be detoured and he needed to concentrate on his one and only goal - making her scream with pleasure. Burying his nose in the fragrant crook of her neck he breathed in deeply, her singular scent wrapping around him seductively. He captured a pebbled nipple into his mouth, laving it with his tongue and feeling her quiver in response. Her nails dug into his shoulders and the pressure built in his lower back. He couldn't hold off much longer.

"I need–"

Seeming to know what he was going to say, Billie nodded and lifted up from the bed to nip at his lower lip with her teeth. "Yes, now. It's been too long."

The temperature of the room had risen and a sheen of sweat covered his body as he positioned himself between her silky thighs. The heavy scent of their arousal hung in the air and his cock ached with need. Pressing into her slowly, he was rewarded with a groan of pure pleasure as her walls stretched to accommodate him. Tight and hot, she was perfection and he didn't stop until he was balls deep, only then allowing himself to breathe.

Those long legs wrapped around his waist, the heels digging into the muscles of his ass urging him with no words to move. Teasing them both, he withdrew slowly, pausing on the out-stroke before thrusting back in, pushing the oxygen from their lungs. He did it again and again, building up speed each time until they were climbing toward the precipice together.

Teeth gritted painfully, the pressure built in his lower

back and he began reciting lines from the *Thunder* movies in his head to be able to hold back but it was too late. Reaching between their bodies, he found her swollen clit and circled it with his fingertips until she was right there with him.

Her back arched and her eyes closed, Billie had never looked so beautiful as she did when she was crying out his name during her orgasm. Her skin was shiny with sweat and her long hair was swirled around her like a halo on the pillow as they both reached their peak. Shuddering and barely breathing, he collapsed on top of her, burying his face in the valley between her breasts and they didn't move for the longest time, content to simply lie in each other's arms. Her fingers stroked the damp skin of his back and tickled the whiskers on his jaw where he hadn't shaved in over twenty-four hours.

Eventually he rolled off of her, letting her breathe easily again but he pulled her close so her head was pillowed on his chest. As wonderful as that had been, there were still a few things he needed to say. They'd been sidetracked but he wouldn't change it for anything.

"Things are going to be different now, Billie," he said, dropping a kiss on the top of her head. "I'm going to put you first from now on. I'm going to be the best damn husband I possibly can. I promise you that."

"That sounds lovely," Billie replied, her voice thick with sleep. He'd woken her at two in the morning and then wore her out with sex, so it wasn't a surprise. He just had one more thing he needed to tell her and then they could sleep.

"I'm not going to take the Zak role either. I'm going to

take some time off and concentrate on your career for year or two. I'll follow you around and make sure you don't fall in love with any of your leading men."

As sleepy as she had been, Billie sat bolt upright, her eyes wide. "What did you say?"

Smiling lazily, Tyler stretched and yawned. "I'm not taking the Zak role. I already told Weller. Frankly, he's a dick and I pity the poor bastard that has to work with him and his gigantic ego."

She shook her head, clearly not getting what he was trying to tell her. "But that was your dream role. We're getting married because you want that role."

"No, baby," he said gently, pressing a tender kiss to her satin lips. "We're getting married because we're hopelessly in love and can't live without each other. As for the role, I've decided to take your advice and believe in my talent. I don't have to play a part that mirrors my own life. I'm a goddamn actor and I'll find the right role but this one isn't it. Besides, I'm going to be pretty busy making you a star."

"I don't need that," she protested but he placed his fingers over her mouth and shook his head.

"I know you don't but you deserve it. You're talented and this movie with Sam could do great things for your career. You're going to get even better offers soon and I'm going to become your biggest cheerleader and fan."

"I don't know what to say." Billie sighed, her expression more than a little worried. "Are you sure? I don't want you to do something because you think I'm mad or that I don't forgive you. You'd make a wonderful Zak."

"No doubt," he said with a cocky grin. "But there are

even more fantastic roles out there that I can explore. Maybe we can do something together."

That smile... Damn if it didn't get him every time. She ran her finger down the middle of his chest, promise in her eyes. "A collaboration of sorts? I like the sound of that. What did you have in mind?"

She was going to send him to an early grave. But what a way to go.

"Woman," he growled, pulling her back down with him. "You're going to be the death of me. I'm only human, not a superhero."

"You're my hero."

Tyler would do anything to make sure that never changed.

CHAPTER
Forty~Five

FOUR MONTHS LATER...

It was a gorgeous autumn day for Billie and Tyler's wedding. The sun was shining, the weather was perfect, and Billie was happier than she'd ever been in her entire life.

Both she and Tyler had shed tears during the ceremony, standing under a flower-draped arbor in an orchard of beautiful old apple trees. Billie's elegant ivory silk and lace gown was an old-fashioned design with a tight bodice and a full ballgown skirt. She felt like a princess in it and Tyler was surely her prince, dressed in a charcoal gray tuxedo with a red rose in the lapel. Everyone kept telling her how beautiful she looked but frankly she couldn't take her eyes off of her handsome new husband.

Tyler was her husband. She was his wife.

It was surreal and yet they both agreed that it had been

inevitable. From their first meeting so long ago, they'd both known that there was...something...about the other. Something different and special.

The reception was beginning to wind down and soon she and Tyler would be jetting off for their honeymoon. Back to that beach house in Hawaii that had seemed so much like paradise. They'd spend two weeks there and then spend a few months in Los Angeles getting ready to film a movie. Together. It was another dream come true.

The script had been in one of those high stacks in Tyler's office and Curtis had found it. He'd started reading the first page and simply couldn't put it down. Several hours later he'd frantically called Tyler on the phone to tell him that he simply had to read it. At first, Tyler had only been humoring his assistant but it quickly became clear that this story was special.

The Zak role forgotten, Tyler had thrown himself into negotiations and the studio was thrilled to have him onboard along with Billie, who was getting rave reviews from the dailies on the set in Paris.

Placing her hand on her gorgeous husband's thigh under the banquet table, Billie leaned over and pressed a kiss to Tyler's cheek, leaving behind a light lipstick mark. Immediately he turned away from Max, who simply chuckled and lifted his wife Carrie out of a chair and whirled her onto the dance floor. Carrie and Max were being awfully cagey when asked questions, but Carrie hadn't touched a drop of alcohol this weekend. Everyone was sure the happy newlyweds were having a baby even if they weren't ready to admit it yet.

Sadly, Nate and Paige hadn't been able to make the

wedding as she was placed on bedrest as they awaited the birth of their twins - one boy and one girl - but that gave them ample time to decide on names. Apparently Paige was still trying to talk Nate out of Balthasar, heaven help her.

"Hello, baby," Tyler said, his soft blue eyes glowing with all the love she'd ever dreamed of. "Have I been neglecting you? I'm sorry."

"You haven't." Billie shook her head. "I snuck out and had a toast with the girls and then came back here. I was just thinking that we need to thank Sam and Dinah somehow. They've been so good to Sierra."

Sierra had landed a small role in an indie production with Dinah and the two women would be flying off to Chicago in just a few days. But it was Sam that had made the movie possible in the first place. It was his production company that was making the film.

Now officially divorced, Billie's sister was fully embracing her life and freedom, although the specter of the past still hung over her from time to time, but she was courageous and determined to move forward.

"It was sweet of Dinah to insist that Sierra be the maid of honor," Tyler observed. "She didn't have to do that."

"She said it was only right but I sort of made them co-maids of honor. I'm not sure if that breaks some etiquette rules but I don't care." Billie's fingertips ran lightly across Tyler's jaw. "The only thing I care about right now is you."

"Agreed," he replied, urgency in his tone. "How soon can we make our escape? I want you all to myself. I've had to share you for two whole days."

"Such a tragedy," she teased, although she felt exactly

the same way. "Are you sure you won't get tired of me after a few weeks in the tropics? Just me, you, and some umbrella drinks. If you read some of the tabloids, they say you will. That you'll get bored and leave me."

They could laugh about it because they both knew it would never happen. They'd worked too hard to get here.

He frowned playfully and shook his head. "That's strange, the other half of the tabloids say that I've been thoroughly tamed by a dark-haired temptress. I know which one I think is right."

"Do you mind that your playboy title has been passed along to someone else?"

She already knew the answer in her heart but it was nice to hear too, especially on a day like today.

"Kirby can have it with my compliments," Tyler grinned. "I hope he uses it in good health. Personally, I feel badly for the poor bastard. The press is going to hound him night and day if he so much as looks at a female. Now, back to the important issues. How do we get out of here?"

"I have to throw my bouquet. Then we can go."

Her ivory and yellow rose bouquet tied with a matching ribbon sat on the table in front of her. Tyler reached for it, twirling it in his hand. "This one?"

"Whoever catches it is supposed to get married next. At least that's what they say."

An evil smile spread across his face. "Does it matter who throws it?"

She wasn't sure what he had up his sleeve but she'd learned to be wary when he wore that expression. "I guess not but usually the bride does. Why?"

"Can I throw it?"

"You want to throw my flowers?" she asked, rolling her eyes. Sometimes he could be so strange. Her big, sexy goof. "Sure, if you want to."

"Thanks, babe." Tyler pressed a quick kiss to her lips before standing up and clanging his fork on his glass. The room quieted down and suddenly every set of eyes in the place was staring at her bridegroom. "I want to thank everyone for coming this weekend. I know it isn't easy to find time in your crazy schedules and it means the world to me and Billie that you did. I'm the luckiest man on the planet to have such great friends and now the most amazing wife too. Now to get to the bouquet toss...according to my beautiful bride whoever catches the flowers is the next to get married. Is that right?"

A very feminine cheer went up from the crowd, affirming his theory.

"Good. So here goes."

Unlike at other weddings Billie had attended there was no buildup, no gathering of the single women. Tyler simply flicked his wrist and the bouquet sailed through the air as the collective audience held its breath. Even Billie found herself not even blinking as the roses seemed to hover for a moment before falling into the arms of the last person she'd ever imagine.

Sam. And not only was he holding her bouquet, he was wearing one pissed-off expression directed at said thrower of flowers. Her new husband.

His hand under elbow, Tyler lifted her out of her chair. "We better get out of here before he kicks my ass."

"You did that on purpose?"

She shouldn't be laughing but she was. Sam was

stomping through the dancers and headed right to them. Tyler was right. They needed to make a quick exit and fast.

"Of course I did. Now let's disappear before he messes up my new tuxedo."

Somehow she and Tyler managed to slip out of the hall and into their suite before Sam caught up to them, both of them laughing so hard they had tears in their eyes. This was what she'd signed up for. Tyler might have grown up a little but he was always going to be exciting and unpredictable.

She couldn't wait for a lifetime of sneaking out of parties. With him.

I hope you enjoyed Tyler and Billie's happily ever after! Check out Sam's story – Love in the Spotlight! Thank you for reading Wild on the Red Carpet!

About the Author

Olivia Jaymes is a wife, mother, lover of sexy romance, and caffeine addict. She lives with her husband and son in central Florida and spends her days with handsome alpha males and spunky heroines.

She is currently working on a new contemporary romance series – The Hollywood Showmance Chronicles in addition to the ongoing Danger Incorporated series and the Cowboy Justice Association series.

Visit Olivia Jaymes at
www.OliviaJaymes.com

www.ingramcontent.com/pod-product-compliance
Lightning Source LLC
Chambersburg PA
CBHW020640030726
47498CB00002B/301